# BOX ONE OF TWO

PAMELA DEAN

BOX ONE OF TWO


**Pamela Dean**

"May you be remembered how you see yourself on your best day."
-Violet Merryweather
1910-1984

# PROLOGUE
## VIOLET



NEW YORK, 1935
Ambassador Theater

"YES, I AM HERE TO AUDITION," I say, holding my head high. *They will choose me, I know they will. This time will be different.*

"Spell your name please," the voice from the darkened room says.

"Certainly. V-I-O-L-E-T," I say, carefully and slowly so they can write it down. They need to do that, you see, so they can contact me for the role.

"Alright, Violet, please read the underlined sentences in the script," the voice commands.

I hold my hand up to shield my eyes from the bright lights and say, "Oh no. Not Violet."

"What? What do you mean not Violet? That's what you spelled." I hear him say to someone else, "Isn't that what you got, Cathy?"

"Yes, sir. That is what I heard as well," a small, female-sounding voice replies.

I straighten my hair and tug on my dress a little, waiting.

"Well, what on earth is your name if it's not Violet, because that is how you spell that name, in case you didn't know!" the man in the dark snaps. He sounds angry now.


"MY NAME IS PRONOUNCED IOLET. The *V* is silent."

"Oh, for Chrissake. NEXT!" he yells, and I am quickly ushered off the stage.

That did not go as I planned.

# ONE
# HEATHER

Chico, California, 1984

SERENITY FALLS

"MISS MERRYWEATHER HAS REQUESTED YOU, Heather. She's in room one sixty-six."

Lionel hands me a list and a few keys.

"Miss Merryweather? Have I met her?" I ask as I adjust my apron.

"I am sure you have." He chuckles and walks back into his office.

"Okay, thanks," I say to his retreating back. Without looking over his shoulder, he shuts his door. God, what a prick.

I check my cart and make sure I have everything I need. I've cleaned for the seniors here for almost a year and I can't remember if I have ever met a Miss Merryweather. They are all nice for the most part. Serenity Falls isn't a nursing home; it's apartments for seniors who just want a community and an easier life.

At least that is what the brochures say. There are a few residents here who make me wonder if they would be better served with more care. Not my job though, so I just clean. Well, and run errands for a few of them. One sweet lady likes a certain kind of yogurt they don't serve in the dining hall, so once a week I drive to Albertsons and pick some up for her.

Of course, when word got out that I was doing that, I ended up with a long list of things for people who don't want to be bothered by going themselves. The bus isn't super reliable here, so I guess I understand. I decide to check in with apartment 166 before I clean the others so I can find out what she wants from me. Each person is different, and what they consider important varies. I have one client who just wants me to fluff her pillows on her bed and flush her toilet if I notice she has forgotten. Another gentleman has me clean his whole place, baseboards and all, every week, even though he is the biggest neat freak I have ever known. I swear he must clean before I get there, but we chat, and I like his stories about being overseas after the war. He was a part of a rebuilding effort, and he is very proud of his involvement.

That's the best part of this job—the stories. These people have led amazing lives. We have veterans and retired teachers, an artist or two, and I think a retired senator. My favorite client is Boyd. He is a true Southern gentleman and always offers me a glass of sweet tea when I am finished cleaning. He has the best stories of growing up in Louisiana. He was a jazz musician and has the coolest black-and-white photos of himself playing in clubs. He has told me the names of some of the other people in the pictures and he acts very impressed, so I try and seem pleased, even if I don't know who Ella Fitzgerald is.

I reach apartment 166 and knock loudly, saying, "Housekeeping" like I always do. I never just let myself in. Once my friend Charlotte walked in on two residents having sex. I shudder every time I think about it.

The door flies open and a very short woman in a leopard-print muumuu stares up at me. She has thick, black-framed glasses that make her eyes look huge. She has a purple turban on her head today, and I see she is wearing her signature pearls.

Oh crap. *This* is Miss Merryweather?

"Hello, Iolet. I heard you needed housekeeping?" I say, hoping to hell she has changed her mind. Maybe I can pawn her off on Charlotte.

She looks me up and down, then leans out in the hall and glances in both directions.

"Does anyone know you are here?" she asks in a hushed voice.

"No. Well, that's not true. Lionel sent me, so he knows—" I start to explain, but she grabs my hand and pulls me in, shutting her door quickly. She looks at the door and yanks it back open, tugging on the handle of my cart and trying to pull it inside.

"Here, wait, Iolet. Let me get that," I say, reaching past her.

"Hurry! Don't let anyone see you!" she whisper-hisses again.

"Okay, I won't," I say, and glance down the vacant hallway in both directions before pushing my small cleaning cart into her apartment.

"So do you want to get on my cleaning schedule, Iolet?" I ask as I look around. All the apartments are pretty much the same. The one-bedrooms like Iolet has are actually pretty big. Bigger than my stupid apartment, that's for sure.

"Yes, I want you to clean for me. Every other day," she announces, and I reach for the clipboard I carry. I tear off the top sheet and hand it to her.

"Iolet, I can clean once a week. That is included in your rent. These are the things I can do for you. Just look this over and put check marks on all of things you would like and make notes at the bottom, like if you have a cat or something." I look around her place and don't see any indication of a pet, but you never know.

"All of it. And every other day. Also let me ask you this." She leans in and whispers, "Can you remove blood from a carpet?"

"Oh, um, sure. Yeah, I think I have something that will work for that. Did you hurt yourself, Iolet? Do you want me to have Lionel call your doctor?" Her eyes get even bigger.

"No! Don't tell Lionel or anyone else about the blood. Good grief, girly. Don't you know how to keep things on the down-low?" Iolet asks, and she jerks her thumb over her shoulder. I glance in the direction of where she is pointing and see a pair of men's shoes tucked under the side table.

"Oh! Right, of course. I can come back. I didn't know you had company. Why don't you fill out the form and you can leave it in my box by the front desk? I can clean for you tomorrow, okay?" I say, backing toward the door. If a naked old man walks out of her bedroom, I will barf.

"No one is here, you twit. Listen, I need your help. Someone stole my banana," she says, blinking up at me like a lost barn owl.

"Your banana?" I am so confused right now.

"Yes, I had it when I left the dining hall, but when I got to my door it was gone. Heather, bananas don't just disappear. It went somewhere, and I think I know who took it!" She thrusts her crooked finger in the air to drive her point home.

"Okay," I say slowly. What does this have to do with the blood she wanted help with?

"Anyway, Frank over by the laundry room said that I can have his parakeet when he dies. Isn't that lovely? I am going to rename it Albert. I have always loved that name."

I just blink at her. Crap, she has lost her damn mind. I try again. "Okay, well, I have to get going. I have some other places to clean, and then I am going to the store. Did you want anything? Maybe another banana?" I ask.

"Someone stole my banana, Heather. Don't think I have forgotten," Iolet says.

"Right, so you want another one?" I ask, inching toward the door.

"Nah, I hate bananas. They are too mushy for my taste. Never did like them. Dear, I really don't know why you keep insisting on talking about bananas. It's just rude." She has crossed her small living room and is now sitting in a very nice upholstered chair. The arms are a deep mahogany wood, carved in a beautiful pattern with only a small patch of soft, cream-colored velvet fabric. The back and seat have the same creamy velvet, and I think it is the most beautiful chair I have ever seen.

She catches me staring at it and smiles. "Do you like my chair?"

"Yes, it's very pretty. Your whole house here is lovely. I don't think I have ever seen inside. You have very nice taste, Iolet."

"Yes, I know. It's all those movies I was in. I developed quite the eye for the nicer things. The set designers were just so talented, and I was good at borrowing them for my own home." She pauses and looks at me with a horrified expression. "The designers, not the sets. You know? The people. Oh, for Chrissake. Do you have Girl Scout cookies or not?"

"Pardon?" I ask, trying to catch up.

"Cookies. Isn't that why you are here?" she asks.

"Yep, but I just realized I don't have any more. Ran out. Sorry. No cookies today," I say, turning the doorknob with one hand while grabbing my cart handle with the other.

"Well, good. I hate those cookies, and you look way too old to be a Girl Scout. Hey, listen. Have you seen a rogue banana around? I am missing one," Iolet says.

"Nope, but if I do, I will be sure to let you know!" I open the door, shove my cart into the hall, and walk quickly behind it. I reach back and pull the door shut. Holy hell, what was that? That woman is off her rocker.

I start down the hall when I hear her door fly open and she yells, "See you tomorrow, Heather. Don't forget my banana!"

Jesus.

## TWO
## VINCE

HOLLYWOOD, California, 1984
    Hugh's Auto Body


"DO you want me to pick up a sandwich for you, Tony?" I have to lean under the Mustang so I am not talking to his legs.

"Sure, where you going? Don't get me a sub if you go to that fucking dive over on Santa Monica. I swear I almost died the last time we ate there," he says.

"You're such a fucking baby. Just don't get the tuna fish again. I can't believe you ate that with how bad it smelled," I grumble. That sandwich stunk up the whole shop for two days.

He laughs, and I hear the wrench clank against the frame as he adjusts his body under the car. "I'll take a turkey club with extra bacon, and grab me some chips too. Hey, I want a Diet Coke this time. I am trying to watch my figure." He slides out from under the car and wipes his brow with a dirty red cloth.

"Gettin' a little snug under there, huh?" I give him shit. It's all we know, and I am not about to be the one to stop, even if he has had a hell of a year.

"Fuck you." Tony reaches for his wallet, and I wave him off.

"Nah, I got it. You paid last time. Just finish the oil change on that thing before Mrs. Foster gets back. I can't deal with her threats to call the manager again," I say over my shoulder.

Tony grabs his crotch and says, "She can speak to this manager."

"Classy, dude. Real classy." I laugh. I know he's just messing around. Tony is one of the most respectful guys I have ever known. It's why I hired him out of all the guys from the old neighborhood. No way I'd let some of those clowns near these high-end clients. My dad worked hard to build the clientele here, and I am not about to let that slide.

I hop into my pickup truck and make my way to the corner of Sunset and Wilcox. Sammy's has the best sandwiches around, and since I always get here a little early, I don't have a long wait. As I walk in, the little bell above the door dings audibly in the nearly empty restaurant.

"What's up today, Vince?" Monica says in her annoying, high-pitched voice. She leans on the counter, making sure to show off her cleavage. I roll my eyes. I know she wants me to say something like I used to, but I am just not into her anymore. She was fun to flirt with and all, but man, she is not bright. A guy needs a little more than a nice rack, you know? Well, at least I do.

"Just working, Monica. Picking up some sandwiches for me and Tony," I say. I stop short of the counter, not wanting to get too close. Hopefully she gets the hint real soon that we are not going to happen.

"Oh. Tony, huh? How is that poor bastard?" She cracks her gum. God, what a gross habit. I can see the green wad every time she opens her mouth.

"He's doing all right. Hey, so Tony wants a turkey club, extra bacon, and some chips, large Diet Coke, and I'll have the same," I say.

She blinks at me. "So two turkey clubs?" she asks.

"Yeah, both with extra bacon."

"Did you want two bags of chips?" she asks with her nose wrinkled like she is trying to understand calculus.

"Yeah," I say.

"And to be clear, you want two Diet Cokes?" she asks.

"Yes, Monica. Thanks." I stare at her, wondering what part of my order was confusing.

She writes all of that down and walks it back to the kitchen, then comes back out with the drinks.

"Here. In case you're thirsty now." She winks, and I force my lips up in an attempt at a smile. I am not known for my cheery disposition.

Glancing around, I see only a few tables with customers. Most people start their lunch break at noon, so getting here at eleven helps. This is a cool place, and I kind of wish it wasn't as popular as it is. Sammy's is that classic diner from the fifties with black-and-white tiles and red-leather covered booths with lots of chrome trim. There are framed pictures of movie stars and a few singers. Some of the pictures have been signed. Those hang by the booths and along the wall to the restrooms. There is a really cool old jukebox in the corner that plays all the good stuff from the forties and fifties.

I can't stand the shit they play on the radio now. That stuff is not music. Give me some Billie Holiday or Ella Fitzgerald any day. Frank and the Rat Pack are high on my list too. My mom says I must be an old soul. I think I just have good taste.

"Order up!" I hear from over Monica's shoulder, and I know it's my sandwiches, but she's just standing there twirling her big hair and smacking her gum. Her uniform is way too tight, and I notice she has her name tag right where her left nipple would be. It's an obvious tactic to get people to stare at her chest. Not like anyone would need help in that area. The buttons are doing a heroic job of keeping those things contained. It defies physics.

"Hey, Monica?" I ask.

"Yeah, Vinnie?" She leans forward, hope dripping from her voice.

"Think maybe you can check and see if that was my order?" I ask.

"Huh?" She cocks her head like I said something in a foreign language.

"The cook yelled 'order up,' and I think it might be the sandwiches, you know, that I ordered?" I know I sound rude, but fuck. How hard is it to get food when it's ready?

"Right! Oh, sorry. I was just thinking about this party I got invited to next week. Want to go with me?" she says, propping her elbows on the counter again. She is swaying her ass back and forth and staring at me with those big, blue eyes. She has a pretty face, but she is really into makeup. Like all the makeup that was ever made is currently slathered all over her face.

"Nah, I'm busy. Hanging with Tony, you know?" I say.

"Oh, right. Sure. You're a good friend, Vinnie," she says, straightening up and sticking her chest out a little.

I don't correct her, but I fucking hate it when people call me that. My name isn't Vinnie, it's Vince.

She finally goes into the kitchen, returning with a big paper bag. She rings me up, and I drop the money on the counter. "Keep the change. Thanks, Monica," I call out over my shoulder.

Traffic is starting to pick up as I make my way back to the garage. I pull into the back lot and walk through the open bay door to find Tony talking to a guy in an expensive-looking black suit.

"Oh, there he is. That's Vince DeLuca." Tony points at me and I freeze, feeling a bit of panic rise in my chest.

"Can I help you with something?" I ask, handing Tony the bag. "Mine's in there too. Don't eat both." I give Tony his drink and wait for the man in the suit to respond.

"Can we go somewhere to talk?" he asks, and I shake my head.

"Nope. What you see is what you get." I don't get a good feeling from this guy, and I am not about to take him upstairs to my office.

He reaches into his suit and pulls out an envelope.

I can see it has my name on it, and I feel my stomach tighten. Am I being served or something? Fuck. I rack my brain trying to think of anyone who would want to sue me and come up blank.

"Do you remember a woman named Violet Merryweather?" he asks. He's tapping the envelope on his hand, and I wonder if my answer will make a difference in what he does with the envelope.

"No, but I have a lot of customers. I can look back through the logs. Is she unhappy with her car repairs or something?" I say.

"No, nothing like that." He rubs his hand down his face and sighs. "Do you know someone who would have spelled their name like Violet but insisted on being called—"

"Iolet!" I say, cutting him off.

"Yes!" His shoulders visibly relax, and a smile crosses his lips.

"Oh fuck, I do remember her. I don't think I ever knew her last name though. I used to mow her lawn when I was fourteen! Wow, now that's a blast from the past. Hey, Tony!" I glance over to my friend, who has his lunch spread out across the chair next to him. "Remember Iolet? She lived a few streets over? We'd mow her lawn, you know, that movie star lady?"

Tony looks at me over his sandwich and cocks his head. "No, but I don't have a memory like you. Plus, I only mowed my lawn; that was your hustle. I was the pool guy, remember?" he says, and I nod, smiling. Man, those were fun summers.

"Anyway, Miss Merryweather has passed away, I'm afraid, and she has requested you come to my office. You are listed in her will."

"What the fuck are you talking about?" I say, not believing that shit for even one second.

"Yes, well, she mentioned you in her will, and I am afraid it took me a bit to find you, but I have something for you at my office." He hands me the envelope and his business card.

"As soon as you are able to stop by, it would be most appreciated. This is a time-sensitive matter you see," he says.

No, I don't see. What the hell?

I open the envelope and see a handwritten letter like those Iolet would leave me under her mat.

*Dear Vince,*

*I hope you remember me. I have thought of you often over the years and wonder if you were ever able to make it big in music. I hope so. You have a lovely voice. Anyway, if you are reading this, I am dead.*

*Please go to the lawyer's office and retrieve what I have left for you.*

*All the best,*

*Violet*

Well, hell. I look up to say something to the man in the suit, but he is gone. Tony is busy with his sandwich, like nothing just happened.

"Dude, did you hear any of that?" I ask. I walk over to the area where people who want to wait for their cars sit. I'd call it a waiting room, but it's really just two folding chairs shoved up against the wall.

I motion to Tony to move his lunch so I can sit, and I wait while he gathers his chips and the second half of his sandwich. I sit and lean back, kicking my long legs out. Tony hands me my sandwich and I take it, unwrapping it and breathing in the wonderful smell of bacon.

"Old lady from Palm Springs left you some money?" Tony asks with a full mouth.

"I doubt it. If it was just money, he could have brought it, right?" I tear into my sandwich. Fuck, it's good.

Tony just shrugs.

I look at the business card and see his office isn't that far from here. Today is pretty slow, but we are slammed for the rest of the week.

"Mind if I head over there after I eat? We only have that Ford with the brake job left."

"I can handle it. Plus, if you leave, Mrs. Foster won't be able to hit on you when she comes to pick up her Mustang," Tony says, waggling his eyebrows at me.

I roll my eyes and he laughs, then I say, "I don't think she is flirting with me. She's married to some big NFL player. What would she want with a grease monkey like me?"

Tony shakes his head and laughs. "Slumming? All the rich chicks dig it. You know like that Billy Joel song, 'Uptown Girl.' She just wants out of her white bread world." He shrugs, then adds, "Haven't you seen the music video on MTV?"

"You know I don't watch that shit," I say. My eyebrows are pinched, and I am about to launch into an angry tirade about today's music when Tony holds up his hands in surrender.

"Chill, dude. Hey, I can handle the rest of the day here. Why don't you go see what Miss Moneybags left you?" Tony says.

After I finish my lunch, I change into a clean shirt. My upstairs office also happens to be my small apartment, another reason I didn't want the suit to come up to talk. It works for me, especially since I don't have to pay rent or anything. It's not exactly nice though, not a place I want other people to see. I just keep reminding myself I didn't choose this, and I am doing the right thing.

Driving over to the attorney's office, it is easy to let my mind imagine all kinds of things she could have left me. I tamp down my excitement as I pull open his door. It won't do me any good to get my hopes up. I have a black belt in crushed dreams, so I fight the urge to wonder what if. I expect to see a secretary at a desk, but I am greeted by the man in the suit buried behind a desk full of papers, folders, and boxes.

"Mr. Daniels?" I say to get his attention.

"Oh, Mr. DeLuca, thank you for coming so quickly!" He stands and comes out from behind the desk to shake my hand. "Sorry I ran off. My secretary quit yesterday, and I didn't want to leave the office unattended. I can't find anything in the mess she left me. I think her filing system was the product of too much coffee and not enough education." He waves his hand around the cluttered office and I nod, not sure if that was an insult about the secretary or a joke.

"Sure, I understand," I say coolly, like I totally know what he is talking about. "So, you have something for me?" I shove my hands in my pockets. I don't want to appear too eager, you know?

"Yes, that I know where to find." He pauses and looks around for a minute before saying, "Ah! There it is!" He bends over and grabs a box off the ground. It's taped shut and has an envelope on the top. I see the side of the box says *Box Two of Two* in Iolet's handwriting.

"So, first thing you have to do is open the top envelope. There are instructions in there for what to do next. Please don't contact me until the end. I really have no desire to be a part of this, and when Violet hired me, I asked as few questions as possible, so I wouldn't be of much help anyway." He looks around and over my shoulder, then whispers, "I am not entirely sure this isn't breaking some laws."

"What?" I ask, but he makes a zipping motion with his fingers over his lips before saying, "Just follow the instructions! Have a wonderful day."

"Wait, the box says two of two. Is there another one?" I ask.

"Yes, but that isn't for you. Instructions!" he says while wagging his finger at me. He ushers me to the door, opens it, and I step back out into the warm LA day.

"Right. Okay, well, thanks I guess," I say to the door as it closes in my face. Through the glass I can see that Mr. Daniels has already returned to the mountain left by a secretary that must have hated him.

This is the strangest fucking day.

# THREE
# HEATHER



"HEATHER, can you come to my office please? There is a man waiting to talk to you," Lionel says from behind me. I hate it when he stands behind me. He is such a creep.

"What man?" I ask. When I turn around, I tuck my hair back behind my ear and wipe my brow. The air-conditioning out in the main area of this place is awful. I am sweating like a pig.

"He said his name is Fred something. I don't know anything other than that and that he wants to speak with you," Lionel says. He leans on the wall while I go back to restocking my cart from the supply closet.

"Okay, thanks. I'll be there as soon as I can," I say. I expect he is just going to stand there and stare at my ass, so I stop what I am doing and straighten up. I turn to look at him and, yep, he is just staring.

"Now?" I ask, irritation clear in my voice.

"Well, Heather, as I said, he is in *my* office, and I would very much like to get back to work. If you aren't too busy, *now* would be great." His voice is slimy and condescending, and I hate him with all the cells in my body.

"Okay, lead the way," I say, knowing he is waiting so he can walk behind me.

"Ladies first." He winks.

I make a low growling noise in my throat that I am sure he hears, but at this point I don't even care. Last week was the worst week of my life, and this asshole didn't even have the decency to give me a day off. I mean it's not every day that you walk in on a dead woman. Fucking banana I bought her was still smeared on the bottom of her shoe. With my luck, it's probably the cops come to haul me away for murder.

"Here she is!" Lionel says with a flourish, like he's presenting the queen to her court instead of the cleaning lady to a stranger.

"Miss Fields?" the man in the suit asks. I see he is holding a box that is taped shut with an envelope on the top. The box says *Box One of Two* in handwriting.

"Yes, that's me. Can I help you with something?" I say. I shove my hands into my apron pockets and start fiddling with my keys.

"Wonderful. Lionel, could you give us a minute? This is a private matter," the man says with authority. I fight a smile as Lionel grinds his teeth.

"Of course." Lionel sneers at me as he walks out of his office. The man in the suit puts the box on the desk and walks over to shut the door.

"Hello, Miss Fields. My Name is Fred Daniels, and I am Miss Merryweather's attorney," he says.

Crap.

"She asked me to buy her the banana. I put it on the counter like she asked, then I left the apartment. I swear," I blurt out.

He just cocks his head at me with a puzzled look, then says, "I am not sure what banana you are talking about, but that is not why I am here. You were listed in Miss Merryweather's will. She would like you to have this box, or rather the contents of this box."

"Oh. Well, I see," I say, trying to regain my composure. I am sure there is sweat running down my face, even if Lionel keeps his office like a meat locker. I am surprised there isn't a little tornado outside his door where the warm air hits this icebox.

"I have not located the owner of box two, but I think I might have a lead. Please just read the letter on top and wait for my call," Mr. Daniels says as he hands me the taped box.

"Do I read it now?" I ask, feeling my nerves start to unravel.

"God, no. Please don't. I really don't want to know what it says. In fact, I want to know as little as possible, if you don't mind. Please don't contact me until the end." He nods at me like this is the end of our conversation.

"The end?" I squeak.

"You'll find her instructions in there. Good day, Miss Fields." He pushes past me and opens the door. I hear him talking to the front desk clerk, Mandy. "Can you tell me if there is steak house nearby?"

I tune them out and stare down at the box in my hands. Iolet left me something? Why? I didn't know her at all. I was in her apartment only twice, and I didn't even speak to her the second time. I just gave her that stupid banana and went in to clean her bathroom.

When I went back to clean the next time, I found her. Thank God I had agreed to clean every other day. If it had been a whole week...I shudder. They are pretty good at keeping track of the residents here. I mean if someone skipped three meals in a day, I am sure a staff member would check on them, right?

I am still standing there when Lionel walks back in. "Why are you still here? Don't you have apartments to clean?" he snaps.

"Um, no. I finished, and I need to go do my shopping now, so right, I need to leave and, you know, shop. I will be back." I spin on my heels, box clutched to my chest, and walk out of his office and past the front desk before he can stop me.

The staff don't have reserved parking spots, but today I was able to find a space close by on the street. I hurry to my car and balance the box under my arm while I dig my key out of my pocket. I lean in and set the box on the passenger seat, then climb in and take a deep breath. I don't even know what to think. I glance over at the box and wonder if I should read the letter now. I only live a few blocks away, but I don't know if my roommate will be home. I push the button to warm the glow plugs on my diesel Rabbit, then turn the ignition and pray. This time it starts.

Thank God.

I shift into gear and ease out onto the street. My car is held together with tape, glue, and prayers. Someday I will be able to afford a nicer one, but there are other priorities right now. Mostly rent, then food with whatever I have left over.

I decide to pull into a vacant lot near Serenity Falls and open the letter. I can't stand it anymore. I stare at the box that is labeled *Box One of Two* and wonder how someone's life can be pared down to just two boxes. All I own can fit in a single suitcase, but I am only twenty-two, and I don't need much. I learned to get by with very little, but Violet with the silent *V* had a whole lifetime to accumulate. Is this all that is left of that wild, over-the-top woman? I imagine her apartment before I found her on the floor. That was fucking awful, and I try not to think about her sprawled out, staring with unseeing eyes at her sparkled popcorn ceiling. Mostly I try not to think about how it might have been me who killed her.

Instead, I think about the beautiful furnishings and unusual art and decor sprinkled tastefully throughout the small space. My heart clinches a little with guilt that I didn't know her better, that I actually avoided her at all costs when I saw her in the main rooms.

She was a bright, shiny, loud bundle that I couldn't handle. People flocked to her, sought her out, and tried to be in her orbit. I wish I had not resisted her pull. I wonder if we could have been actual friends. What lessons could she have taught me?

*Dear Heather,*
*Thank you so much for offering to help me.*

WHAT? I did not offer to help her with anything, did I?

*It takes a special woman to take on a task like this, but I know you are up for the challenge.*

*When my attorney finds Vince, I am sure you will have no problem taking care of my wishes. Please wait and open the boxes together. It will make sense, I swear.*

*Remember what I told you about New York, and dear, please be careful. Danger lurks behind every corner.*

*One last thing, please feed Albert, my parakeet.*
*With love,*
*Your friend in heaven (I hope),*
*Violet*

I turn the page over, hoping there is more, but of course there is not. What the hell? I know that man promised her his bird, but he is very much alive in his apartment by the laundry room. As far as I know he still has his bird.

I take a deep breath and read it again. New York? She never said a damn thing about New York! I would remember that. I know I would. Danger?

What the hell is she talking about?

Who the hell is Vince?

FOUR

VINCE

BURBANK, California
Glendale-Pasadena Airport

I FEEL like such a goddamn idiot. I am leaning against my truck holding a stupid box waiting for someone to walk out holding the same box. Mr. Daniels said her name is Heather but didn't feel the need to give me a description.

Her flight arrived twenty minutes ago, and I can't stay in this spot much longer. I blow out an irritated breath and lower my gaze to the box. I have almost opened it a hundred times since Mr. Daniels left it with me. The suspense is killing me. I just want to get this over with, see what the old gal left me. It's hot today, and the smog is laying low, making me feel claustrophobic and agitated. I really want to get back to the shop, finish out my day, and head to the beach.

I look up at the new wave of people pushing through the doors and see a girl about my age looking around. I look down at her hands, and thank all the gods in heaven, she is holding a box like mine. Nice job, Iolet. Very nice indeed.

I smile and lift my box a little, waving at her. She looks down at her box, then at the one I am holding, and I see her shoulders relax a little. She crosses to me quickly, a big, beautiful smile on her face.

"Are you Vince?" she asks. Her voice is soft and sweet.

"Yeah. You Heather?" I say like a fucking idiot. Who else would she be, for Chrissake?

"Yes. Oh my God. I totally worried you were a forty-year-old man with a bald spot. I almost threw up on the plane, and again when I walked out here," she gushes, and I can't help but smile. Damn, she is cute.

"Not a forty-year-old. I am twenty-four. Also, I have nice hair," I say for some stupid reason. Maybe she won't notice I'm wearing a tank top and my work jeans. I've got grease smeared on my arms and probably my face, but when I got the call that her flight was today, I couldn't move things around. We are so busy right now, and this little "adventure" isn't too high on my priority list. I have to keep things moving at the garage, but I agreed to pick her up, so here I am.

"You do have nice hair." She is smiling at me, and I actually feel myself smiling back at her. What the hell? I don't fucking smile at people. Damn, she has big brown eyes, not a stitch of makeup, and her hair doesn't look like the Valley Girls here in LA. She has it in a fancy braid with bangs and some side pieces that must have come loose on her trip here.

"Where did you fly in from?" I ask as I open the door of my truck for her.

"Sacramento. I don't live there though. I live north of there in a town called Chico," she says.

I cringe a little at the name. That's a town I know all too well. What a small world. Of course she is from Chico. The universe hates me and likes to remind me all the time of what I missed out on. I grind my teeth and say, "Oh, I know where that is. A buddy of mine went to Chico State to play ball." I motion for her to climb in, and she does. I don't bother mentioning *I* was supposed to go to Chico State to play ball. That dream died a long time ago. I am about to go around and get in on the driver's side when I notice that she doesn't have any luggage with her.

"Did you not bring luggage?" I ask, leaning in her window.

"Oh, I did. Do they just deliver it? I put Mr. Daniels's address on the tag because I wasn't sure what I was supposed to do," she says, and I fight off a smile by rolling my lips. This fucking girl is too much.

"Um, no. You are supposed to pick it up at the luggage carousel," I explain.

"Baggage claim? Is that what they were talking about?" She blinks and looks like she might cry.

"Yeah. Do you have a bag?" I ask again.

She nods and looks back at the airport. I see tears forming in her eyes, and she says, "I am so stupid. I have never flown before. I didn't know how to do any of it. They let me hold this stupid box because I cried when they tried to take it from me."

"Hey, you aren't stupid. It's okay. What does your bag look like?" I ask, and she explains. She tells me her flight number again, and I run in and find her carousel pretty quickly. Her bag is one of only three left, so I grab it and make my way back to the truck in a slow jog.

"Got it!" I say as I toss it in the bed of my truck.

"Thank you so much. I am sorry. I really haven't traveled much, and by that I mean ever." She laughs, and it's light and sweet and I can't help the corners of my mouth tipping up again. Damn it. I climb into the driver's seat and buckle up. Looking over my left shoulder, I ease out into traffic.

"So, Heather, how did you know Iolet?" I ask as I slow to squeeze behind a bus.

"I work at her senior apartment complex. Well, where she used to live," Heather says.

"Were you close? I am sorry for your loss," I say, but she is shaking her head before I can even finish the sentence.

"No. Listen, this whole thing is just super weird. I, like, didn't know her at all. I mean I cleaned her apartment twice and maybe bought her a banana." She squeezes the box with her hand when she mentions the banana.

"Oh, really? Weird. So not like your favorite resident or anything?" I ask, and she shakes her head again.

"How about you? Did you and Iolet have a good friendship?" she asks. I notice her looking around at the wide freeways and tall buildings. Her eyes are huge as she cranes her neck and ducks down to look out the window of my beat-up Ford truck.

"Well, when I was fourteen I mowed her lawn one summer," I say, then wait.

"And that's how you became friends?" she asks.

"Nope. That is it. I mowed her lawn once a week in the summer of 1974, and now I am the proud owner of a box." I glance over my left shoulder to see if the lane is clear.

"So fucking weird," she says, shaking her head. She then looks over at me. "Sorry, I . . ."

"Don't apologize. It is fucking weird," I say with a laugh. I have been thinking that same exact thing all week.

"Mr. Daniels said she didn't have any children, and she never married. He said she was in some movies and mentioned something about a Vegas show. Do you know anything about her life? When I met her, she was kind of, well, interesting," she says, and I think she is trying to be respectful.

"From what I remember of Iolet, she was a wild card. Some days she and I would talk about things like movies or the Rat Pack, and other times she acted like I was in the way. We didn't get close or anything," I say. I need to get over so I can get to the exit, and the guy in the next lane is being a prick so I slow even more to get behind him. Fucking LA traffic.

"The Rat Pack? What's that?" she asks, and I shake my head.

"Oh, Heather" I say solemnly.

"What?" She laughs.

I push a tape into my stereo and press play. "Fly Me to the Moon" by Frank Sinatra fills the cab of my truck, and I tap my fingers along with the beat. My smile is wide as I turn to her and see her eyes drift closed and a smile form on her beautiful face.

"Oh, I think I have heard this song. My friend Boyd, one of the residents at the place I work, played music in his younger days. He loves jazz, but I know I heard this is his apartment once or twice.

"Oh, jazz is amazing. Don't even get me started on that. Ella Fitzgerald and Billie Holiday? Hands down my favorite," I say excitedly.

"Wait, I know those names!" She twists in her seat and faces me. She puts her hand on my arm, and I feel it straight to my gut. Her fingers are soft and warm, and they curl into my forearm just a little.

"Boyd has pictures in his room of him playing the saxophone with people, and he pointed out one lady in the photo, saying her name was Ella Fitzgerald! Is she famous?" Heather asks.

I bark out a laugh. "Oh yeah, super famous. Who was your friend? What's Boyd's last name? Maybe I have heard of him!"

"Shit, I don't know. I didn't know Iolet's last name either. They all wear name tags, but just with their first names," she says.

"That's okay. I didn't know who Daniels was talking about because he called her Violet," I say, and Heather laughs.

"Yeah, I have never met anyone like her. Was she pretty when she was younger?"

I think back. At fourteen, I am sure I would have noticed if she was like Marilyn Monroe pretty, but nothing is coming to me. I shrug. "I don't know. I think she was alright."

"She looked like a barn owl when I knew her." Heather laughs again and reaches for me. She squeezes my forearm, then says, "She wore a long muumuu every day and a turban, and these black cat-eye glasses that were so thick her eyes looked like bowling balls! I saw her in the dining hall a lot, but she only became my client a week before she passed."

"Client? So what do you do at the senior apartment complex?" I ask. I like her. She is open and nice, so different from the girls here.

"I clean the apartments and some of the main areas. It's a big place. Almost two hundred people live there. I think of it as a land-locked cruise ship," she says with a shrug.

A laugh escapes me before I can stop it. Fuck, she's funny too? "Sounds like you like it there."

"I do." She sighs, then continues, "I need more hours, and that's been hard, but I started doing some shopping for a few of the residents and they pay me directly, so that helps."

She turns toward me and puts her hand on my arm again. Why is she touching me so much? Is this what the girls in Chico are like? Touchy?

"She gave me some money, Vince, and she bought my plane ticket. I don't know what to think about all of this." She bites her lower lip. I need to stop looking over at her or I am going to crash into the back of someone.

"I know. I was surprised by the money too. What did Daniels call it? A stripend?" I ask.

"A stipend," she corrects.

"Right! I had never heard that word before," I say, liking that she didn't make fun of me for not knowing that.

"What do you do, Vince?" Heather asks.

"I am a mechanic. I run my dad's garage over in Hollywood," I explain.

"Hollywood? Like where all the movie stars live?" Her eyes are big, and her hand is back on my arm. My stomach is flipping out of control now. Fuck. I really wish she'd stop doing that.

"Well, mostly they live near there, like in Beverly Hills. There is more to it than the movie industry. It's just a regular town. Can you tell me the address of the hotel you are staying at again? Daniels said it wasn't in Hollywood, but he didn't tell me where it was."

"It is on Daly Street in a town called Lincoln Heights. Do you know where that is? I had no idea where to stay, so I just called a chain motel and asked for Los Angeles," she says as she removes her hand from my arm and places it in her lap.

"Fuck no, you are not staying there," I say, instantly pissed.

"What? Why not?! Vince, I don't have another place to stay." She sounds panicked, and I don't like that one bit.

"Well, you aren't staying in fucking Lincoln Heights. I can't believe Daniels didn't help you." I shake my head and try to think of hotels near me. I merge over to get to the freeway I need to take to get back to the garage.

"Well, I can't just not show up! I used my friend's credit card to rent the room!" She's twisting her hands again, and I hate to see her upset.

"It's okay. We can call them when we get to the shop. You can stay somewhere near me in Hollywood," I say, glancing over at her.

Her eyes get big again, and she shakes her head no. "I can't afford that."

"Heather, it's not all glitz and glam. It's a normal town with cheap motels." As soon as I say that, I picture her in one of the run-down, rat-hole places and shake my head to clear the image.

Damn it.

"Okay, I am sure you know since you live there." She lets out a big sigh and says, "I wish I could have called you before this. It would have been easier. I have never been out of Chico, so I wasn't sure what to expect."

"What? You've never gone anywhere? How is that possible?" I ask, stealing a quick look at her. I want to reach out to touch her like she has been touching me, but it's just not me. Instead I rest my hand on my leg, keeping the other hand on the wheel.

"Wait, that's a lie. I have been to Oroville!" she says brightly.

"Oh yeah? Is that a nice place to visit?" I ask.

"Not at all." She laughs. "It's about a half hour away from Chico, but that is where the county seat is, so when we needed to meet with my mom's parole agent, we would go there."

"Your mom have some trouble with the law?" I ask, trying to keep my voice casual. Who the fuck just says something like that?

"Yeah, she didn't make the best choices when I was in high school. She was only in for about ten months." She shrugs.

Most people would try and hide something like that, but she seems totally at ease about the subject. I don't get this girl at all. What do you say after someone casually says their mom was in jail?

"Do you have brothers or sisters?" I ask, and she shakes her head.

"No, how about you?" she asks.

"Nah, just me. My mom and dad tried to have more, but they learned pretty quickly that I was enough," I say, using the line my mom told people when they asked why I didn't have any siblings. Most Catholics we knew had a lot of children, so it was a sore subject for Mom. Maybe that was one of the reasons she and my dad split, but what do I know? I tried to be enough. That I fucking know. I tried.

"Are you close with your parents?" she asks, and before I can answer I have to slam on the brakes to avoid an idiot on a crotch rocket-type motorcycle. Fuck, I hate those things.

She screams and covers her face with her hands, so I reach over and touch her leg. She's wearing a denim skirt and it's riding high on her thigh. God, her legs are spectacular. Her skin is soft and warm, and I curl my fingers in a little, unable to help myself.

She peeks out between her fingers and looks down at my hand, then up at me. I try and give her an easy smile, but I feel like I swallowed a bunch of butterflies. My hand feels like it weighs a hundred pounds, and I want to move it, but I also never want to move it. I turn my gaze back to the road and slow with the traffic that is coming to a crawl. Not uncommon here; it always bottlenecks, and people like the guy on the motorcycle make it worse.

"You okay?" I ask, patting her leg like an idiot. I finally move my hand off her leg. She probably thinks I am a major creep.

"Um, yeah, did you almost hit that guy?" Her eyes are wide, and she licks her lips. Damn, she is so hot. Not just cute. Hot.

"Nah, he's fine. The traffic just slows down a lot through here, and he probably knew that. He can split the lane and zip around all this, but I have seen them get hit doing that. Not everyone is paying attention," I explain and think, *Like me. I am not paying attention because a distractingly beautiful woman is sitting in my truck.*

"Oh," she says in a small voice. "I don't know how you drive here every day."

"I don't unless I have to go pick up a part or something. I don't have a commute to work or anything."

"You live at your job or something?" She laughs, and I nod.

"Actually, yeah. My dad's garage has a small apartment above the shop, so I am staying there. He had a major heart attack a few years ago and I, um, kind of had to take over." I swallow the bitter feeling and try a smile.

"Oh, man. Is he going to be okay?" she asks, and I shake off my anger enough to answer her.

"Yeah, he's doing better now. Thanks for asking," I say, even though that's not the whole truth. His heart is better, but the stuff that happened after the heart attack still has him all fucked up. I don't mention all that because I just met this girl. No need to take a deep dive into my depressing life.

"That's nice. I hope everything works out. I had to take a leave of absence from work, and I have no idea when I will be back. I have never done anything like this in my whole life. I gave my roommate two months' rent. I hope she doesn't rent out my room while I'm gone." She blows out a breath like she's frustrated.

"She would do that?" I ask. I flip on my blinker and try and move over so I can take the surface streets the rest of the way. It might take a little longer, but I am in no hurry to get out of this truck.

"Maybe. I really don't know, but it took me forever to find a place I can afford. I am sure she's worried I won't come back. That's why I gave her the money. I thought it would make her happy, but now I realize she can still rent it out and have twice the amount. She's kind of a jerk," she says with a little shrug.

We grow silent for a few blocks, and my nerves are starting to get the best of me, so I ask, "Did you peek in the box?"

She answers just like I thought she would. "God no. I have been on edge since I got the damn thing. The letter from Iolet made no sense, and when she talked about danger at every turn—"

I cut her off. "Wait, what danger?"

"I don't know. She was a bit strange. I mean, God rest her soul and all that. I don't want to speak ill of the dead." She pauses and looks around like maybe someone else is in the truck with us.

"She said someone stole her banana, Vince. Like she was convinced of that. Then in the letter she said I had agreed to help her with this matter. I don't know what she was talking about." Heather shakes her head, and a little more of her hair falls free of the braid. She reaches up and tucks it behind her ear, and my fingers itch to do the same.

"Oh man, do you still have the letter?" I ask, curious because mine was pretty run-of-the-mill.

"Yeah." She digs around in her big purse and pulls out a folded piece of paper. She reads what Iolet wrote to her, and I laugh.

"Wow, she really was nuts. What did she tell you about New York?"

"Nothing!" She throws her hands in the air. "I have a really good memory, and I know I would have remembered something like that."

I shake my head and say, "Well, maybe when we open the boxes it will make sense, like she said."

"God, I hope so. Hey, Vince?"

"Yeah?" I glance over at her.

"Thanks for being so cool and stuff. I was really nervous to meet you. I mean this has all been so bizarre, and I gotta admit, I thought you might try and kill me or something," she says with a small smile.

"I promise I won't. I was a little worried too. I thought you might be an old lady friend of hers or something," I say, and she laughs. I was not looking forward to this at all. But now? At least she is easy on the eyes and seems nice.

"So we are about ten minutes from the shop, but I am realizing I don't really have anything to offer you for lunch. Want to stop and get something to eat?" I ask, flipping on my blinker to turn onto the street that leads to my favorite place to eat.

"Um, sure, yeah, as long as it doesn't cost too much. I am on a pretty strict budget," she says with a small smile.

"Nah, we will go to Sammy's. It is a diner, nothing too fancy," I explain.

"Sounds great. I am very hungry. I didn't eat breakfast because we had to leave Chico so early to get to the airport."

I glance at my watch and see it's after one. Shit, I'd be on the floor crying right now if I hadn't eaten yet.

"Well, let's get some food in you." I pull to the curb, grateful for a spot right in front. I know this area is pretty safe, but I still like to see my truck if I am sitting to eat.

I hop out and go around to open her door for her. She moves her box to the floorboards and scoots mine over to put it on top. When she slides out of the truck, I grab her suitcase and put it on her seat before closing the door and locking up.

"Think they will be okay?" she asks, and I nod.

"Yeah, we will sit right there." I point at the big window. "There's a table there, and it looks like it's open. Come on."

I lead her in, holding the door for her, and as she passes by, I pick up her crisp, clean scent. She smells like honey and apples. I wish I had a reason to give her a hug or something. I don't hug people, but I also don't fucking smile, and that seems to be happening a lot today.

I wave at Monica, who is at the register again today, and point to the booth by the window. She smiles and nods, making her way around the counter. I see the moment she realizes I am with a girl, and I want to laugh.

"Hey, Vinnie. Boy, you sure are coming in here a lot lately. Can't get enough of me, huh?" Monica says, smacking her damn gum. She looks at Heather, who is adjusting her purse on her shoulder as she looks around the restaurant.

"Yeah, well, a guy's gotta eat, and it's close to the shop. Plus you have the best food in town." I shrug and motion to the booth for

Heather to see where we are going. She is looking around like she did on the freeway—big, wide eyes and a really fucking pretty smile on her face.

"Gosh, this place is so cool! Look at your uniform! It's so cute. God, you are so lucky to work here!" Heather gushes at her, and I can tell it's genuine. Even if I just met her, I know. She is just a nice person.

"Yeah, sure. So, you want menus or something?" Monica glares at Heather before turning to me with a big smile. Like I didn't just see that. God, she is a bitch.

"Yeah, two menus, and I want a Coke, regular, not diet. Heather, you want a Coke?" I ask.

"No, I'll just have water. Thanks," she says to me and Monica.

Monica spins on her heels and stomps off. I am grateful that Heather didn't seem to notice how rude she was.

"Thanks for bringing me here. So you come here often?" Heather asks.

"Yeah, me and my friend Tony get our lunches here a lot, but usually I get the food to go, and we eat at the shop," I explain.

"Oh, that's nice. There aren't any places to eat by my work, and if I forget a lunch, I am just out of luck. I mean they let us buy meals from the dining hall, but it's kind of expensive," she says.

Monica brings our drinks and two menus, and I see her top button has come undone on her shirt. Probably on purpose. I wonder if Heather noticed, but when I glance over at her, I see her looking at the menu. She starts to chew on her bottom lip as her eyes dart around.

"The sandwiches are really good, but so are the burgers. If you feel like going all out, the root beer floats here are pure heaven," I say as I slide my menu back towards Monica. "I know what I want, but Heather will need a little more time." I hope Monica will leave, but she doesn't.

"Gosh, I am sorry. It all looks so good, but I want to stick to my budget. I'll just have the side salad and maybe a slice of toast?" She closes her menu and smiles up at Monica.

Damn, that's not enough food. I know she is starving, but I don't want to embarrass her or make her uncomfortable.

"I'll get the hamburger and the chicken sandwich. Hey, can I get French fries too? The big size, with maybe some ranch on the side?"

Monica squints at me like she does when I have confused her. I wait, folding my hands on the table in front of me. I press my lips together and let them roll out slowly while I wait for Monica to catch up.

"So, like you want two whole meals? With fries?" she asks as if she is pondering the creation of man.

"Yep. Burger well done please," I say, and Monica pinches the bridge of her nose.

"Do you want the chicken well-done too?" she asks.

I fight off a laugh and nod.

"Okay, coming right up. Hey, you didn't come to the party the other night. I missed you," she says with a pout.

"Yeah, I am pretty busy these days. Parties aren't really my scene anyway." I am trying to be polite but all I can think about is how Heather hasn't eaten yet today and I wish Monica would just leave and put the order in. I glance over to see if there are any cracker packets on the table, but there aren't.

"Well, you better come next time. Jessica and I will make sure you have a good time." She winks and walks away, her ass swaying with each step.

"Boy, you must be really hungry to order all that food!" Heather's laugh sounds like she is nervous or something.

"Well, I am a growing boy, plus whatever I don't eat I am sure you will help me with, right?" I say.

"Oh, I couldn't take your food. It's okay." She gives me that small, sweet smile.

"It's fine, Heather. Let's just see how it goes, but I might bite your finger off if you reach for a fry." I wink at her, unable to help myself.

She giggles, and I know right then, I am in big trouble with this girl because my heart just started beating faster.

FIVE

## HEATHER

GOD, I have never been this hungry in my entire life. That Monica chick was so focused on flirting with Vince, I didn't think she'd ever put our order in. Besides almost dying of hunger, I must say this restaurant is the absolute coolest place I have ever seen. There are pictures on the wall of movie stars and some of them are even signed! I will absolutely drop dead if someone famous walks in. I mean I might die of hunger before anything like that happens, but I am trying to take my mind off the fact that my stomach has started to rumble loudly.

The waitress seems to have more than a little crush on Vince, but I can tell he's not into her. She is really pretty but wears way too much makeup for my taste, and I have no idea how she makes her hair that big. I kind of can't stop staring at it. It reminds me of cotton candy. Big, delicious, fluffy cotton candy that melts in your mouth. I like when you get a little bit that has hardened. The sugar crystals are lumped together like rock candy. God, those were my favorite when I was a kid. The kind that was on a stick, and the wooden stick had a tiny little ball at the end. Jesus, those were awesome.

"You okay?" Vince asks me, and I realize I have drifted off in thought again. It's worse when my blood sugar gets low, and if I am honest right now, I am tempted to eat my own shoe, I am so hungry.

"Oh, yeah, I am fine. Sorry. I do that. I was just thinking." I smile at him, and he smiles back. He is so easy to talk to, and that smile is to die for. I want to see it all the time. He has a freaking dimple, and his teeth are so nice and straight. He's got dark hair that is a little curly, and it's longer in the back than on the sides or top. I want to run my fingers through it, but that is a super weird thing to do to someone you just met, right?

"I was just saying I am going to go wash up. I am covered in grease from work," he says, and I look down at his arms. He is very muscular, and I didn't notice when we were in his truck, but he does have grease on his arm and some on his shirt.

"Okay, sure." I watch him slide out. He has an old, faded pair of 501s on with a worn spot on the back pocket from his wallet. He is wearing a pair of work boots, and the bottoms of his jeans are kind of half up and half down around them. His tank top is tight, and I can't help but notice how nice his body is. Damn, he is way out of my league. Is that what all guys look like around here?

The waitress, Monica, comes over to set our food down and seems disappointed that Vince is gone.

"You his girlfriend or something?" she asks, and I glance down at my salad, wondering if she spit it in.

"Me? Oh no. We just met. We are not dating or anything," I say. I grab my slice of toast and take a huge bite. It's perfect, soft in the middle with glorious butter and crispy on the edges. I close my eyes without meaning to and let out a little moan.

"Hey, you started without me," I hear very close to my ear. It sends a hot spike right through me.

He slides in on my side, nudging me out of the way with his hip. I am about to ask what he's doing when I look up and see a very angry Monica glaring at us.

Oh.

"Sorry, I couldn't wait." I lick the butter off my lips, and I see his eyes dart to my mouth. He puts his arm around the back of the booth and trails his finger on my arm.

"Sure, just met. You could have just told me," Monica says in a huff as she walks away.

"Sorry about that," Vince says sheepishly. "I knew if I tried to scoot past her to get to my side she would try and grab my ass or something. She is kind of a lot. I was nice to her when she first started here, and I think I gave her the wrong impression. Now I can't seem to shake her."

He hasn't moved away, and he is still tracing little circles on my shoulder, which is doing things to my breathing. I am trying to play it cool, like hot guys are always stroking little patterns on my arm. Was that a heart he just drew? A circle? Is he spelling out *where have you been my whole life*? I look past him and see she is leaning against the counter watching us.

"So, I shouldn't have told her we aren't dating? Damn, you could have given me a sign or something! I'd help you out," I say. I am trying to ignore the way my stomach is bottoming out, or how I feel like I can't breathe right.

He leans his head back and closes his eyes. "Did she ask if you were my girlfriend?"

I nod, and he groans.

"Well, damn. I thought maybe I could get rid of her today." He pulls his plate over with one hand, leaving the other one draped over the bench seat behind me.

"Chicken or burger?" he asks, pointing at them.

"What?" I ask. I am still distracted by him being so close. I take a steadying breath and square my shoulders.

"Do I eat the chicken or the burger first?" he asks.

"Um, that burger looks like it was made in heaven, so that is where I would start," I say, forcing myself to act normal. I pull my salad plate over and stab a few pieces of lettuce. There is a hunk of radish and a few strips of carrot. Pretty lame salad, but it was cheap, so that's all that matters.

I see Vince pull the chicken sandwich over to him and he pushes the burger in front of me, nudging the small plate that holds the lettuce masquerading as a salad away.

"Enjoy." He turns his head and gives me a quick peck on the cheek, and I suck a breath in and may even squeak a little.

"Sorry," he whispers in my ear before pulling back.

"Here's your fries." Monica drops the plate on the table, sending French fries everywhere. "And your ranch!" She drops the cup of ranch next to the fries, and I am impressed none splashes out.

I wait for her to get back to the counter where she is helping someone with their to-go order before I say anything.

"'Hell hath no fury like a woman scorned, or something like that," I say quietly.

Vince laughs and finally moves his arm so he can use two hands to eat his sandwich.

"I'm just going to sit here next to you if that's okay. I feel like it would be weird if I got up now," he says, but he's not looking at me.

"It's fine, and I don't want to eat your burger, Vince," I say, but my mouth is literally watering at how good it looks.

"Listen." He puts his sandwich down and wipes his mouth with the napkin. "You have two choices: you can eat the burger or I can feed you the burger. I am pretty sure if we do it that way, they will have to call an ambulance for Monica over there." He nods his head in the direction of the register, but he doesn't take his eyes off me. I peek over his shoulder and catch her death glares aimed directly at me.

"Well, we can't have that, now, can we? Come to momma!" I say, grabbing the burger with both hands. I take a bite, and the flavors explode in my mouth. I haven't had a burger in a long time, and the last one was a sad, little fast-food patty on a bun that had gone stale.

I close my eyes and moan. I feel Vince shift in the seat next to me, but I don't even care. He can scoot over. I was here first. It's like I am all alone in this place, just me and the best fucking burger I have ever eaten. I don't want to be dramatic or anything, but it's like a spotlight just narrowed in on me, making the rest of the room disappear. I am in a one woman play called *Heather and Her Burger*. People are already clapping and hooting for me. I can hear it.

"Oh my God," I say, chewing and swallowing the next huge bite. I know I have sauce all over my face, but I can't stop myself long enough to grab a napkin. One more bite and then I will wipe it off, I swear. I take another huge bite, and this one has the perfect combination of onion, pickle, and tomato. I'd say the only thing missing is cheese, but I would probably have a heart attack right here if it had cheese. That would be too much. Too perfect. The meat is seasoned perfectly, salty the way I like it, and there is some kind of magical sauce covering the whole thing. I want a tub of this sauce. I would bathe in this sauce. This sauce is my new favorite thing. It's my life now.

I groan again and finally set the burger down, realizing there is only maybe one bite left. Well, that's embarrassing. Fuck, I don't even care. I grab the napkin off the table and wipe my face before reaching for the last bite. I stare at it like it's my long-lost friend, then shove it in my mouth.

"Oh my God," I say again, this time a little louder. I close my eyes to chew because I need to concentrate on the flavors that are bouncing around in my mouth. I finish, swallowing my last bit of culinary delight, and look up to see the man in the booth next to ours staring at me. He winks and I scrunch my nose. I look over at Vince and he seems a little uncomfortable. He picks up a napkin and wipes his face.

"Good burger?" he asks in a deep rumble that bounces off my chest like when a car drives by and they have the bass thumping.

"Um, yeah. I haven't had anything that good in my mouth in a long time," I say, leaning back in the booth.

He makes a strangled sound in his throat and shifts in his seat. He looks down at his plate and says, "I am glad you liked it."

"It was so good. Like so fucking good. I am going to dream about that burger tonight." I reach for a fry. I am quick about it since he did threaten to bite me if I stole one.

"Me too," he says, and I look at him for the first time since I inhaled his burger.

"I'm sorry. I should have offered you a bite. That was so rude. I guess I was really hungry." I devoured that thing like my life depended on it, like I had been stranded on an island for years without food. Good grief, I should have offered him some. Crap, that was so rude of me.

He shakes his head and clears his throat. "It's fine. Do you want another one maybe?"

He looks hopeful.

"No, I think I am good. I feel like I'm going to need a nap after eating that!" I say.

"I need a cigarette," the guy in the other booth says, and Vince bristles.

"Hey, watch it. Why don't you mind your own business there, sport," he snaps.

The man holds up his hands like he's surrendering. "Hey, sorry. Next time maybe your girlfriend could not have an orgasm while I am trying to eat my lunch."

Vince goes to stand up, but I grab his arm and pull him back down.

"Don't. Please, it's okay. I am sorry. I didn't mean to make a scene," I say and think about explaining to the man that I was just really fucking hungry, but it probably wouldn't help.

"Don't apologize. That guy is a prick." Vince sits back in his seat, but this time puts his arm around me instead of the bench. He pulls me into him, and I allow it, not sure what else to do.

Thankfully the man gets up and pays his bill, leaving long before we finish our lunch. I don't say much, even though Vince has tried to keep the conversation going with questions about Chico or my flight. He finally gives up and asks, "Hey, you sure you're okay?" I nod and force a smile.

Monica comes by and drops the bill on the table, but I am still so wrapped up in my embarrassment that I don't notice until Vince slides out of the seat to go pay. I scramble out after him and grab my wallet from my purse, but by the time I get to the register he has already paid for lunch.

He walks to the door and pulls it open for me, waiting with that big, handsome smile of his. I feel my shoulders relax a little as I blow out a breath. It's going to be fine. This is fine. I just need to make sure I am never that hungry again. I will put granola bars in my purse or something.

He puts his hand on my back, guiding me to his truck, and I wait for him to unlock it. He leans past me to grab my suitcase, putting it in the back of his truck. I try and act normal when his arm brushes mine. It would be super weird if I held the spot where he touched me to trap the warm feeling I just got, right?

Instead of being a creep, I move the boxes up onto the seat, then climb in and sit. When I look down, I see I have a huge drop of that burger sauce on my white T-shirt. Damn. I love this shirt. It's a plain one, but I like how it's cut, and it has a cute little pocket over the left breast. Now it also has a pink stain. Ugh.

The drive to his shop isn't very long at all, and I have relaxed a lot more, probably because I'm no longer starving. He points out all the shops and tells me gossip about the store owners and what celebrities he has seen on his street. I think he is uncomfortable that I was upset, so I try and shake it all the way off. This poor guy has to pick me up at the airport, rescue my luggage, then deal with me having an orgasmic reaction to a burger. The best fucking burger ever made, but still not the best way to make a first impression.

"Well, here we are! Hugh's Auto Body. Hollywood's best garage." He pulls behind the tall, grey building into a lot with various cars and a motorcycle or two. He kills the engine and hops out, pulling the boxes out with him. He sets them on the hood, then goes to grab my suitcase from the back of the truck. I climb out and offer to take my bag, and he lets me only because he needs to carry the boxes. I get the feeling that Vince is always a gentleman.

"Hey, Tony! I am back but I am heading upstairs. You doing okay?" he yells to a pair of legs under a Lincoln.

A muffled voice comes back. "Yep, all is good here. You pick up that chick?"

"He did!" I say loudly and hear a clank against metal and a curse.

The legs start to slide out from under the car, and they are attached to a tall, very muscular, blonde man. He sits up on the roller and wipes his face with a dirty red rag that was in his pocket.

"Oh, sorry. Hi," he says. I notice he's lowered his voice to sound deeper.

I try not to smile as I say, "It's okay. Hi. I am Heather."

"Hi, Heather. I'm Tony. Nice to meet you. This clown treating you okay?" he says, and I swear his pecs just jumped. I look down at my chest and wonder if I could pull that off. I am so going to try that later.

"He's been very nice. Took me out to lunch and everything," I say with a genuine smile. My belly is so happy to be full. I feel like I could kiss everyone. Can you be drunk off a burger? Full belly drunk? That's me. I kind of want to dance around the shop singing my version of *The Sound of Music*—the hills are alive with the taste of burger—throwing my arms out wide like that chick on the mountain did.

"We went to Sammy's," Vince says. He's leaning the boxes on a simple wood railing that leads up to what must be his apartment. The stairs are made of unstained wood like the rail, and I can see the years of use on each tread.

I take a deep breath in, loving the smell of gas and oil. I don't know why I like it, but I always have. I used to roll down the window when Mom was getting gas just so I could get a big whiff. I think there is probably a health warning against that sort of thing, but you only live once, right?

"Oh, that must have been fun. Monica working?" Tony says with a laugh.

"Yeah, she about had a heart attack when she saw Heather, but hopefully she will back off now. Hey, lock up when you are done, alright?" Vince says.

"Just finished. Thanks for your help with that brake job earlier. I was able to handle everything else," Tony says. He seems to be slightly flexing in my direction. I fight off a laugh by rolling my lips together.

Vince looks around the shop and shakes his head before saying, "Terence come by and help?"

"Fuck," Tony says, then snaps his head to me and says, "Sorry, Heather. Yeah. He was in the neighborhood, and he was bored. I'm heading over to his place now."

"Okay, but watch yourself, man. Don't get into any trouble. You know your ex might stop by," Vince says, and even though I don't know him, I can hear concern in his voice.

"I know." Tony straightens up and stretches his arms above his head. and I marvel at his size; he is a big boy. Like over six foot easily, and his arms are like tree trunks.

"Well, call if you need me, but hey, Tony?" Vince says.

"Yeah?" Tony answers, stepping toward us. He tucks the rag he was holding in his back pocket.

"Don't need me," Vince says.

Tony rolls his eyes at Vince and walks over to us. He takes my suitcase from me without asking, and they both walk up the stairs. I have no choice but to follow.

# SIX
# VINCE

HOLLYWOOD, California
Hugh's Auto Body

I DON'T KNOW why I am so nervous. She's just a chick, and it's not like she's some rich Valley Girl who is going to look down her nose at me. I just wish I had a nicer place. I also wish this wasn't my fucking life, but now is not the time to dig into that. I balance the boxes while I fish out my key, and I smile when I hear her ask Tony if he works out. That just made his whole day, I'm sure.

I get the door open and walk in, setting the boxes down on the little table. My apartment is two and a half rooms. The main room is a living room-kitchen combo, then a small room where I have my bed. There is a bathroom, but it's tiny, just a shower stall and toilet with a little sink. There is also a closet with a washer and dryer, so I don't have to wash all the shop towels and my clothes over at the laundromat. My dad didn't plan on anyone living here, but when he and Mom split, this was his only option. The few times I came to stay I slept on the couch, and it wasn't bad. I guess I am lucky that they split when I was in high school. I don't think I could have dealt with it when I was little. The summer I met Iolet I was able to get out of staying here because I had a job. That was something my mom and dad really pushed, so it made things easier. Once school started back up though, I had to spend some weekends here. Dad and I got along fine, it was just weird.

I turn around to find Tony flexing for Heather, and I roll my eyes. I say, "Fuck, dude. She doesn't want to squeeze your bicep. Save that for the girls at the beach."

Tony shrugs and waves goodbye, heading back down the stairs, calling out, "Sorry, Heather. I gotta get back to work. My boss is a real dick."

"Fuck off," I yell, then I shut the door. I move her suitcase over a bit so she can step all the way in, then watch her as she scans the room. Her eyes are huge as she takes in the space. I follow her gaze to the walls that are painted a slate grey like the outside of the building. I have a few pictures of muscle cars hung up on the walls. The table where I put the boxes is from my mom's place. It was the only piece of furniture I had to bring. I don't know how my dad ate meals without one. I like this table. It holds a lot of memories of me and my friends playing games and drinking things we weren't supposed to. It's a small wooden table that needs to be refinished, and the top is scuffed and stained, but I wouldn't change it for anything. I watch her eyes travel to my couch and coffee table, and I shift on my feet nervously. I wish she would say something.

"You live here all by yourself?" she finally asks, and I nod.

"It isn't much, but I don't have to pay rent or anything, like I mentioned, so that helps." I shrug and stuff my hands into my pockets. I haven't brought a girl up here in a long time, and it feels weird to have someone other than my friends see my personal space. Hell, even Tony and Terrence don't spend a lot of time here. It's really just for me.

"Gosh, you are so lucky. This place is so nice, Vince! My apartment back in Chico is only a little bigger than this, but I share it with someone. My bedroom is supposed to be an office. There isn't a closet, that's how you can tell," she says, tapping her finger to her temple. "I'm smart like that." She laughs, and I can't help but smile.

"You don't have a closet? Where do you keep your clothes?" I ask.

"In there." She points to her suitcase, and I look at the luggage she brought with her, then back to her to see if she's joking.

"Made packing for the trip easy!" She smiles and glances over at the boxes.

"Can we sit on your couch and open those, please? I think I might die if we don't do it soon." She takes a tentative step toward me.

"Yeah, for sure. Sorry, come on in." I move out of the way and watch as she walks over to the brown plaid couch that has been in here for years. I honestly don't know how my dad got that thing up here, but it's comfortable as fuck, so who cares.

She sits and sinks into the worn couch and sighs. "Oh, this is nice. Do you ever just fall asleep out here? I bet you do. This is a nap trap."

I watch as she rubs the couch cushion with her hand like she's petting a dog. Her fingers are long and dainty, but I notice she doesn't have fake nails like a lot of the girls here.

"I have a time or two." I grab both boxes and set them on the coffee table, realizing too late that I have a *Playboy* sitting out. Crap. I grab it and stuff it under the couch, praying she didn't notice.

"Okay, so should we open the envelope on top first?" I ask. Under the first envelope there was another taped more firmly to the box.

"Yes. I think that is what Mr. Daniels said to do. Oh God, I am so nervous. I feel kind of sick." She pauses, then covers her face with her hands. "What if it's something awful, like body parts?"

I laugh loudly. "Body parts? You think Iolet was a murderer?"

"She asked me to get blood out of her carpet the first time I was in her apartment! I don't know what she got up to!" she says, throwing her hands in the air. That little gesture of hers is just about the cutest thing I have ever seen.

"Let's just start with the envelopes and we will go from there," I suggest.

"Okay, you first," she says and puts her hand on my arm again. God, what is it about her? These little touches are driving me crazy.

"Alright, here we go." I pull the envelope off the box and open it, taking my time to unfold what appears to be a list.

"It's a list of old movies," I say, a little confused.

"What? Really?" She leans over to look, and I am ashamed to say I sniff her hair. Fuck, she smells good, like apples and honey, or cantaloupe maybe?

"I wonder what mine says." She pulls her envelope off and tears into it, revealing another list.

"I don't recognize these titles. Are they movies too?"

I scoot closer to her even though I could have seen it from where I was. Reading down the list, I scratch my jaw. How odd. Some of them sound familiar but not all of them.

"Maybe those are plays? I know she said she did film and theater," I say.

"Oh! Maybe. So these could be the plays or movies she was in?" she asks, and I look back at my list.

Wow. If that is true, Iolet was in some big movies.

"I bet that's it. Man, she was in *Casablanca*? Fuck, that's a great movie. I don't remember seeing her in it though, but I haven't watched it in a while," I say.

"I have never seen it." She leans over and presses her chest into me as she scans my list. The end of her braid is tickling my arm, and I don't want to move, ever. How fucking weird am I?

"*Gone with the Wind, It's a Wonderful Life, The Maltese Falcon, Breakfast at Tiffany's, Gentlemen Prefer Blondes.* Wow, you think she was in all of those?" she asks and looks up at me with those big, brown eyes. I want to brush the hair out of her face. I want to lean in and kiss her lush, full lips. I want to press my chest against hers as I claim her mouth, then slide my hand up...Wait, did she ask me a question?

"Huh?" I say like a complete idiot as I tear my gaze off her mouth.

"Do you think she was in all those movies?" she asks again, but I think she knows I was checking her out because she smiles and looks down. I catch a bit of pink rising on her cheeks.

"Yeah, probably. I mean we all knew her as one of the movie stars in the neighborhood. I never thought to ask her what she movies she was in when I was a kid." I tear my eyes off her and look at my list again.

"She talked about being a star all the time in the dining hall. A few other guests fell all over themselves to sit with her. Maybe she was famous with her generation?" Heather says.

"Let me see your list again." I hold out my hand. She passes it to me and leans in again to read over my shoulder. I wish she wouldn't do that. I can't think.

"*Notorious*," I say, tapping my chin. That is one I have never seen. I'll have to ask Henry about that one. I glance down and read the next line.

"Holy shit!" I yell as I scoot forward on the couch a little.

"What? What is it?"

"*The Copa Room*. That's not a play, that's a place," I say, feeling a little like the room has been tipped on its end.

"Where is the Copa Room?" she asks, scooting forward with me.

"In Vegas. It's where the Rat Pack played in the fifties. Oh my God, was she there on stage with him?" I say, not really expecting an answer.

"Iolet sang?" Heather asks with a cute little scrunch to her nose.

"Not that I know of. She had kind of a nasally speaking voice from what I remember."

"What about the other ones?" Heather asks, tapping the list.

"Well, *Harvey* was also a play and a movie. I know that one. *I'll Be Seeing You* was a movie. Then there is *Gone with the Wind*. I know that was for sure a movie. I haven't ever heard of this one, so it might be a play." I point to the last title on the list, and she leans in to look again. I hand it to her and stand up. I can't be that close to her anymore. This is all too much.

"This? *Killed Before My Time?*" She looks up at me and I nod. I think I just licked my lips like a fucking creep.

"So, I don't get it. What's in the boxes that would be dangerous?" Heather says. She has moved her box into her lap, and I pull it together by doing some deep breathing, then sit back down and do the same with my box.

"Only one way to find out." I take my knife out of my front pocket and slice through the tape on both of our boxes, then fold it back up before putting it on the coffee table.

She opens her box and peers in. I glance at her, then do the same. Huh.

"I still don't get it," Heather says, pulling out a bell. She rings it and sets it on the table. Then she pulls out a pair of men's shoes and looks at them closer. She shudders and drops them back into the box.

"Nope. No. Not going to look in there anymore," she says. She has pushed herself back into the couch, and I glance at the shoes. They are a nice pair of wingtips with what appears to be a drop of blood on one.

"You okay?" I ask, and she shakes her head no.

"Is it that?" I point at the dried red spot on the top of the left shoe. "Might just be stage blood or something." I reach for the shoes. Man, these are like a size thirteen.

"Those were in her apartment the day I went to see about cleaning for her. They were under the side table, and I thought she had company, you know, like a man friend paying her a visit," Heather says.

"Oh! Ew, gross. That happens there?" I ask.

"I told you, it's like a landlocked cruise ship. Those old people are living out their dreams and my nightmares," she says.

"Interesting. Please never speak about that again. I want to be able to sleep at night," I say, and she laughs.

"Want to keep going, or should I pull something out of my box?" I ask.

"You go," she says with a sigh.

I reach in and pull out a man's gold pinky ring. It has a black, flat stone, and the sides are kind of etched or carved. I pick up something that looks like a chicken foot. I look closer at it and almost smell it for some ungodly reason, but then I drop it back in the box before Heather can see it. It *is* a fucking chicken foot, I am sure of it. What the hell? I nudge it aside and pick up two small boxes, each labeled with a number. I turn one of them over and see an address card taped to the back. I open the box marked with a one and find a key that says A22.

"This is for a storage shed, and I bet the other one is too."

"So your box has a key to a storage unit, another small box, and a ring?" she asks.

"Yeah, that's it. Let's look in yours again," I say, not wanting to freak her out with the chicken foot.

"You go right ahead. If there is a banana in there I am flying back home tonight!" she says, crossing her arms over her chest.

What is it with this girl and bananas?

"Okay, so you have a bell, a pair of men's shoes..." I pause and pull out a pair of long, pink gloves. "And these." I hold them up.

"Looks like a pair of women's gloves." She reaches for them and smiles. "Oh, these are nice! Do you think she wants us to keep these things?" She slides one of the gloves on and it goes all the way past her elbow.

"I guess." I look over the lists again and then at the stuff. I don't really know. I do know I'll be throwing that dried chicken foot in the trash the first chance I get.

"Maybe we could look this stuff up at the library or something?" she says with a shrug. She is still wearing the glove, and she looks so cute. She has on dirty white Keds with no socks, a denim skirt, and a stained T-shirt, topped off with a long, satin, pink glove. Damn, she can totally work that look. She could start a trend down here, I am sure of it.

I am just about to say something to her about how cute she looks when she takes the glove off. She reaches for the other one, then puts them both back in the box.

"Should we call Mr. Daniels?" Heather asks.

"No, he said not to call until the end. I don't think this is what he meant." I wave to the boxes. "I don't think we are done."

"Well, I don't understand what we are supposed to do with all this stuff. Are these things from the movies or something?" she asks, and it hits me.

The bell. Of course. *It's a Wonderful Life.* Every time a bell rings, an angel gets its wings!

"Heather, you are so smart. That's it!" I grab the bell and ring it, smiling. "An angel just got its wings." She laughs, and it's prettier than any bell.

"Vince, what are you talking about?" she asks.

"The movie *It's a Wonderful Life.* In the movie, they talk about how when you hear a bell ring, that means an angel got its wings. This bell must be from that movie!" I say excitedly.

"Oh my God! Well, that's kind of cool!" She takes the bell and rings it, grinning like a little kid.

"These must be props from the films and plays and stuff that she was in!" Heather says, and I have to agree. But now what? I look in my box again and feel around in case I missed something. I slide the chicken foot to the corner and grab the other small box. It's like one you would use to hold jewelry, like a necklace, but when I open it, inside is what looks like a house key and a folded-up piece of paper.

Heather sees me unfolding something and leans over again.

"What's that say?" She points at the note. "Is that another key?"

"Yeah, the note just says, 'GTB, start here,' and nothing else." I turn over the paper to make sure I haven't missed anything.

"What? What does that mean?" she asks.

"No idea, but I guess we need to start at this address." I hold out the paper to her, pointing at the address in case she thought I was making it up.

"Is it another storage place?"

"No, I know this address. This is an old movie theater over in West Hollywood. They show all the classics, like the movies Iolet was in." I scratch my jaw and say, "I guess we should go."

"Can we? Like right now?" Heather jumps up and claps her hands like a little kid. "Wait, can I change? I have a stain on this shirt."

"Sure, you can take your suitcase in my room there," I say, then freeze. "Wait, let me just check to see if it's clean. I wasn't expecting to bring you back here," I say, and she winks.

"Is that why there was a *Playboy* on the coffee table?" she asks.

"Damn. You saw that, huh?" I cringe.

"It's okay. I get it. Those girls are really pretty," Heather says, and I know not one of them is as beautiful as she is. Probably shouldn't say that to her yet. Maybe someday. I scratch my jaw again and try to focus.

"Yeah, well they also have really good articles," I say with a smile.

"Sure, yeah. I have heard that before, Vince." She rolls her eyes and walks toward her suitcase. I really hope she was exaggerating when she said that bag is where she keeps all her clothes. Is that all she has? Man, I thought I was poor.

I dart into my room and pull up my comforter, then fluff the pillows for the first time in my life. I look around frantically and see more than one pair of underwear on the floor. Jesus, what is wrong with me? I grab the underwear, tossing it in the hamper next to my dresser. I notice the dresser top is kind of dusty, so I try and use my hand to wipe it off, which of course doesn't work. I spot the underwear from the hamper and swipe them across the top. It's not perfect, but not much I can do now. I sigh and toss the underwear back in. Maybe she won't care.

"All clear," I say, casual as fuck, like I didn't just dust with dirty underwear.

"Thanks, Vince. I really appreciate this," she says with a smile.

I nod. While she is changing, I look down at what I am wearing and groan. Why didn't I change when I was in there?

Heather comes back out wearing a pair of faded jean shorts and a baggy T-shirt. It's a light yellow color faded from years of use. It looks so soft, I wish I could touch it. Hell, I wish I could touch her, if I am being totally honest. The color makes her skin look even more tan.

"I'm ready! I hope it's okay I put my T-shirt in your bathroom sink to soak, and I used a bit of your shaving cream on the stain," she says, seemingly unaware that my eyes just traveled all over her beautiful body.

"Oh, sure. That works?" I clear my throat and try to focus.

"It can. Not always, but a girl can dream. That was my favorite shirt, so I really hope that stain comes out." She glances back at my room.

"I'm sure it will be fine. Hey, do you want to call that hotel now or when we get back?" I ask.

"Oh! God, I totally forgot about that. Can I call now?" she says.

"Sure." I point to the phone on the end table and duck back into my room to change. I pull off my tank top and give my pits a sniff. I wish I had time to shower, but this isn't a date or anything, right? I pull on a clean black T-shirt and spray some cologne. I walk back out just as she is finishing up.

"Okay, well, thanks for understanding. So you won't charge the card? Okay, yeah. Gosh, Mr. Lind, I really appreciate your help. I hope everything works out with your knee. Yeah, next time I will stay with you for sure. Thanks again." She hangs up and looks up at me.

"Get it all sorted out?" I ask, wondering how long I was in my room. She seemed to have formed a friendship with the guy on the phone.

"Yeah, Mr. Lind was super understanding. I think I would have been fine to stay there, but I understand you know the area better than me," Heather says.

"Yeah. Maybe it's in a good pocket, but that area is gangland. I don't want you there," I say, feeling stupidly protective over this girl I literally met only a few hours ago.

"Okay. You have to help me find a place when we get back!" she says with that big smile of hers.

"Deal," I say, knowing damn well I will be making her stay here. She is too nice for this area, too trusting.

I lead her back downstairs and through the shop. Tony hasn't left yet, so I lean under the car he's working on.

"Hey, still not done? I thought you were headed to see your buddy," I say.

"Decided I didn't want to chance seeing her. I'm getting a head start on tomorrow. That's better, right?" He slides out and stands to his full height of six foot two.

"You okay?" I ask. I glance over my shoulder and see Heather waiting by the door.

"Yeah, I'll be fine. It's no big deal. One day at a time, right?" he says, pulling on his shirt like he does when he's upset.

"Right," I say and yank him into a hug. Well, a manly side hug with some aggressive back patting.

"You kids heading out?" Tony asks when he sees Heather by the door.

"Yeah, we need to head over to West Hollywood. You know that old theater over on Hawthorn?" I say, knowing he will give me shit.

"The one that only plays old movies? Fuck, dude, you need to work on your dating game. She doesn't want to see that crap. You are the only one that thinks the forties and fifties were cool, man." He chuckles, and if he wasn't in such a dark place I'd push back. Instead I just shrug and smile.

"See you around," I say, heading for the door.

"You working tomorrow? We have that Corvette to figure out. I am not going to attempt that on my own," Tony yells after me.

I freeze in my tracks and run my hand through my hair. "Fuck, I forgot about that. Yeah, of course. I'll be down early, like seven?"

"I'll be here." Tony leans over and waves at Heather, flexing his huge arm at her. I roll my eyes.

# SEVEN
# HEATHER

HOLLYWOOD, California
Past Times Theater


WE CLIMB into Vince's truck again and I try not to take a deep breath. He must have sprayed on cologne because he smells like heaven. I wish I could curl up in his neck and breathe his air. Wow, that sounds creepy even in my own head. I need to get a grip. This guy is way out of my league. I am here to do a job and that is it. A weird job, but a job nonetheless.

It doesn't take long to get to the theater, and he parks a few blocks away, maneuvering his truck like a pro in a spot where I wouldn't have tried to park my Rabbit. I go to climb out and Vince is already at my door, holding it open. I smile at him, and I swear I see him blush. How cute is that?

We make it to the front of the building where the movie theater is, and I feel my heart drop. It looks like it's closed.

Vince reaches for the door that is covered in newspapers and cardboard and pulls it open easily.

"After you." He motions with his hand, and I walk through the door, expecting a run-down place. The wonderful smell of buttery popcorn hits me, and I wait for my eyes to adjust to the dim lighting. Rich red velvet curtains cover the walls, and the flooring is an intricate pattern of gold and white tiles. In the center of the room is a small ticket booth that appears to be empty. I glance around at the movie posters that hang from the ceiling and rest against the velvet. They aren't in plastic frames like the movie theater back home. No, these are framed like works of art.

"Oh my God. This place is so cool," I say, and Vince beams.

"It's my favorite place to see movies. Come on." He grabs my hand, pulling me toward the booth. His hand is rough and calloused but so big it swallows mine.

"Henry? You in there?" Vince says as he raps on the counter with his knuckles. He drops my hand, and I wish he hadn't. It was too brief.

I see a bald, liver-spotted head slowly appear and expect it to keep rising to reveal a face, but it never does.

"Vince, how are you doing, young man?" a tiny, creaky voice says.

"I'm good. Hey, I brought my friend with me and—"

Henry cuts him off. "Is it a girl?"

Vince laughs. "Yeah."

"Hold on!" The top of Henry's head disappears, and I hear things being moved around. Suddenly a mop of black hair reappears in the window and then, with a few clicks of a chair, a face rises up to eye level.

"Hello, young lady. It is a pleasure to see you. Vince doesn't bring girls here, so you must be pretty special," Henry says with a wink. Now it is my turn to blush, and I scramble to explain but Vince jumps in.

"Hey, Henry. Listen, we are kind of on a mission. A mutual friend of ours has passed away and she left us some things." Vince pauses and pulls out the key and the note that reads "GTB start here." He hands it to Henry, who turns the key over in his hands a few times, then studies the note. He lets out a big sigh and hands them back.

"She finally met her maker? Sorry to hear that. I think part of me thought she would live on forever once she left her heartbreak behind. I didn't know you knew that crazy old bird," Henry says with a sad smile.

"You knew Iolet?" I ask, unable to contain my surprise.

"Oh, sure. She was old Hollywood through and through. Lots of fun, and a little nuts." Henry pinches his fingers together to illustrate. A sad smile flickers across his wrinkled face.

Vince shuffles his feet. Maybe he is as uncomfortable as I am. He clears his throat and says, "We both only knew her for a short time, but she wanted us to come here. Any idea why?"

Henry nods. "Yep. Good thing I outlived her, I guess, since I am the only one who knows about this. Give me a second." I watch as his little head disappears again, and then a door swings open and he steps out, rising to his full height of five foot two. He is dressed impeccably in a three-piece suit, wing tip shoes, and—oh my God, I might die—a pocket watch chain is visible in his vest pocket. What a dapper man. Everything about him screams style. Well, except for the sad jet-black toupee perched on his head like a dead cat.

He reaches for my hand and I give it to him, delighted when he bends slightly and kisses my knuckles. He pushes the toupee back just as it slips down to his eyebrows.

"It is a pleasure to meet you . . ." He pauses, waiting for my name, so I tell him.

"Miss Fields," he says, bowing again. He stands up and tugs on his vest. "Follow me." He walks off down the hallway, and Vince and I follow.

He turns at what appears to be a wall of curtains and pulls back a panel of fabric, revealing an archway to another hall. He holds the curtain back and motions for us to step through, then takes the lead again. This hallway is filled with doors and appears much more utilitarian than the lobby.

"Here we are." Henry stops at a door that has a sign that says, "Caution: Poison."

"I need to get back to the front. Have fun." Henry bows again and takes off back down the hall, disappearing through the curtain. I hope Vince was paying attention, because I am sure we are lost in here forever.

"So the key fits a closet full of poison? This must be the danger she was talking about," I say to Vince, only slightly joking.

"Maybe. Let's find out." He puts the key in the lock and turns it. The door is a little stuck, like it hasn't been opened in years, so he has to push hard. We both peer into the dark space. "I didn't think to bring a flashlight," he says as he squints into the dark room.

I reach in and feel by the door, thankful when my hand hits a switch. I flip it up and we hear a buzz, then a light bulb struggles to life above us.

Holy hell.

"Shit," Vince mutters.

"What is this?" I ask.

"I am not sure. Costumes? Maybe stuff she wore in movies she was in?" Vince steps in and cranes his head to look up at the shelf above jam-packed with racks of clothes. There are hatboxes and shoeboxes all labeled with size and color. The clothes range from simple white shirts to colorful sequined gowns. There are men's clothes too, suits and pullover wool sweaters, even long trench coats.

It smells faintly like mothballs, but as I run my hand across the sequined gown on my right, I get a whiff of old cigarettes and rosewater perfume. It smells like the people at Serenity Falls.

"I bet these were clothes from the movies she was in. Do actors get to keep their costumes after a movie?" I ask Vince. He has pulled a suit from the rack and is admiring it.

"I don't think so. I think maybe she stole these things, like the stuff in the boxes. I think our friend Iolet was a bit of a kleptomaniac." He sighs and puts the suit back on the rack.

"Come on, let's go talk to Henry." He grabs my hand again and pulls me out of the storage closet. He flips the light off, then closes the door and locks it back up, slipping the key into his jeans pocket.

I follow along behind him, loving how his hand feels in mine, and wonder why he's not let go. I am not going to overthink it if this guy wants to hold my hand—he can have it—but I do wonder.

"Henry?" Vince calls as we step back out into the lobby.

"Yes? Vince, is that you?" the voice from the booth calls.

"Yeah, man. We are done back there. Do you have any insight for us?" Vince leans on the small counter and peers into the booth where Henry sits.

"Sure, I might I have some insight. As much as anyone can when dealing with Iolet Merryweather. I am just guessing, Vince, but I think she wants you to watch *Casablanca.* It was her favorite film. She's in the bar scene. See if you can spot her." Henry chuckles, then raises his chair up a few clicks again so we can see him.

"It's in theater two, down on the left. I'll start it in a minute. Do you want popcorn and drinks? I think Krystal is back at the concession stand, although she might not be. I can't keep up with her crazy schedule."

"I'll handle it, Henry. Thanks." I watch as Vince slides a twenty-dollar bill through the little window. "Ready?" he asks me.

"Yes! But, Vince, you can't keep paying for things," I say.

"Sure I can." He squeezes my hand like that is the end of the conversation. We walk down the hall, and he stops at the vacant concession stand. Dropping my hand again, I watch as he steps behind the counter and opens the popcorn machine. He expertly fills two large bags. He hands them to me, then gets out two cups. "Coke okay?"

"Sure!"

He reaches in a cooler and scoops ice, then fills the cups with the tap from the soda machine. He carries the drinks, so I follow him with the popcorn, dipping my head to breathe in the buttery goodness. There is a part in the curtains, and he motions with his head for me to step in.

A small room with no more than fifty seats opens up before me. The lights are all on, but dim. I can see the deep-blue velvet seats and the matching curtain hiding the movie screen. The railing is shiny, like it gets polished daily, and the room is spotless. It smells like popcorn and cigar smoke and time. I'm not sure how it's possible, but it smells the same as Boyd's apartment. It makes me feel safe and welcome. I breathe in deeply and smile to myself. This place is amazing.

Vince steps up behind me and, very close to my ear, says, "Looks like we can take our pick of seats."

A chill runs through me, and I feel my pulse rise at how close he is. He hasn't moved yet, and I find it difficult to speak, but I manage to say, "Wherever you recommend."

Vince steps to my side and moves down to the second row until he is in the center. I follow him and sit, delighting in how comfortable the chairs are.

We juggle the drinks and popcorn until we both have one of each. In a heart-stopping moment, I almost pour the entire Coke right on Vince's lap. Once we are settled, we stare at the curtain, and I start to feel nervous for the first time since meeting him.

"So, we just wait?" I ask, looking over at him.

Vince tosses a piece of popcorn in his mouth and smiles. "Yeah, Henry will start the film in a bit."

"You come here often?" I ask, remembering what Henry said about Vince never bringing a girl here. I shouldn't care about that, but my heart doesn't understand logic, and it makes me unreasonably happy.

"Yeah, a couple times a month. More often if I hear they are playing one I haven't seen. I really like the classics. My mom says I was born in the wrong time. I guess she might be right." He gives a cute little one shoulder shrug.

"I don't go to the movies ever, and I don't think I have seen an old movie. Wait, that's not true. I have seen *Miracle on 34th Street* on television at a slumber party I went to in the sixth grade, so it's been a while."

"Oh, man, these movies are great. They rely more on plot than the films today. I swear now everything is about the special effects and blowing things up." He shakes his head, then continues, "These actors and actresses are so good at the subtle, you know?"

"I don't, but since you are so excited about it, I can't wait to see it," I say, and a smile dances in his eyes. God, he is cute.

The lights dim even further, and the room falls into complete darkness. Vince shifts in his chair next to me, and I swear he moves his head closer to mine. I freeze and breathe in slowly, letting the butterflies take flight in my stomach. I will never be able to prove this, but if I was brave just now and turned my head slightly, I am sure my lips would collide with his. God, what it would be like to kiss him. He has these full lips that look so soft, and he smells so good. My whole body feels hot, and I take another deep breath this time, trying to calm down.

The curtain opens, and the music starts as the room fills with light from the screen. I turn to look at Vince and he is studying me. His eyes dart to my lips, then he leans in and whispers, "I hope you like it."

I swallow hard, unable to take another breath. "Like what?" I ask, staring at his mouth, those lush, wonderful lips. His tongue peeks out and rolls across his bottom lip.

"The movie, Heather. I hope you like the movie," he says, moving a little closer to me.

I hold my breath, unsure what to do or say because my brain has stopped working. There is just a steady buzz humming through my veins. I am aware of my chest rising and falling, and I see him glance down and watch as I struggle to get air. He winks at me and flashes that smile before moving back out of my space. I am both sad and grateful to have my air back.

EIGHT

VINCE

HOLLYWOOD, California
Past Times Theater

I KNOW I SHOULDN'T, but once I realize the effect I have on her, I can't help myself. I move in close enough to smell her clean, crisp scent. I see her breathing change, her chest rising in the most seductive way. I have to remind myself and my dick that this isn't a date.

The movie starts and I settle in. I have seen this movie probably ten times, but watching it with someone like Heather makes it all feel new again. She is leaning forward a little in her chair, eating her popcorn, completely oblivious to my stares. I love that she is into the movie, that she gasps and laughs at all the right places. As the movie comes to a part where I think we might see Iolet, I reach over and put my hand on her arm.

"Okay, here we go! This is the first scene where there are people in the bar . . . Oh shit!" I gasp. Literally gasp. How have I not noticed Iolet before? "Right there! By the door!" I almost yell. Thankfully we are alone.

We watch Rick walk into the bar, focused on Sam playing that song, and there she is. Iolet is right by the door talking to two men. I have never paid attention to the background characters before, especially not this scene, because it's when Rick first sees her. The slight smile that crosses his lips is my favorite part.

I look away from the screen and at Heather. Her mouth is hanging open, and she looks over at me and smacks me on the arm.

"Oh my GOD! That was totally her! Man, I would have missed it! How did you see her?" she asks.

"Well, I have seen this a lot of times, and I know all the scenes where there is a crowd, but," I pause and shake my head before I continue, "I have missed seeing her every other time I watched it."

"Wow. Just wow," Heather says, with her eyes back on the screen.

We continue to watch the rest of the movie, and I think I catch a glimpse of Iolet in a few other scenes, pointing her out each time. Some of them are just the back of her head or her from the side and very far from the camera. The best part for me is watching every time Humphrey Bogart looks at Ingrid Bergman. I glance over at Heather, trying to read her reaction. I wish I could stop the film and ask her what her thoughts are on each scene.

When the movie is over, the room falls into darkness again, and the house lights come up slowly, allowing us the ability to walk back out safely.

We head straight for the ticket booth to find Henry. He has his chair lifted all the way up but has fallen asleep with his arms folded across his chest. I tap lightly on the counter, causing him to jump a little.

"All finished?" He wipes his hand down his face.

"Yeah, we saw her. That is pretty cool, Henry. I have seen that movie a bunch and never noticed her before," I tell him.

"You'll find that is true for most of Iolet's films," Henry says. "So did she give you a key to a storage unit?"

"Yeah. How do you know about that?" I ask, and I feel Heather step closer to me.

"Well, I know what she did." Henry winks at Heather.

"Do you know what she meant by the initials *GTB*?" Heather asks.

"What do you think it means?" Henry asks, being evasive and annoying.

"Give them back? The props and things? There was a bell, and we think it is from *It's a Wonderful Life*. She wants us to return that?" Heather's voice is a little higher pitched, and I am guessing she is nervous at the prospect of being in possession of all these stolen items. I'm not going to lie, it's kind of making me nervous as well.

"Well, she might have meant that, but maybe not. I wouldn't be so sure that's what it stands for. Listen, Iolet was a good friend of mine back in the day, but the woman was bonkers." Henry leans forward in his chair. "The one thing I can say with certainty is that you can't trust your instincts with this. You'll be wrong at every turn."

"So, we should go to the storage unit?" I ask Henry, feeling very confused.

"Yep, you'll find something from that film in there. Maybe wait a while before you act on anything. Take your time." Henry looks between me and Heather and adds, "It all makes sense if you step back far enough. Think backstage. I mean I can only assume. I really don't know anything. That's what I told the cops all those years ago, and that's what I will tell them again."

Heather and I share a look, and I am about to ask what I can expect to find in the storage unit when a group of tourists comes in through front door and Henry waves me out of the way. "Come back anytime, but keep me out of this."

I grab Heather's hand, leading her to the doors and out into the bright afternoon sun. We are both quiet as we walk back to my truck. I unlock her door and pull it open for her.

"Thanks." She climbs in and pulls the seat belt across her hips. I pause a moment too long, watching her getting settled, and she looks up and catches me. A big smile spreads across her face, and she reaches up and tucks some hair behind her ear.

"That was incredible, Vince. Thanks for taking me here," she says shyly.

"I am glad you liked it." I shut her door gently and make my way around to the driver's side, glancing in as I pass the front of the truck. Fuck, she is so cute. She is rolling her lips and looking down at her lap. I climb in next to her and start the truck up before turning to her.

"Want to go to the storage place now or tomorrow?" I ask, hoping she wants to go now.

"Now! Oh my God, I can't sleep without knowing what's in there!" she says, and I chuckle.

"Awesome. I was hoping you'd say that." I flash her a smile and pull onto Hawthorn, making my way to the storage facility that is only a few miles from my shop.

She seems deep in thought, and I wonder what is going through her head right now. I am just about to ask when she says, "I really paid attention to what you said about the subtle things when I was watching the movie."

"Yeah?" I like that a lot, and my voice sounding so damn hopeful makes it obvious.

"Yeah, like especially when Ingrid's character was at the piano and Sam was playing that song. You could see the memories and pain dance across her face, through her eyes. It was like a whole story unfolding in just those few moments before he comes in." She looks at me thoughtfully and adds, "Thank you."

"You're welcome?" I laugh, then ask, "Why are you thanking me?"

"Because I wouldn't have noticed that. I would have just been focused on what was happening next, you know?"

I feel my heart expand a little and say, "Yeah. I know."

"She has the most beautiful eyes and how they always looked like she was on the verge of tears was just so, oh gosh, I don't know that I can even describe what it did to me." Heather blows out a little breath.

"That's how I felt the first time I saw it," I say, remembering how

I tried to do the math the first time I saw Ingrid Bergman to see if I could ever ask her out. My dad took me to see *Casablanca* when I was about ten. That was back when I thought everything was good in my life. Before I knew what kind of a man he really was. Maybe that's why I like watching that movie. Damn, I wish I had known Iolet was in it when I mowed her lawn. I guess it wouldn't have changed very much, except maybe I would have asked her for her autograph.

Maybe that is why she liked me, because I didn't fawn all over her? Sounds like Heather didn't either. Is that it? Is that why she chose us?

We pull into the lot and drive around for a few minutes before I locate A22. It's a unit in the far back, not up front like I expected and it's big. Hell, Iolet, what did you take?

"Ready?" I ask, looking over at Heather.

"So ready." She climbs out before I can make it around to open her door. I dig the key out of my pocket and fiddle with the lock several times before it finally gives up its secrets and falls to the cement.

I look over at Heather and smile as I grab the bottom of the roll-up door and hoist it up.

Fuck.

That's a fucking car.

Holy shit.

That's the car at the end of the movie!

Oh, Iolet. How?

"Is that a car?" Heather asks from over my shoulder.

"Yeah, not just a car, it's a 1940 Buick Model 81C Phaeton. It's the car they rode to the airport in at the end of the movie. Remember?" I take a deep breath, trying to steady myself.

"Holy shit," Heather breathes.

"Yeah." I step in further to peek in the window.

"So do we just start it up or what?" Heather says, and I chuckle.

"Nah, this has been here for over forty years. I am sure Iolet didn't bleed the lines or disconnect the battery. This isn't going to be driven without some work," I say, and walk back out. I reach up and pull the rolling door shut, sliding the lock back in place.

"Come on. Let's go back to the shop and figure out our next step." I walk over to my truck, opening the door for her.

She climbs back in, and I quickly make my way around to the driver's side.

I am silent on the drive back to my shop because I can't believe that tiny lady was able to steal that fucking car.

# NINE
# HEATHER

<br>

HOLLYWOOD, California
Hugh's Auto Body

<br>

WE WALK INTO THE SHOP, and Vince bends slightly, checking under a car. Looks like his friend finished for the day. He motions for me to follow him, then heads up the stairs to his apartment. I wait while he unlocks the door and smile when he steps aside for me to go in first. He is such a gentleman.

"So do you think it was hard for Rick to lie like that at the end?" I ask.

"Oh, I am sure it was, but he wanted to keep her safe. I think I would have done the same thing," Vince says. He digs his keys and wallet out of his pockets and sets them on the table. He's been pretty quiet since we left the storage place. Maybe he is just worried about how we are going to return a car that won't run.

"Excuse me, I'll be right back. Please make yourself at home." Vince smiles at me, then walks to his room and closes the door. I glance around, taking in his little apartment. It's such a cool place.

None of the furniture matches, including the two chairs by his kitchen table, but it's clean. The dishes that are out are stacked neatly on the drying rack, and the dishrag is folded and draped over the side of the sink. I noticed that when I got here earlier. You can tell a lot about a person by their home, especially when they weren't expecting you.

Oh shit! I glance at the clock. It's a little after six and I still don't have a place to stay tonight! I walk over to the phone and pull out the phone book from the shelf below it. I guess if I look in the Yellow Pages I can just ask them what the price will be. I can also ask if they will take cash since I don't have a credit card.

I take a deep breath and sigh. Flipping the book open, I run through the pages until I get to the motel section. Oh, wow. There are a few that rent by the hour. Gross.

I am so lost in the ads I don't hear Vince come back out, so when he says my name, I jump a little.

"Sorry, didn't mean to startle you. What are you doing?" he asks, sitting next to me at the table.

"I need to find a place to stay. What about this one? It's called the Golden Slipper. That's probably nice, huh?"

"Fuck no. It's not safe, Heather." He shakes his head and scrubs his hand over his jaw.

"Well, shoot. Okay, what about this one?" I point to another ad, and he shakes his head again.

"Damn, what about this one? Wait, no, it says they have a pool. I bet that will make it cost more," I say, fighting off the tears I feel forming.

"Heather, just stay here. I'll sleep on the couch. You can have my room." Vince slides the phone book away from me and closes it.

"I can't ask you to do that!" I say.

"You didn't ask, I offered. I just put clean sheets on my bed. I am totally fine sleeping out here. That couch is just as comfortable as my bed. What did you call it? A nap trap?" he says with that heart-melting smile.

"Yeah, but then at least let me take the couch. I don't think I would feel right about taking your bed," I protest.

"Not a choice." He stands and walks to the fridge. He takes out a package of hamburger and then moves to the cupboard and pulls out a few cans and a bag of pasta. He sets the items on the counter, then pulls out two pots.

"Vince, please. I don't want to kick you out of your bed," I say, trying again to convince him.

He turns and raises his eyebrows at me, then smiles again. "Do you want to share my bed, Heather?" he asks in such a deep voice I feel it in bounce around in my chest. I know I am blushing based on the look on his face.

"That's not what I meant. I just feel bad," I explain, feeling my face turn five more shades of red.

"Please don't. Look, if you are here, I won't have to drive to pick you up or drop you off each day. You'll save money, and I'll have it easier, okay?" he says.

I sigh and say, "That does make sense, I guess. Okay, but maybe we can take turns with the bed?"

"Can we stop talking about my bed?" Vince says with a wink.

I roll my eyes and laugh. "Okay, what are you making? Can I help?" I stand and cross to him.

"Sure. Here, you can cut the onion." He reaches into a basket on the counter and picks a white onion, then opens the fridge and pulls out mushrooms and fresh basil and parsley.

He bends to get out the cutting board, and I am ashamed of myself for gawking at him. Damn, those 501s fit him so good. I step up next to him at the counter and get to work on the onion, and he instructs me to slide it into the hot skillet. We work like this side by side until the pasta with red sauce is done.

"Sorry I don't have French bread or a salad to offer you. If my mom ever asks you, I fed you a full meal, okay?" he says.

"Okay, that is a deal. I doubt I will ever meet your mom, so I feel safe in saying I'll lie for you." I wink at him.

"Ouch. Here I thought we were friends," Vince says.

"Oh, we are. Gosh, I am sorry. I was thinking you meant..." I stop talking because I realize how pathetic I am about to sound.

Vince looks at me puzzled, then I see understanding cross his face. "Oh, you thought I meant like if we were dating and I took you home to meet her?"

I nod, embarrassed.

"Don't want to date me?" Vince asks. He sets his fork down and leans back in his chair, letting a slow smile spread across his face.

"Stop. I am sure you have a girlfriend, or lots of girlfriends," I say nervously. I twist some pasta onto my fork and fight off a moan as the flavor bursts on my tongue. I watched him make this. How in the hell does it taste this good?

"Not currently seeing anyone. How about you? Is there a guy back in Chico waiting for you to get back?" he asks.

I laugh before I can respond. "Um, no. Not a lot of guys beating down my door, Vince."

"Well, Chico is filled with very stupid guys," he says with a little more force than I think he expected. He blushes, then he stands and gets out two wine glasses, then opens a cupboard, pulling out a bottle of red.

"Wine?" he asks nodding toward the bottle.

"Sure." I feel my stomach flip as he smiles again at me. If I didn't know better, I would say this feels like a date. It's not a date. It's not.

He pours us each a glass, then brings it back to the table, setting mine down in front of me. I have had wine exactly never times; I am usually a beer girl. I don't want him to think I am lame though, so I smile.

"It's not the best wine, but at least I remembered I had it. We always have wine with dinner at my mom's." He picks up his glass and tips it toward me, so I grab mine and do the same. He clinks our glasses together and says, "Here's looking at you, kid."

I swoon. I swear to fucking God, right then and there, I swoon. I put my hand on my chest to calm the racing and tip my glass back, taking a sip. I hope he doesn't notice that I just went up in flames.

As I get the first taste of wine on my lips, I expect that I will hate it. To my surprise, I don't. I actually like it. It tastes like cherries and chocolate and something else I can't place.

"Oh, that is very good." I close my eyes and take another sip, allowing the flavors to soak my tongue. When I open my eyes, Vince is staring at me over his wine glass. His eyes are darker than before, and they are focused on me.

"What?" I ask, suddenly feeling very nervous.

"You aren't like the girls around here," he says. He takes a drink of his wine and sets the glass down.

"How are the girls around here?" I think about the waitress at Sammy's Diner and wonder if he means her.

"They are all just so made-up all the time. Big hair, tons of makeup, you know?" he explains.

"Yeah. I mean there are girls like that back home too. I don't have that kind of time or money. If I ever had any extra cash, I sure as hell wouldn't waste it on a tube of lipstick," I say, rolling my eyes.

"What do you spend your extra money on?" he asks.

"Extra money? That's funny. Although, last week when I bought groceries, I did splurge," I say, with a smile.

"Oh yeah?" He leans forward and says, "What'd you get, Heather?"

Oh God. When he says my name, it sends chills up my spine. I smile and take a bigger drink from my wine and say, "Vanilla ice cream. A whole gallon. Not the fake gross kind, but the vanilla bean kind with the little black flecks."

"Oh, fuck yeah. That's good stuff. Do you put anything on it, like chocolate syrup?" he asks, and I see the joy in his eyes.

"No, I am a pure vanilla gal. What's your favorite?" I ask.

"You'll think I am just copying you," he says with a chuckle.

"Vanilla? Really?" I laugh. "No one ever likes that. I get told all the time how boring I am because that's my favorite. My friend in high school said it wasn't even a flavor but a base for other things."

"You have terrible friends," he says, shaking his head.

"So what are we going to do about the car, Vince?" I ask, because I want to return the focus to why I came here. It would be so easy to get my hopes up with this guy, continue talking like this and pretend. That pretending is something my heart can't take. That is just not my life. I know my place.

"Well, I have a flatbed tow truck out in the back lot. I think if we just tarp it really good and bring it here to the shop, I can fix it. Then we have to return it to the studio, I guess. I don't know who she stole it from, but they probably would want it back," he says.

"Right. Do you know where that studio is?" I ask.

Vince shrugs. "Probably. Most movies in the era were filmed at the Warner Brothers studio over in Burbank. But we can check it out to be sure. The local library here has a great section on all things old Hollywood. I bet we can look it up."

"Okay, I am about to say something that may make you judge me," I say, taking another sip of my wine. I feel warm all over, and I don't know if it's from the wine or him.

"Never. I don't judge," Vince says. He finishes his wine with a tip of his head.

"Okay, ready?" I ask.

He nods and smiles at me, and I know I'm blushing.

I lean forward like I am telling him a secret. "I love libraries." I take a breath in and close my eyes before saying with a little more drama, "A lot."

He bursts into laughter. "Okay, that is not at all weird. I go to the library all the time. You are going to have to try harder if you want me to think you are weird or something."

I smile and dig back into my pasta, finishing it and my wine as we fall into a comfortable silence. I take my dishes to the sink, then turn to reach for his plate just as he stands up from the table. I may have grabbed his crotch with my hand. I know I did, but part of my brain wants to pretend that didn't just happen. I look up into his face and his eyes are wide, and it appears he is fighting off a laugh.

"Oh, gosh. I am so sorry," I say.

"Totally fine. I am sure you were reaching for the plate, right?" he says, and he clears his throat. "Here, I can help."

He takes his plate and wine glass to the sink. We work together and get the kitchen clean, and I start to feel more relaxed. He has that effect on me. I have to remind myself that I just met this guy this morning. I feel so comfortable around him, like we have made dinner together a thousand times.

He finishes wiping dry the last plate and puts it in the cupboard, then turns to me and says, "It's kind of wild that we just met this morning. I feel like I have known you for a long time."

"I was just thinking the same thing. I can't believe how scared I was when I left Chico this morning. When my friend drove me to the airport, I kept thinking this is the last time anyone who knows me will see me alive," I say.

He barks out a laugh. "And yet you got on the plane anyway? I am questioning your judgment, Heather."

"Desperate times call for desperate measures, I guess. Plus I would have died if I couldn't open that damn box."

"Yeah, I almost cracked a few times too. Want to sit and go over things again or are you tired?"

I don't want to admit it, but my full belly and probably that wine have made me so sleepy. This has been quite a day. Before I can give him an answer, a big yawn escapes my mouth, and he laughs.

"Let me just grab some stuff from my room, then you can go to bed." He winks at me, and I feel the butterflies that live in my stomach now take flight.

"Okay, I guess I am pretty tired," I say with a weak smile. I don't want this night to end, but I really am spent.

He says, "Don't worry about it. I need to get up early anyway. I'll be quiet, so sleep as long as you want. When you are up you can just come downstairs."

He disappears into his room before I can answer and comes out wearing shorts and a T-shirt. He's holding a pillow and a blanket, and it's probably the cutest thing I have ever seen.

"Okay, it's all yours, Heather."

"Are you sure?" I ask one more time, because I have a feeling once my head hits the pillow, I will fall fast asleep.

"I'm sure." His voice is soft and sweet.

"Thanks again for today, Vince. I had a lot of fun. I'll see you in the morning." I head into his room and pull the T-shirt I sleep in and my toothbrush from my suitcase. Stepping into the bathroom, I twist my hair up and use a scrunchie to hold it up. I have always slept hot; maybe because I have never lived in a place with air-conditioning, but I have learned ways to cope. I wear almost nothing and make sure my hair is off my neck. After I brush my teeth, I walk back out to his room and climb into bed. I crawl under the comforter and snuggle into his pillow. It smells like him, and I drift off to sleep with thoughts of his dark-chocolate eyes watching me over a glass of wine.

TEN

VINCE

HOLLYWOOD, California
    Hugh's Auto Body

THE NEXT WEEK flies by with me working my ass off trying to get caught up on all the cars I have on the schedule. Heather splits her time between the library and my apartment. She has hung out with us down here in the shop too but never stays very long. I think she is worried she is distracting Tony. If I am honest, she is distracting me, but I don't tell her that. We have our next big project on Monday, and Tony called me on Sunday night to remind me that it will probably be an all-day thing.

Monday morning, I am downstairs bright and early as promised. I get in my coveralls and get right to work. Tony arrives a few minutes later and we tackle the Corvette that was dropped off on Friday afternoon. Should be an easy job, but so far it's not making sense. We take a break from discussing the car and are bullshitting about who the Dodgers are going to have in their starting lineup when Heather comes downstairs.

"Are you sure you don't mind me using your car again today? I can totally take the bus," Heather says, walking towards us. She is wearing the same pair of shorts she had on yesterday but with a bright pink tank top on that is cut low. I swear the top of a white, lacy bra is peeking out, but I am trying to be a gentleman here, so I look away.

"Totally fine. If I need to go get a part I can use the truck or Tony can go get it. You think you'll be okay to find the place again on your own?" I ask.

"Yeah, I think so. If I get lost, I will just find a gas station or a pay phone and call you," she says, and with that and a little wave she walks out the door, my eyes glued to her ass as she goes.

"You think she has any idea how fucking hot she is?" Tony asks.

"Oh, hell no. I wonder if all the girls up in Chico are like that?" I say, still staring at the open doorway.

We both watch my beat-up VW Bug putter out of the gravel back lot and we shake our heads in unison.

"So, what's your best guess?" I ask, wanting to get back to the problem sitting in front of us. "What do you think is causing that noise?" This is a brand-new Corvette, and the owner said it makes a weird sound when he's driving. It's worse on the freeway at high speed.

"I have no idea. I have checked the belts and that isn't it." Tony scrubs his hand over his jaw. "Do you want to take it for a spin and see if that helps?" he asks. Normally I would think he is just trying to take a car for a joyride, but this really isn't making sense. We are going to need to take it out to see the problem, or rather, hear it.

"Yeah, I'll drive." I lower the bright yellow hood, letting it snap into place.

"This car is so fucking cool, but I can't understand what is making that racket. How many miles does he have on this thing?" Tony asks as we make our way out the back bay door and through the gravel lot.

"Only like six thousand, and most of that is freeway out to

Vegas." I put the car in park and wait while Tony hops out and pulls the gate shut, locking it with the chain and padlock.

"Vegas, huh? So is it anyone I know?" He waggles his eyebrows at me, and I laugh.

"No, and I am not telling you who owns this car." I pull out onto the street. We head to the freeway and immediately hear the rattle. What the fuck is that? It's like metal on metal.

"Something is hitting or grinding. I can hear it better now that we are out here. Is something hitting the crankshaft?" Tony asks. He has his head cocked so his ear is toward the engine.

"Fuck, maybe. That is what it sounds like. Let's check it out." I take the first exit and head back to the shop, relieved we have something to look at. "I need to do an oil change too while we have it, so let's start with that, and when it's up on the lift maybe we can see what's hitting."

"Sounds good, boss," Tony says.

About two hours later, I wipe my hands on my coveralls and shake my head. "Who the fuck makes a dipstick that long? The bottom of that thing looked like a rat chewed it up."

"No quality control over at Chevy I guess," Tony says with a shrug. "I totally wanted this car when I saw it this morning. I was like, yeah, that's my dream car right there. Now you couldn't pay me to own this car."

"I feel the same way," I say. I tuck my shop rag into my back pocket and walk over to the shop phone. I need to call the owner and let him know we figured it out. It's getting warm, so I open the front bay door to let a breeze in. Once it's all the way up, I slide the pin to lock the door in place.

"Still playing with cars, Vince?" a familiar voice says over my shoulder, and I tense, squeezing my hand into a fist before turning slowly around.

"Giovanni. Didn't know you were back in town," I mumble and walk over to my little desk. It's nothing fancy, just a metal box with a Formica top that you can never see because I have invoices and manuals scattered across the top of it. I pick up the phone and dial like he isn't even here.

Tony calls out to our old friend, so I make my way around the desk to the creaky wooden chair and sit, praying my customer answers so I have an excuse not to talk to that fucker Gio.

"Hey, Lenny. Glad I caught you," I say into the phone as soon as I hear a hello. I watch as Gio and Tony do some bullshit handshake fist bump thing. I roll my eyes and spin so my back is to them. Why the fuck is he here?

I take my time giving the owner a detailed explanation about the oil dipstick being too long and hitting the crank shaft. He asks if I noticed the problem with the power windows not working or the oil temp getting too hot. Damn, this is basically a new car and it's a total lemon. Literally and figuratively since it's the brightest yellow I have ever seen on a car. I promise to look at his other issues and reluctantly hang up the phone. I dig through the invoices and decide now would be the perfect time to work on getting this desk organized. I grab a stack of invoices and start putting them in order by date. That should work. Or maybe I could put them in order of cost. Or by car type...

"Fuck, no fucking way! Are you serious? Dude, that is so radical!" Tony bellows, and I glance over at them as they hug. I roll my eyes again like a goddam teenaged girl and go back to the invoices.

"When do you start?" Tony asks, and I feel my gut tighten. No, this can't be happening.

"Well, they want me to finish up my degree. I am working with my professors to take finals early so I can train. I'll be in the blue and white before you know it," Gio says, and of course he is looking right at me. I grind my teeth and keep sorting, I refuse to give him the satisfaction of seeing me angry. I am trying to regulate my breathing before I have to go and congratulate that idiot.

"Did you hear that, Vince? Gio got picked up by the Dodgers! Fuck, man. I knew you could do it. I just knew it." Tony is beaming like he just gave birth to this baseball prodigy.

I walk over to Gio with my hand extended. "Congrats, man. That's really awesome." I can do this. I can be happy for him.

"Dude, it's the dream. Too bad you weren't up there in Chico with me when the scouts came. We were quite the amazing duo. I miss catching for you, man." Gio flashes that million-dollar smile of his and I clench my fist at my side so I don't put my knuckles through his face.

"Yeah, that would have been cool," I say, because that's the truth. I should have been up there. I should have pitched for the Wildcats, then the Dodgers or Giants. Instead I am digging around elbow deep in a car built by people that don't know how long to make a fucking dipstick.

"How long you in town for, Gio?" Tony asks, and even though he is my best friend, I kind of hate him right now. He looks like a golden retriever prancing around begging for a pat on the head for Chrissake. If he mentions the city league I play for after Gio dropped his Dodger news, I will kick him right in the nuts.

"I just came down to sign some papers. I have to get back up to Chico tomorrow," Gio says.

"Hey, isn't that Heather chick from Chico?" Tony asks, and I grind my teeth harder. I am going to break a fucking molar if he doesn't leave soon.

"Who's Heather?" Gio asks with his big, stupid smile. Fuck, I still want to hit him.

"Yeah," I bite out, shooting Tony a glare that of course he misses because he is busy staring at Giovanni like he hung the moon.

"So who is this Heather chick?" Gio asks, and I realize I didn't answer him.

"We are working on something for a mutual friend. She lives up there but is staying with me until we get things sorted out," I say, trying to be as vague as possible.

"Great, can't wait to meet her. Does she go to college up there? Maybe I have already met her if you know what I mean." He turns to

Tony because he knows Tony will appreciate the wiggle of his eyebrows.

"She doesn't go to college there, dipshit. She lives there," I snap before I can stop myself. Heather would see right through this guy. I mean I hope she would.

"No need to be a dick." Gio laughs, holding his hands up in a defensive pose, then adds, "Bring her by Gold Run tonight. If I have met her, I am sure we will both remember."

"No," I say without any hesitation.

"You not hanging out there anymore?" Gio looks to Tony for support, and I see my friend bow his head and take a deep breath.

"No, Tony and Mandy broke up. We don't go there anymore," I explain, because I have Tony's back no matter what.

"Oh fuck, man. I thought you got married. The wedding was a few months ago, right?" Gio asks like a fucking asshole.

"It was. She never showed," Tony says. This time he holds his head up and straightens his shoulders, squaring them to face whatever is coming. I move away from the desk and stand next to him.

"Oh, man, that's fucked up. I can't believe she did that," Gio says, and it actually sounds sincere. I don't know anyone we went to school with that took Mandy's side on this, but if anyone would have, it would be Gio.

"Yeah, well, I guess it is better than getting a divorce." Tony shrugs, repeating what we have told him over and over.

"So she still works there?" Gio asks, and I take over.

"Well, her parents still own the place, so yeah, Gio, she still works there. None of us go anymore, not even Terrence." I hope the weight of that hits Gio right in the chest.

"Fuck, man. If her cousin Terrence isn't even going, I guess I will find a new place. Where is everyone hanging out these days? I miss the old gang," he says, and I know immediately he misses all the adoration. He wants to brag about getting picked up, that's it. He doesn't care at all about the old gang. When Tony got stood up at the altar, or when Michael was in the hospital, none of us heard even a peep from this asshole. He sure as hell didn't check on me after my dad's heart attack or the stroke. Tony was there almost every fucking day.

"We have been going to Burt's over on Santa Monica. They put in a dance floor, and the back room still has the dart boards," Tony says.

"It's way better, and there are a lot of really cool people that hang out there," I say, trying to sound supportive, even if I hate going there.

"Cool, bring that Heather chick tonight and I'll check it out," Gio says.

"No, we have stuff to do tonight. Sorry, man. If only I had some notice that you were going to be in town, I might have been able to move things around." I slap him on the back—hard. I let a small smile dance across my lips when I see him wince a little at the smack.

"I'll call a few people, Gio. I think Michael might want to go. I can see if Robin and Dave are free," Tony says, still trying his damnedest to please this fucker.

"Sure. Sounds great, Tony. Whoever you can get. I'd love to see my old friends," Gio says. I bite my tongue because I bet he doesn't even know Michael is in a fucking wheelchair now. Wonder what he will say when he sees him. It would be worth going to see his jaw hit the floor.

I walk back to the desk and shuffle through the invoices again while Gio and Tony continue to talk. Tuning them out as best as I can, I actually make progress on the mess. I should hire someone to do this. When I first took over for Dad, I was sure it was temporary. I'd be here a few months, maybe miss a semester of college tops. Now two years later and this place is like a chain around my neck, getting tighter every day.

ELEVEN
# HEATHER



VINCE'S DIRECTIONS were super easy to follow, and I found the library the first few times without any problems, but today I missed the turn and ended up driving around in a panic for about a half hour. I pulled over and took a few deep breaths and got my bearings. I'd like to say it is the first time that has happened, but it's not. This past week I have been running around on my own, and I feel like I am getting the hang of it, but when I couldn't find the Safeway I had been at just the day before, I tried to be more careful. These streets all look the same to me, and they have similar names. It's not my fault I turned on Wilcox Place and not Wilcox Avenue.

I didn't mind too much that I got lost, since driving Vince's car is pure heaven. It smells like him and gives me glimpses of who he is. All the personal things about someone's car delight me. I see he has another cassette tape of the Rat Pack in his stereo, and the ashtray is open and filled with change. The gear knob is custom, a beautiful, smooth wood with the grain almost black. Each number and the R are cut deep and filled in with a pretty blue paint. He has a pair of sunglasses tucked in the visor as well as a map.

I swear I pictured all of LA like I see on television. I guess it didn't occur to me that there would be neighborhoods just like those in Chico. I still don't want to drive on the big freeways, but the library is tucked into a nice neighborhood. Parking in the lot in back, I make my way to the front doors of the biggest library I have ever seen. I am in heaven. This is the mother ship.

I make my way to the front counter and ask for Margaret. She offered to help me when we spoke on the phone, but she has been out of town visiting a sick relative. I came here on my own, but I wasn't able to find very much. I did manage to get my own library card and check out a book about Hollywood.

The woman at the desk smiles sweetly when she sees me, and I am told to wait by the card catalog, so I walk over to the beautiful oak cabinet. I want to run my hand along all the tiny drawers. The Dewey Decimal System is doing things to me, and I take a deep breath in. This place must have a million books or more. I should have spent more time just looking around.

"I hear you need some help?" a familiar voice says from behind me. I turn and take in the short woman who must be Margaret. She is decked out in what looks to be a handmade button-up dress. The fabric is a beautiful green and covered in whimsical, cartoon versions of books. She is wearing a long, colorful bead necklace that picks up the blues and greens of the print. She has her hair up in a tight bun with a pencil behind her ear, and big, oversized glasses rest on the end of her nose.

"I'm Heather. I believe we spoke on the phone?" I say.

"Oh! You're the young lady that was interested in the classic movies?" Margaret says with a big, beautiful smile.

"Yes, a few specific ones. I have a list. Do you have time now? If not, I can walk around if you just point me to the right place," I say, hoping she will help.

"Oh, honey, I always have time for people like you. Sorry I was out last week. Couldn't be helped. Well, it could have if that sister of mine hadn't smoked two packs a day and then acted like a victim when she got sick, but that's neither here nor there. Come on, let me show you our 'Old Hollywood' section. Is there an actor or actress that you are interested in?" She sets off, and I follow quickly behind her, surprised at how fast she is.

"Yes, a Iolet Merryweather. Her name is spelled like Violet, but the—"

Margaret pauses and grabs my arm, saying, "V is silent! Oh my God, I met her a few times. She was a hoot!"

"You did?" I am surprised, but I guess I shouldn't be. Before Iolet moved to Chico, this was her home. She was bound to have had friends and known people.

"Oh yeah. We auditioned for the same role more than once. I think we were even at a few of the same casting calls. She got lots of jobs because she was willing to be an extra or just have one or two lines. Me? I held out for the big roles!" Margaret says, puffing out her chest as she walks on quickly.

"Oh? What films were you in?" I ask, struggling to keep up with her.

"None. Not a damn one!" She spins on her heels and thrusts her finger at my chest. "Let me tell you, missy, take whatever they offer. That's what I learned after living here for years. I mean, look at me. Am I an Ava Gardner or a Marilyn Monroe? No! No, I am not. Did I know that back then? Also no." She smiles, and I like her even more than I did on the phone.

"Well, they missed out if you ask me. You would have been great. I am sure of that," I say, my smile genuine.

"Aren't you sweet. My acting was crap, and because I am only about five foot one on a good day, there weren't a lot of roles that would have worked. Can't have a leading lady who only comes up to the leading man's belly button. That doesn't look proper!" She wiggles her eyebrows at me.

"Oh sure. Well, I bet you had fun at least, right?" I ask.

"The best times." She finally stops and says, "Here we are, dear. This row here all the way down will have what you are looking for. All the seven hundreds are Arts and Recreation, but I know for a fact there is a great book in the nine hundreds about the history of film here in Hollywood." Margaret stops and waves her arm toward the massive row of books.

I take a moment, then ask, "So is there a way to look up these?" I hand her the list of the plays and movies that Iolet was probably in. I keep my face neutral since I am basically holding a crime scene list. If I think about it too much, I know I will break out in a sweat.

"Oh sure, the Screen Actors Guild has books. I bet she is in a few of those. Here, I'll show you where those are." Margaret leads the way, and I follow, overwhelmed and excited.

A few hours later, I lift my head from the pile of books. Holy shit. I thought it would be difficult to find what movies Iolet Merry-weather was in, but it would be easier to find movies she was *not* in. She had to have been the busiest woman in Hollywood in the forties and fifties. She did slow down a bit in the sixties, but I am betting she did things that weren't listed in these books. I didn't find anything that matched the "Killed Before My Time" reference. In fact, there isn't a single movie or television show with that title from what I can tell.

After I take a break and eat my lunch outside on a bench, I find Margaret in the stacks and wait for her to finish talking with another patron. When she turns to find me leaning on the books, she smiles and says, "How'd ya do? Find what you were looking for?"

"Some, but I was wondering if this last one sounds familiar to you. There are no movies listed with the name, and I checked a few books for plays, but I came up with nothing." I hold out the list and point to the bottom line.

Margaret taps her chin with her stubby finger and makes a few humming noises before her eyes go wide. "It's not a movie or a play!" She grabs my hand and pulls me down the row of books, abandoning her cart in the middle of the aisle. We weave down a few more aisles until we reach a room filled with big grey machines and filing cabinets. Margaret drops my hand and rushes over to the far wall, then bends down, pulling the bottom drawer open. She rifles through some small reels, and I know the moment she finds the one she was after because she yells, "Eureka!" She immediately shushes herself and looks around for witnesses. I laugh and join her at the machine she approached. I watch as she threads the microfiche into the giant metal viewer. When it's all set, she turns to me and says, "Okay. This is the *Hollywood Times* from 1935. That is the year Iolet came here from New York."

I interrupt her. "Iolet lived in New York?"

"Oh yes, dear. She tried to be a Broadway star but didn't make it, at least that is what I remember people saying. Anyway, when she moved here there was a reason. I can't put my finger on it, my memory isn't what it used to be, you know, but I know there was a story. Something big. You'll find it, I am sure." She pats my cheek and walks off.

I take a deep breath and pull a tall chair over to the machine. The reel starts on January 1st, 1935, and includes every day of that year. I groan and think, *I am going to be here forever*. I scan the headlines, then find the arts and entertainment section, assuming this is where news of Iolet Merryweather's arrival in Hollywood would have been documented. I get to March before my eyes give out. Nothing, no mention of her at all in those sections. I stand and stretch from side to side, feeling the cracks and pops up my spine. I do a few jumps in place to get the blood flowing in my legs and check my watch. It's three o'clock, so I really should give this another two hours. Vince will be working in the shop until then. I sit back down and dive in, making it to April when something catches my eye.

ALBERT MILTON, STAR OF THE HIT MOVIE *YOU AND ME*, SEEN WITH A NEW GIRL ON HIS ARM. SOURCES SAY SHE IS A BROADWAY STARLET.

There are no pictures unfortunately, but this might be a lead! I read the short article, but it doesn't name the woman he was seen with, only states that she seemed to love the attention he was lavishing on her. Well, who wouldn't? He was a movie star, wasn't he? I write down his name, thinking I can look him up later in the Actors Guild books. I realize this is going to be a lot of research. I groan at all the time I wasted last week. One day here at the library isn't going to cut it. I take a deep breath and scroll through a few more months before hitting gold.

## Albert Milton, star of stage and screen, found dead in his north Hollywood home

I READ THE ARTICLE QUICKLY. It states that he was found face up in his living room with a single bullet to his head. There were no suspects, and the police had no leads. They asked the public to please call if anyone had any information. Holy crap. Did Iolet murder this man?

Was that the danger she was talking about? I need to tell Vince. This is crazy! I write down the date of the murder and also where I stopped in the reel so I can find this part again quickly. I rub my eyes as the reel rewinds, then stand and pull it free from the machine just as Margaret walks back in.

"Albert Milton!" she shouts, then looks around, shushing herself again.

I snicker and say, "Yeah, he was murdered. Was Iolet the Broadway starlet that he was seeing?"

"I think so. They dated, then she got the part opposite him in a movie. The name escapes me at the moment. They had just started to film when he was killed," Margaret says, shaking her head. She takes the reel from me and returns it to the drawer.

"I didn't know any of this when I was auditioning alongside Iolet, and to be honest, I had completely forgotten about it until you started asking questions," she explains.

"When did you learn about it?" I ask.

"I think about four years ago. There was a college student doing a paper on unsolved Hollywood murders. He and I looked through tons of information, and I remember him finding that little tidbit." Margaret smiles at me, then says, "You should talk to that boy. He did a lot of research. Let's go to the front desk. I bet I still have his number!"

I sigh, relieved that maybe someone else will have information and I won't be spending the next week scrolling through old newspapers. She ducks behind the big wooden desk, nudging another woman out of her way.

"Sorry, Ruthie, I need to get in that bottom drawer," Margaret says in a loud whisper.

Ruthie steps away but looks over at me quizzically. I smile and give her a little wave, but she just glares and stomps off.

Margaret pops back up with a big smile. "Here! I knew I had his number." She hands me a three-by-five card with a name and number written in the neatest handwriting I have ever seen. There is also a date in the corner, and on the back of the card is a little note about what he was looking for at the library. I wonder if she has a card like this about me somewhere.

"Thanks, but this card is from a few years ago. He might not even live here anymore," I say, taking the card and tucking it in my bag.

"Can't hurt to call, dear!" she says, then walks off after that grumpy Ruthie woman.

I pull the keys to Vince's Bug out of my purse and head out to the parking lot. I have so much to tell him. I hope he is done with his work for the day. I think about that card and what I will even say to the man if he answers. What if he wants to meet me? I wonder if Vince would be able to go with me. I know he is busy at his shop, but I am nervous about doing all this on my own.

As I drive back to Hugh's Auto Body, I let my mind wander. This has been such a surreal experience. This past week has also been a bit of a vacation for me. It's the longest I've gone without speaking to my mother since she got out of jail. I have a mixture of feelings that have been swirling since the plane lifted off in Sacramento. I feel free and lighter, but the tug of my years of responsibility yanks at my heart. I have almost called her every night, but I told her I wouldn't call until I knew something. She has to be able to stand on her own, and I have to be able to let her try. I have been on my own since I was sixteen, but that's different. I am not an alcoholic. I don't have the pull that she has to the bottle.

Chico is a small town, and it was easy to get around on my bike or just walk. When Mom went to jail, I told no one. I just took over all the things people thought my mom had done on her own. I paid the rent, went grocery shopping, paid the bills, and kept up the appearance of her being home. She had been gone so much before she was arrested for drunk driving, the neighbors were used to the fact that they didn't see her a lot. I want to blame that idiot boyfriend of hers, but I know it doesn't matter who she is with. She just makes horrible choices. Always has, always will.

If it wasn't for Allen Richie, no one would have known about my mom. Allen's dad is an attorney in town doing mostly family law. Unluckily for me, Allen took some papers to his dad at court on the very day that my mom had a parole hearing. I had borrowed my friend's car, lying and saying that I had a doctor's appointment and our car was in the shop. Well, that part was true. If by shop you mean impound yard. Apparently when you don't pay the registration, they can tow your car. The fees to spring it from the tow yard were more than I could afford, so I just rode my bike everywhere, even when it was raining. But I couldn't ride to Oroville. It was too far away.

I remember pulling in the parking lot and being so determined to get inside, see my mom, and show her I was there for her, even if she didn't know how to be there for me. I ran into the courthouse and found the room I needed. The doors were open, and there was Mom sitting with her thick, brown hair up in a high ponytail, her shoulders narrow and thin. She looked young until you got close and saw the effects of the booze.

"Hi, baby. I am so glad you came." She held out her hands to me, and I sat and grabbed them, turning so our knees were touching. She was sober, through no choice of her own, but I liked it. Her eyes looked clear, and she didn't smell like vomit and vodka. I was lost in conversation, questions about how she was doing, what the lawyers thought about her getting out soon, and if she needed anything.

I didn't see Allen come in. His father was at a table on the other side of the room. He wasn't there for my mom's hearing. He was just waiting for his case to be called. There were several other groups in the room, and to be honest, I am kind of surprised Allen even saw me.

I had just pulled Mom in for a hug, and I opened my eyes and found him staring at me. A slow, evil grin spread across his face, and I know he saw the fear in my eyes. I refused to push my mom away. I pulled her in tighter and whispered in her ear that I loved her.

Later, after the hearing and a tearful goodbye, I drove back to Chico, praying the whole time that Allen would keep his damn mouth shut about what he saw.

The next day as I walked through the hallway to my locker, the snickers and leers confirmed what I already knew in my heart. Allen had a big fucking mouth.

It's one thing to be the poor girl, never having the latest thing to wear, or having a backpack that was falling apart. It's a whole other thing to have people know your mom is in jail. By last period I had heard all the rumors. My mom robbed a bank, my mom murdered someone, my mom sold drugs to kids, my mom was in on a plot to murder a local politician. None of those things were true, but I didn't have the energy to stop the lies.

My good friend Dee tried as best she could to stop the rumors, but I told her to stop. It wasn't worth her time either. I held it together pretty well until I climbed on my bike to go home. I only had a half hour before I had to ride down to Taco Bell for my shift, so I rushed to get back to our apartment. Allen pulled his car in front of me, blocking me in the crowd of kids leaving school.

"How's Mommy, Heather?" he sneered.

"Great. She's getting out next month. Thanks for your concern," I snapped and pulled my handlebars up and maneuvered away from him before he could say anything else. I let the tears fall as I raced home and allowed myself a few more tears as I rode to my job, but tears are for people who can spare them, and that was not me.

God, I hated him so much. He was one of those people who just decides to fuck with you one day, like you did them wrong or something. I had seen him turn on other kids over the years, and I wondered how he had any friends.

Thankfully for me, a new girl came to our school, and the attention switched to her. She was very sweet and pretty and had traveled the world. Little old me with a mom in jail suddenly wasn't so interesting. I should send that girl a thank-you note. I wonder what happened to her.

I park Vince's Bug in the back lot of his shop and climb out with all my papers and a book I checked out. It is after five, but I can hear Vince and Tony talking still, so I pause and take a deep breath in, letting it out slowly. It has been years since I thought of that asshole Allen. I don't know why it still gets to me, or why it was on my mind today. Maybe it's that tug of guilt that I don't have to be responsible for anyone but myself down here.

As soon as I walk in, Vince turns to me and I see a small smile cross his face, but then his eyes dart to Tony and he resumes his normal serious scowl.

"Find anything out?" Vince asks, but I don't answer right away. Instead my eyes follow Tony as he walks away from Vince. He strips out of his coveralls. He's wearing a tight tank top and a pair of board shorts. I have never seen a guy that muscular up close. I have to admit it kind of freaks me out. I don't find it attractive at all. His back is huge. I didn't know guys could make their back spread out in an expanse of muscles like that. And his thighs. I think his thighs are the same size as my waist. I bet he could wear my jean skirt on his leg. I really want to ask him to try it, but that is a weird thing to request, so I don't. I blink, mesmerized by the way Tony's muscles flex and strain as he sits and pulls his work boots off. He reaches under the chair and grabs a pair of flip-flops, sliding them on his feet.

"I'm hitting the beach. See you later," Tony says, walking off without another word. When the shop door shuts, Vince turns to me and asks, "Like what you see?"

"What?" I ask, shaking my head to clear the thought I had of poking Tony with a knitting needle to see if he would pop like a balloon.

"You were checking out Tony. You like that? Muscle heads your thing?" He kind of sneers at me, and I turn to see if someone is behind me.

"What is your problem? I wasn't checking him out like that. I just haven't ever known someone that into body building. It's not like I am going to hit on him or something," I say, my voice pitching higher than I wanted.

Vince stares at me for a beat, then I see his shoulder sag a bit before he says, "Fuck. Sorry." He shoves his hand through his hair and looks down at the floor. "Tony has just been through a lot. If you are interested, you should know that. He's more than just a body-builder."

"Well, I am not here to try and find a boyfriend, Vince. I am here to figure this shit out, and guess what? It got a lot more fucking complicated today." I push past him and stomp up the stairs to his apartment. I wish I could slam the door and keep him out, but this is his place, and I really hate fighting with people. I set my stuff down and head into the bathroom to splash some water on my face. Maybe that will help me calm down.

When I come back out, Vince has a beer in his hand and he's sitting at the table, waiting. He looks up when I walk in, and his expression softens. He is all over the place today. I'm not sure what I am going to get.

"Tony got hurt pretty bad by a girl he was seeing. I guess I am kind of protective of him. I shouldn't have snapped at you like that," Vince says while picking at the label of his beer.

"It's alright. I understand. But next time give me the benefit of the doubt, okay? I am here to do a job. I want to finish this and get back home. It's not like I asked to be here, you know?" I say. He looks down like he's ashamed, then raises his gaze to me and nods with a small lift to one side of his mouth. Not quite a smile, but close enough.

"What did you find out?" he asks. He goes to the fridge, grabbing another beer for himself and one for me before sitting back down.

I could use a drink about now. I used to worry that I would develop a problem like my mom, but I don't crave it like she did. I don't think I have a vice like that, but I am careful. I grab the bottle and use my shirt to cover the top as I twist it off. I flick the metal cap into the trash can. I look back at Vince, who has a little smile on his lips.

I ignore it. This guy is driving me crazy, and not in the cute way like yesterday when he purposefully let his arm brush against me as we made dinner, or how he walked in his room just as I had pulled my shirt off. I felt the heat of his stare as I quickly turned and grabbed my shirt off the floor. The way his voice was all strained as he apologized made my stomach flutter with something like hope. Then he switches to this grumpy asshole. What the hell is his problem?

"Okay, so I don't even know where to begin." I blow out a breath. "Iolet Merryweather was in a bunch of movies, television shows, plays, and even some commercials in the late sixties," I explain.

"Really? What were the commercials?" Vince asks with a chuckle.

"A toothpaste commercial, a coffee commercial, and a commercial for chocolate," I say, rattling off what I remember.

"That's wild. I wonder how many times I have seen her on television or in a movie and not known it was her?" Vince's voice is soft and almost apologetic. Maybe that's just my imagination.

"Yeah, that's a real possibility. She was in a lot of things. There is something else, though," I say. I set my beer down and reach for my bag, pulling out the card that Margaret gave me. I slide it across the table, and Vince grabs it and reads the front, then flips it over, scanning the back where Margaret had written what this John guy was looking for.

"I don't get it," he says, handing the card back to me.

"The reference to 'Killed Before My Time.' It's not a movie or a play. It's about this guy Albert. He was a movie star that was killed in 1935, the same year Iolet came out from New York."

"No shit? Did she whack him or something?" Vince asks, and I shake my head.

"I don't think so, but I wonder if she knew who did. I think that is what this is about. I could be wrong, but I think she wants us to find his killer," I say. It's the only thing that makes sense.

"This guy John was a college student who was doing a paper on unsolved Hollywood murders. Margaret helped him with his research, and he found a link between Albert and our Iolet. Margaret knew her, did I tell you that?" I say, realizing that little bit of information is important.

"Fuck, really? That's wild," Vince says, taking a swig of his beer. He wipes at his mouth and asks, "So she wants you to call this guy?"

"Yeah, she said he might have more information. All she remembered was that Iolet dated Albert when she arrived in LA and they were set to star together in a big movie. Filming had just started when Albert was murdered."

"Wow, that sucks. Poor Iolet. I mean poor Albert too. Was he famous or just starting out like her?" Vince asks.

"Apparently he was a big deal. There was an article about him that mentioned he had a Broadway star on his arm. I assume that was Iolet. It seemed like the press followed what he did, so he must have been famous. I was so tired I couldn't keep going, but I plan on calling that John guy and going back to the library tomorrow to look up more stuff about Albert Milton."

"So Iolet was big on Broadway before coming out here? I guess that explains the New York comment she made to you, huh?" Vince says. He finishes his beer and tosses it in the trash can behind him, then opens the second one he got for himself.

"No, Margaret said she heard Iolet didn't make it on Broadway and that's why she came out here. The newspaper thought she was a big deal, and I am betting Iolet let them think that. I could totally see her playing that up, even if it wasn't true," I say. As we talk about this, something isn't sitting right with me, and I can't put my finger on it.

# TWELVE
# VINCE

HOLLYWOOD, California
    Hugh's Auto Body

HEATHER WAS WORRIED that Iolet had killed someone, and it seems she wasn't too far off. Someone was killed, but I doubt Iolet did it. This is fucking nuts. Two weeks ago, that crazy lady wasn't even on the outskirts of my memory, and now my whole life is turned upside down because of her.

"Want me to call him?" I ask, reaching for the three-by-five card again.

"No, that's okay. I know you are busy. I can do it. I appreciate the offer, but I can't really help with the car or anything, so this is only fair," she says. She takes another drink from the longneck beer bottle, and my eyes enjoy the sight a little too much. Why does she have to be so fucking pretty? I don't need this distraction in my life, or my apartment. She stands and walks over to the couch where the boxes Iolet left us have been sitting on the floor since we opened them. She picks her box up and brings it back to the table.

"I just don't know why she left us the things she did. At first I thought she just wanted us to return these props, but I am inclined to agree with Henry. That might not be it. These might be clues to whatever happened to Albert."

She pulls the lid off and reaches in, bringing the long, pink gloves out. As she sets them on the table, we both hear a dull clunk as something hits the wood. She cocks her head and grabs the gloves, stuffing her hand in one, then the other. Her expression changes, and she pulls out a key on a ring with a small metal tab attached. She sets it on the table. She pushes her hand back in and pulls out a tiny, folded piece of paper. She opens it, and her eyebrows furrow.

"What's this?" she asks as she hands me the paper.

"It's an address," I say helpfully. Because I am one helpful motherfucker.

"No shit," she deadpans. "Do you know where this is? Or rather what it is?"

"No. That street is not too far from here though. You could go by tomorrow?" I say as more of a question.

"Yeah, okay. I can do that." She sighs and takes a big drink of her beer, and I have to look away so she doesn't catch me watching her swallow like some fucking creep.

She reaches back in and pulls out the box that holds the man's ring. She turns it over in her hand, then slides it on her thumb. She sighs and says, "I was hoping I'd figure this out. I wonder if it was Albert's."

I hold out my hand, and she slides the ring off her thumb and hands it to me. It only fits on my pinky, so I put it on and shrug my shoulders. "I don't know, maybe it was his. I mean, the car and all those costumes weren't his, or even from his movies, right? She collected all these things after he died, right?"

"Yeah, I guess, but I think that ring is his. Jewelry is personal, and I could see her hanging on to something like that, you know?" Her eyes go wide, and she reaches into the box. "Or these are his!" She pulls out the size thirteen wing tips.

She sets them on the table, and we both stare at the drop of blood on the top on the left shoe. Shit.

We both look up. Our eyes lock, and we say at the same time, "Fuck."

She scoots back like the shoe might come after her, then pushes up out of the chair and starts pacing. She goes to her purse and pulls out the envelope with the letter she got from Iolet and rereads it.

"There isn't anything in this damn letter that is helpful," Heather says as she plops down on the couch. She covers her face with her hands, and I walk over to her. I can tell she's upset, but I am not good at this shit. I am not the guy people go to when they have problems. Except Tony. He comes to me all the fucking time with his problems, or rather problem. It's always the same thing, and I doubt I ever give him good advice, but he hasn't tried to get back together with his ex, so maybe I do.

Heather drags her hands down her face and groans. "I am hungry. Are you hungry, Vince?" She looks at me through those impossibly long lashes.

"Yeah." I am about to go to the kitchen to make something when Heather stands up and grabs her purse.

"Come on. Let's go out. I need to get some fresh air. I'll drive." She spins the keys to my VW Bug around her finger. I shrug rather than answer. I am tired, and if she wasn't here I'd probably make myself a simple sandwich, have another beer, and pass out on the couch watching TV. Damn, my life is sad.

I force a smile and hold the door open for her, breathing in her sweet apple scent as she passes. See? Sad little life. Sniffing girls who would never consider me if they weren't forced to live with me. I hang my head and follow her downstairs and out back to my car.

"Where to?" she asks as we pull out of the lot. I don't really want to go anywhere, but I do need to eat. Maybe food will help pull me out of this funk. I'm like Grand Master Funk or whatever. Tony loves that band. I can't stand them, but it seems fitting for my mood. I sigh and answer her.

"Sammy's is fine. They have a dinner menu, but it might be crowded," I explain, a little bit of me hoping she says we can just go back home.

"No problem. I turn at this light here, right?" she asks, and I nod. At least I am starting to feel a little better about her directional skills. I lean back in the seat and sigh again. I am like a fucking hormonal teenager wearing a blanket of angst. I can't get Gio out of my mind. Fucking Dodgers.

When we were in high school together, baseball and playing for the Dodgers was all we talked about. I'd pitch and he'd catch and we would bring the team to the World Series in our rookie season. Dumb dreaming teenagers, but now he is on his way, and I am stuck here playing for the Hollywood Heyday city league. We are actually pretty good, and even if I am the youngest guy on the team, playing has kept me sane. It's weird how fast the time has gone by since he left, and there have been long stretches of time when I didn't think about college or Giovanni Mancini. I worked hard separating my love of baseball and my hatred for Gio, but as soon as I saw him, it all came back. I clench my fist and wish I could put it through the windshield. I need to go for a run or work out. Something to alleviate this rage I feel building.

"Vince? Are you listening to me at all?" Heather says with a soft hand on my arm.

"What? No, sorry. I had a bad day. I guess I was thinking about that. What did you say?" I ask, stealing a quick look over at her. Fuck, she is so pretty. No way in hell I would let her meet Gio. He'd swoop in with his million-dollar smile and soon-to-be huge paycheck. He could offer her a real life, an escape from poverty. I can offer her shit. I close my eyes against my own thoughts and shake my head a little. I have got to stop. I turn and look at her again. Did she say something to me?

"I asked if you want to be there when I call that John guy in the morning," she says again, but her voice is different. It's lower and sweet, and she is rubbing my forearm like she is trying to comfort me.

The only reason she stops is so she can shift the car into first as we roll to a stop at a light. She turns to look at me, and I am lost in her eyes the moment they connect with mine. Her sweet smile is like a balm, and the way she is looking at me washes over my soul.

"No, that's okay. I am sure you can handle it. If he is even at that number still. There is always the chance you won't reach him there," I say, trying to sound like a normal person.

"Well, I know I can handle it, but I thought maybe you'd *want* to be involved," she says and smiles again. I am about to say something, but the light changes and we drive the rest of the way to Sammy's in silence.

# THIRTEEN
# HEATHER



I PULL up to the diner, pleased that there is a spot right in front that I can drive into. I am not terrible at parallel parking, but I have a feeling with Vince in the car I would do something wrong and mess it up.

"Sorry you had a bad day, Vince. I am here if you want to talk about it," I say, then vow to myself to drop it. I have learned that guys don't like to be nagged about their feelings. It's best to just let him talk when he's ready. Me pushing him is just going to make that mood worse, and I do not want that. I like the guy that picked me up at the airport, not this grump.

"Thanks," Vince says. He climbs out and heads to the door, so I lean over and lock his door, then get out and use the key to lock my side. It is so nice to have access to a car. I am embarrassed to admit I pretended it was mine when I was driving back to the garage. I have missed driving and the independence that goes along with it.

Vince is at the door waiting for me, and when I approach, he opens it and gives me a small smile. I smile back and step through the door. I jump a bit when I feel his hand on my lower back guiding me a little. It startles me, but it also sends a zing right through my gut. I wish my body didn't react like this around him. He isn't someone who would be interested in a girl like me.

"Two, please," Vince says to an older woman who has walked up. I glance around, looking for Monica, but don't see her. I thought maybe that is why he touched me.

I lean over as we are walking to our table and say quietly, "If you need me to pretend we are together, I got your back this time."

He chuckles and moves his hand across my back again, letting his fingers curl a little around my hip. He pulls me into him, and I get chills because I am unable to stop these feelings apparently.

"I appreciate that, Heather," he says. He turned his head so he could whisper that in my ear, and the whole room goes a little hazy.

My chest is rising, and I lick my lips to steady myself before I say, "Do you see that Monica girl? I didn't notice her when we came in."

"Nah, I don't think she is here." He lifts his hand off my hip and slides it up my spine, sending chills to chase his touch. He grips the back of my neck in a little squeeze, then lets me go, and I immediately miss his hand on me. Damn it.

"Here you go. The waitress should be over soon to take your order. Do you want some waters?" the hostess asks, and we both tell her yes, please. I said yes because I need something to douse the fire that has consumed me from one stupid touch. I am that desperate, a fact I find quite annoying.

I sit, and Vince slides in across from me, slumping down a little in the booth. I wish he wasn't so moody tonight. I fight the urge to ask him if he wants to talk about it again. The hostess brings our waters, and I grab the two menus, sliding one over to Vince.

"Let me get dinner since you tricked me and bought lunch the last time we were here. Now that I don't have to pay for a hotel, I am not as worried about my budget," I say, hoping he will let me do this. He looks up with fight in his eyes but gives a smile instead.

"Okay, Heather, if it's that important to you. You can buy me dinner," he says, letting that softer side emerge just a bit.

We are silent while we look over the menus, and once the waitress comes over, Vince seems more relaxed. He orders another beer with dinner, and I stick with water since I am driving us back to the shop later.

"So what did you think of that librarian? Was she able to show you stuff you didn't find on your own?" Vince asks, finally breaking the silence.

"Oh my God. She was amazing. Like so fucking cool. Our library in Chico is small, nothing like that. Hollywood has all the best things, I guess. Margaret was super helpful too, and if my eyes didn't feel like they were going to roll out of my head, I would have stayed longer," I explain in what sounds to me like a rush of disjointed thoughts. I don't know why I feel so nervous around him tonight, but I bet it's because of his bad mood.

"You found a lot of stuff it seems. I can't believe Iolet might have been involved in a murder like you thought." Vince shakes his head. He has folded his hands on the table, and I notice he's still wearing the pinky ring from Iolet's things. I hold out my hand, and he looks at me questioningly.

"Can I?" I say, my hand still extended, open, waiting.

He lifts his hand and places it in mine, and I move my other hand over his and start to massage around the base of his thumb. I turn his hand so the palm is up and work around his wrist and then back to his thumb and fingers, taking my time to rub deeply at each joint. I chance a glance up to his face and see he has his eyes closed, and his mouth has fallen slightly open. His calloused hand is relaxing slightly at my touch. I don't speak or even look at him, I just grab the other hand and do the same thing, starting at the base of his thumb. This is his dominant hand, and I see him wince when I dig near the pinky base.

"Sorry. Too much?" I ask quietly.

"No, it's fine. God, that feels good. I have never had someone do this," he says with a slight rasp to his voice.

"I just thought you might need something like this. Boyd would ask me to massage his hands sometimes. All the years of playing saxophone were hard on him. I bet the work you do on cars is like that, huh?" I say, and he shrugs slightly.

"I guess." He pulls his hands back a little. He leaves them on the table though, and for some reason that makes me happy.

"Did you hurt your pinky today?" I ask.

"Nah, that's an old injury. Caught a pop-up ball without my mitt and broke it."

"Oh, sorry if I hurt you," I say. I wonder if I should have asked before just rubbing his hands like that. God, was that a weird thing to do?

"Don't apologize. It was one of those hurts so good kind of things. You have a nice touch." He takes a deep breath, then says, "Sorry if I have been an ass. An old friend from high school stopped by the shop and it kind of bugged me." I notice he still hasn't pulled his hand away, so I reach out and take his hand in mine again. I start to rub, this time a little more gently.

"Oh? You don't like him?" I ask, and just as Vince is about to answer, the waitress walks up and sets our meals down. Vince pulls his hand back, and he looks from me to his food and decides he'd rather eat than talk. He gives a quick answer that does nothing to quell my curiosity.

"I used to," is all he says.

I drop it and dig into my pasta. Vince is quiet too as he eats his burger. I glance over at the wall where a black-and-white picture hangs. It is framed in a gold-colored metal and really isn't anything special, just a man and a woman at a table. I almost look back to my dinner when something catches my eye.

Holy shit.

"Vince!" I yell, unintentionally loud.

He jumps a little and sets his burger down, grabbing a napkin to wipe up sauce that dripped out when I startled him.

"Sorry, I didn't mean to yell. Vince, look at the picture," I say in a whisper, this time because I am floored. Flattened. "Who is that?" I squeak.

Vince turns his head and looks at the picture, smiling as he turns back to me. "That is Frank Sinatra and Ava Gardner. Great picture, huh? This is my favorite place to sit in here. It's like I am having dinner with him."

"No, not them. The lady in the hat behind him! Isn't that Iolet?" I whisper-hiss.

Vince turns and looks again, then scoots down the booth toward the wall to get a closer look. "Holy shit, that *is* Iolet!"

He reaches up to touch the picture and I squeak again, louder this time. I sound like a mouse, a shocked-as-hell mouse. I put my hands over my lips and stare at his hand in disbelief.

"What?" Vince asks, looking at me, then back at the picture. His eyes dance around the picture and land on exactly what made me squeak. He looks at the picture of Frank's hands resting on the table, then slowly down at the ring on his own finger.

He says in a low deep rumble, "Fuuuck." He doesn't just say the word, he drags it out so it is not just a single exclamation but rather a whole sentence. I feel it in my bones.

Fuck is right.

"That is this ring? On my finger? Frank's ring? Heather?" Vince says in a whisper, and if I wasn't in shock I would find that incredibly cute.

I squeak again in response because I have nothing else anymore; this is my new voice. Vince looks back at me, eyes wide and mouth slightly open. "What the fuck, Heather? I am wearing Frank Sinatra's ring on my fucking finger?" He has scooted away from the picture and is pointing at me now, like this is somehow my fault.

"It appears that way, Vince," I say when I finally find my voice. Now it's my turn to move closer to the picture. I stare at Iolet sitting just behind Frank and Eva. This picture exemplifies everything I learned about Iolet today. She is a background person. She's just everywhere, all the time. I will never be able to look at another picture without looking for her. I literally have to fight the urge to run around the room and scan all the pictures in the diner for her. I bet she is in more than just this one. She was everywhere.

"So we can check the Copa Room off that list. I understand that one now," Vince says.

"Is this picture from there?" I ask, and he shakes his head.

"No, I don't think it was taken there. Can you see if they have this picture in a book or something in the library? We need a copy of it," Vince says. I notice a new gleam in his eye and a spark of something.

"Why?" I ask.

"Because we are going to Vegas to give Frank his ring back!" Vince's smile is huge now. I have never seen him this happy, and holy hell, he is so handsome when he smiles like that.

"Vegas? How?" I push my empty plate to the edge of the table and lean in toward him, mesmerized by his smile. Right now I would follow him anywhere. When he is charming and happy, I want to fling myself in his arms, kiss him on the lips, and tell him I'd go anywhere with him.

"Yeah, it's only a four-hour drive from here, or I guess we could fly, then rent a car or something." He pauses, then says, "No, we should totally drive. I think my Bug is up for the trip, but I will do an oil change and check the brakes before we go."

"When are we going?" I feel overwhelmed. My head is spinning, and my heart is beating out of my chest. Vegas?

"This weekend. You don't have plans, do you?" He winks at me, and my insides turn to liquid.

# FOURTEEN
# VINCE

HOLLYWOOD, California
Hugh's Auto Body


I CAN'T STOP BOUNCING my leg as we drive back to the shop. I know I am making Heather nervous, but I have Frank fucking Sinatra's ring on my finger.

I can't breathe. I might throw up. We need a plan, I need to calm the fuck down, and we need that picture. If I can show that picture to him, he will understand why we have his ring. Maybe I can bring the letter from Iolet too. Yeah, that would work. He— and by he, I mean *Frank Sinatra*—would know we knew the same zany lady, and funny story, she stole his ring.

Jesus.

"Are you going to be okay?" Heather asks as she pulls up to the gate. I nod and hop out to unlock it. I slide the big metal frame in enough for her to pull the car past, then push it closed behind us. Once it is locked again, I head to the door of the shop and fumble to get it open.

She walks up behind me and places her hand on my arm, making me pause and look at her.

"Vince, I am worried about you. Are you okay?" she asks, and all I can think is that her hand is so soft. When she was massaging my hands earlier it took all my strength not to moan like a fool. Thank God the table covered what she was doing to me.

"Yeah, sure, Heather. I am okay. Let's get upstairs. I want to book a room in Vegas," I say. I pull the door open for her, and she walks through, allowing me some space to take a deep, cleansing breath.

As soon as we are upstairs, I am on the phone calling to get a room. Heather walks past me and into my bedroom. I close my eyes and try to picture the billboards I have seen around town. I am almost positive Sinatra is playing at the Gold Nugget, so I start there. Since luck is a lady tonight, the nice gal on the phone helps me snag a room and tickets to the show. It cost me an arm and a leg, but fuck, it's Frank. I can't believe I get to see him perform, and maybe even talk to him. My leg is bouncing again, and I stand up and pace back and forth in my small living room. Heather emerges from my bedroom wearing what she calls pajamas—that damn thin crop top and a pair of shorts that should be illegal.

"So? Did you get it all sorted out?" she asks. She has braided her hair in one thick braid down her back, which only makes me stare at the gentle slope of her shoulders. Her graceful neck and ears that I want to nibble on are on full display.

"Yeah, got a room and tickets to the show on Saturday night. We can leave early Saturday morning and get checked in, then walk around and check out the sights. Vegas is something else," I say.

I sit on the couch, finally feeling a little more settled. I stare at the ring on my finger and spin it around, rubbing the smooth stone.

"Great! I will go by that address I found in the glove in the morning and then over to the library. I think Margaret could help me find that picture in a book, or maybe we can even ask the owner of Sammy's where they got it," Heather says. She comes over and sits next to me, and I can smell that sweet scent of hers.

"Is that a perfume or lotion or something? Why do you always smell like apples?" I say, the words flying out of my mouth before I can stop them.

"What?" She raises her forearm to her nose and sniffs herself, then cocks her head at me like she is confused.

"Apples. You smell like green apples," I say, digging myself in deeper, because every girl likes to know you are fucking smelling them.

"Oh, I guess it's my lotion. I'm sorry. Does it bother you? I have used it for so long I can't smell it anymore." She sniffs her other arm, then shrugs.

"No. It's fine," I mumble.

"Okay." She draws out the word like I have lost my mind, and as I sit here spinning the ring on my finger, I wonder if I have.

"I'll also call that guy tomorrow," Heather says, and I snap my head over and look at her. What guy? Why is she calling a guy? Then I remember the card.

"Oh, right. Yeah. Maybe call him first, you know, in case he wants to meet us or something. I need to change the oil in the Bug and check the brakes, so unless you want to drive my truck, you'll need to be here for a little bit in the morning," I say. I really don't want her meeting up with some random guy without me. I wasn't thinking earlier when I agreed to her contacting him.

"Okay, I can do that. Man, I am all worked up. Is there any more beer?" she asks, and I immediately think of another way to burn off some steam. But thankfully, before I can make an ass out of myself, she gets up and walks over to the fridge. I need to get a grip, and as I am telling myself that very thing, she bends over and rummages through the contents of my refrigerator trying to find beer. Her long, toned legs and perfect ass on full display.

"Want one?" she asks, looking back over her shoulder, and I groan. Hopefully she didn't hear it, but her looking back at me while bent over was just too much.

"Sure, if there are two in there," I say, hoping I sound like a normal human and not a fucking weirdo.

"AH-HA!" she says victoriously, pulling two longneck bottles out. She pops the tops and walks back over, handing me one before settling on the couch next to me. She puts her bare feet up on the coffee table, and I notice her perfect pink toenails.

"Cheers." I tip my bottle toward hers. We clink, then both drink. I lower mine and notice Heather is still gulping hers down. She finally stops, lowers the bottle, and lets out a wall-rattling burp, then sighs and leans back into the cushion.

"Feel better?" I laugh.

"So much. Do you know a month ago I was cleaning old people's apartments, ignoring my mom's phone calls, and trying to figure out how to take a class or two at the local junior college? Now I am sitting in your apartment trying to solve a murder." She tips her beer back and quickly finishes the rest. She leans forward and puts the empty bottle on the coffee table, burps again, and settles back into the couch.

I roll my head to the side and study her. I think again how she is nothing like the girls here. I can't quite put my finger on it, and I don't even know where to start. If I didn't find her so damn attractive, I'd say she was one of those girls who likes to hang with the guys, not into girly things like makeup and fussing with her hair. But that doesn't describe her right. She takes care of herself, she always smells so fucking good, and her hair is nice; not in like the latest style or anything, but that's cool. She has only a suitcase full of clothes, so she wears the same thing a lot. I realize I don't really care about any of that. I can't stand materialistic girls like Monica, but I don't think I have ever met anyone like Heather. I don't know what to do with her, or what to think about her.

"You are staring, Vince. Do I have my pasta dinner all over my face or something?" She tilts her head to mirror my own.

"Nah, just thinking." It comes out quiet, almost a whisper, and I didn't mean for it to sound that way.

"About what?" she asks, not moving at all or giving away her thoughts. Her face is impassive, and I wish I knew what was going on in her head.

"You, I guess. This. It's wild. A month ago I was doing pretty much the same damn thing I am doing now, but there wasn't a beautiful woman on my couch," I say.

She laughs, and it's not a dainty giggle. She snorts and covers her mouth a little, then says, "Thanks. You're not so bad yourself."

"Thanks." I tip my beer and chug the rest like she did, setting mine down on the coffee table next to hers. I kick off my boots and put my feet up, feeling relaxed and comfortable.

"We will figure this out, right? There has to be an end to all of this. I keep replaying that first time I was in her apartment. She was really rattled, like she thought someone would see me coming into her room. She talked a lot about bananas . . ." She trails off, and I jump on it.

"Yeah, what is that? You mentioned it when you first got here. What happened with the banana?" I sit up and turn on the couch to face her. I hook my leg up so I am more comfortable, and she turns to me and does the same.

"Okay, so when I first went to see about cleaning for her, she told me someone stole her banana," she explains.

"Why the hell would someone do that?" I ask.

"No idea, they wouldn't. Those are out on the counter in the cafeteria for anyone to get anytime they want. I really have no idea what she was talking about. She also rambled on about some bird she was going to get, and she was going to name it—" She freezes mid-sentence, and her eyes fly open wider. She raises her hand to her mouth.

"What? She was going to name it what?" I ask, leaning in, because fuck, I am invested in this story, like it's happening to me too.

"Albert. She was going to name it Albert. She said she always loved that name. Oh my God, Vince!" Heather grabs my arm. She squeezes, and my whole body reacts to how strong of a grip she has. My dick jumps a little, like he's asking to come out and play.

I look at her hand on my arm and take a breath. "How did you find out that she had passed? Was it like me, the attorney showing up with a letter?"

"No, I found her," she says in almost a whisper. She relaxes her hand but leaves it on my arm.

"Oh, fuck, Heather. I am sorry," I say, wondering how this is the first I am hearing of this. Why didn't I ask her more questions when she got here? Because I am so caught up in feeling sorry for myself, I don't know how to be a normal fucking person anymore, that's how.

She shrugs a little, and I expect her to turn her head away, but she doesn't. She holds my gaze and tells the story of how she knocked to let Iolet know she was there to clean, then let herself in with her key when no one answered.

"She was lying there in her living room, and at first I thought she was just resting or something because she looked so normal. Well, normal for her. But then I saw the bottom of her shoe, Vince." Heather closes her eyes and takes a deep breath, then continues. "The day before I brought her a banana because I assumed she wanted one, you know?"

"Sure," I say, knowing where this is going.

"The banana I bought her was smeared all across the bottom of her shoe. I found the peel in the kitchen and I—" She puts her hands over her face, and I wait.

"I put it in my purse," she whispers and lowers her hands, then looks at me with the saddest eyes I have ever seen.

"Well hell, Heather," I say, not sure what one says in this kind of a moment.

"I covered up a crime, Vince," she says, and before I can stop it, a laugh bubbles out of me.

"Don't laugh. I killed her with that stupid banana, then I covered it up. I don't even know if they can get fingerprints from a banana skin, Vince, but I wasn't taking any chances!" Heather tuns so she is fully facing me, and she pulls her legs up to sit cross-legged on the couch.

I am shaking, silently laughing at the image of poor Iolet wiped out by a banana. It's too much.

"Stop, Vince. It's not funny." Heather pushes me a little. She cracks a slight smile, and I reach up to wipe my eyes and try to stop laughing. It's no use.

"Her big ole glasses were all askew, and her eyes were still open, you know, so one eye looked huge, like a horse's eye, and the other small." She drops her voice to a whisper and adds, "Like a marble." Her hand goes to her mouth to cover a smile.

"I'm sorry. That must have been awful," I choke out, and she relaxes a little.

"It was," she says, then she cocks her head and asks, "Do you think I killed her, Vince?"

"No," I say without even a thought.

She sits up a little taller, and her shoulders ease.

"Heather, even if she slipped on that banana, it wouldn't be your fault. I mean unless you put it on the floor or something," I say with a chuckle. Then I give her a questioning look, because she is kind of a wild card.

"No, I left it on her counter. I know I did. Okay, well, thanks for that. I guess I can't keep blaming myself." She bends her head forward and picks at her nails, something I have seen her do a lot.

I grab her hand, squeezing it a little. "Heather, you are not to blame, and she clearly liked you. She trusted you with whatever the hell this is, right?"

She looks up at me and laughs a sweet little chuckle that warms me up. "I guess. Thanks, Vince. I am going to head to bed. Do you need to get in there first?" she asks, nodding toward my room.

"Yeah, thanks. I'll just be a minute." I stand and grab our empty bottles, tossing them in the trash before I go to my room to change.

I walk back out wearing just my shorts, because that is how I sleep, and if she can walk around with no bra and a thin crop top that reveals her gorgeous nipples, then she doesn't get me in a T-shirt.

With my arms held wide, I say, "All yours," wishing she would get my double meaning. She doesn't, of course. She just smiles and says good night.

I grab the pillow and blanket I have folded up on the side of the couch and settle in. Hopefully, I can fall asleep before my willpower slips.

# FIFTEEN
# HEATHER





I DON'T KNOW how I fell asleep. I felt like I was going to vibrate right out of my body from all the nerves bouncing around. Iolet's friend Albert was murdered, and she hoped Vince and I would be able to solve it all these years later? Is that even what she intended? How hard would it have been for her to just leave a note saying what the hell she wanted us to do? Instead there are weird clues and notes about New York that make no sense at all. As soon as I wake up, my mind is racing.

I roll to my side and watch as Vince tiptoes in to take a shower. It must be about six in the morning. He glances over at the bed like he has every morning since I got here, and I wonder what he would do if I was just lying here naked one morning. I imagine his reaction and try not to laugh. I hear the water turn on and the shower curtain getting pulled back. I flop onto my back and sigh.

I wonder how different things would be if I had stayed at a hotel instead of here. I wouldn't have been able to afford it for more than two weeks, so I am grateful for this arrangement. Vince is so confusing though. Sometimes he is so sweet and thoughtful, and I think I have a crush on him, but then he snaps at me for something stupid, like looking at his friend's big dumb muscles.

I should get up. I have a million things to do today, but this bed is so comfortable and the breeze from the fan feels so good. I wait until the shower shuts off, then I groan in disappointment and reach over the side of the bed to grab my shorts. I slide them on and sit up, waiting on the edge of the bed for Vince to come out. When the door opens, he steps out in nothing but a towel wrapped low on his hips. His friend Tony may work out a lot, but Vince has a much better body, if you ask me. He isn't too bulky or cut. His muscles look like they are born from hard work, not hard workouts.

He has a nice patch of chest hair and a delicious line of dark hair that disappears into the towel. I'd really like for that towel to slip, but he has one hand holding it, so the chances seem low. If I didn't think he would see me, I might put my fingers to my temples and try a Jedi mind trick: *fall towel, fall.*

"Sorry, I forgot to grab clothes. I thought you'd still be asleep," he says when he notices me sitting on the edge of his bed. For a moment I see and feel his eyes travel over my body like they have done several times in the past two weeks. I stand and take a step toward him, or rather the bathroom. He turns and leans against the dresser, watching me walk toward him, and I wish I was brave enough to walk up to him and run my fingers across his chest, maybe trail them a little lower, let them dance across the flat, firm stomach he keeps hidden under tank tops most days.

"It's okay. I'll just grab my clothes and take a shower," I say, but for some reason my feet have stopped moving. My eyes are glued to his bare chest, his tight stomach, and that damn towel that refuses to fall.

"Okay," he breathes out, and I feel it down to my toes. His gaze falls to my legs, and I swear I get goose bumps as he moves up my body, his eyes raking over every inch of me. I know by the time he reaches my chest, my nipples are sticking out, saying hello. *Hi, cute boy. Notice me. Notice me.* God, they are so needy. I fight the urge to put my arms across my chest and decide to just own it.

I move to where I stashed my suitcase and grab a pair of shorts and a T-shirt I haven't worn yet. Seeing the sad bunch of clothes I own makes me shoot back up and spin around. His eyes dart up like he is trying to hide that he was checking out my ass.

"Crap! Vince, I don't have anything nice enough to wear to a Vegas show. Isn't everyone all decked out at those things?" I try not to sound panicked, but I have one skirt, and it's denim, and I have zero nice shirts. I own cotton and denim. That's it.

"Well, I guess so. I don't really have anything nice either." He scratches his chin. "Why don't you go take a shower so I can get dressed, and we will figure this out." He glances down, and I notice the death grip he has on his towel.

"Right! Sorry," I say and scurry into the bathroom and shut the door.

By the time I am done with my shower, I can smell bacon cooking. This guy. I do not understand how he is single. He's handsome, has a great job, and he can cook. This makes no sense to me.

I walk out to the kitchen to find him glaring into the skillet.

"Do you want eggs or what?" he barks.

Ah, there is clue number one. His charm and unpredictable nature.

"Sure, eggs are good. I can make it myself if you want to get down to the shop," I say. I half expect him to snap at me, but his shoulders relax a little and he shakes his head.

"Sorry, no, I can make it. I have to go out real quick before I start work. I got a phone call from my dad's facility," he says quietly.

"Is everything okay?" I ask. I know his dad had a heart attack and couldn't work, but it must have been worse if he is still in a care place. Vince has never brought it up, not since that first day, so I haven't either.

"I am not sure. They were kind of vague on the phone. They just said I need to come down," he says as he slides two perfectly cooked fried eggs onto a plate. The toaster pops, and he grabs the bread and butters it quickly, then pulls two pieces of bacon out of the pan. I watch, mesmerized by his kitchen skills.

"Here you go. I'll be back in about an hour. I think I heard Tony's truck, so I am going to go downstairs and explain what I need him to do, then head over." He pauses and looks around the room. I watch as storm clouds pass over his face. His lips are tucked in, making two thin lines, and he drags his hand through his hair.

"Do you want me to go with you, Vince?" I ask.

"No, you go ahead and eat. You can call that guy if you want. I'm going to have Tony start on the oil change, then I'll check the brakes and stuff when I get back. I am sure you can have it by noon," Vince says, and I feel like he is speaking from a million miles away.

"Okay, sure. Thanks, Vince. I am sure that will be fine." He's standing there like he is lost in his own home. I cross over to him and pull him into my arms, meaning to give him a quick "you got this" hug, but when I wrap my arms around him, he melts into me. I hold him little tighter and pat his back, unsure what to do. He turns his head and buries his face into my neck and wet hair. We stay like that for longer than a hug between friends.

"Thanks," he mumbles as he finally steps back. He drags his hand through his hair and stares at me like he wants to say something else.

"I'll be here if you need anything, Vince." I give him a small smile, wishing I knew him better, or knew better what to say.

He says nothing, but he gives me that weird chin nod thing that guys do, then walks out. I sit and stare down at the masterpiece of a breakfast that he made me.

After I eat, I start a load of laundry and clean the bathroom and kitchen before I work up the courage to call John. I don't know why I am nervous about it. It probably isn't even his number anymore.

I dial and wait as the phone rings and rings. I am just about to hang up when a woman answers.

"Hello?" she huffs, and I hear what sounds like a cabinet door slam.

"Hi. I am sorry to bother you, but I am looking for John Fitzpatrick. Is he still at this number?" I ask.

"Oh no. He's moved, but I can get you his new number. Do you have a pen and paper?" she asks.

"Yes, thank you so much," I say.

"Sure." She rattles off the new number, then adds, "Tell him to call his mother more often when you get a hold of him." She laughs.

"Sure, I can do that!" I say, then thank her and hang up.

I sigh. "Trying to tell me something, God?" I ask the ceiling. I lean forward and rest my forehead on the cool wood tabletop. I could call my mom and just check in. I don't need to give her Vince's number. I don't need to reattach the cord that has been wrapped around my neck my whole life. I sigh and dial my mom's number.

"Hello," a man slurs into the phone. I almost hang up. I should have hung up.

"Is Francis there?" I ask, not even sure which answer I want.

"No, that bitch moved. Took all my beer money too. You tell her to bring it back when you find her, okay?" the man slurs. I think his name is Greg, but to be honest, I try not to pay too much attention to the men in my mom's life.

"Sure thing," I say and hang up before he can say anything else. I call my apartment, letting my knee bounce to release some of my energy.

"Yeah?" Kristen says when she picks up. I have always hated the way she answers the phone. It's just so fucking rude.

"Hey, Kristen. It's me. I just wanted to—" I start, but she cuts me off.

"Yeah, she's here," she says, and I hear her set the phone down and call for my mom. Wait, what? What the hell is my mom doing there?

"Hullo," my mom says. It sounds like she just woke up, her voice all gravelly with sleep, or she is hungover. I don't ask which one.

"Why are you at my apartment?" I ask instead.

"That's a fine way to speak to your mom. Don't I get a hello?" She coughs and clears her throat.

"Hello. Why are you in my apartment?" I ask again, praying for strength or the ability to turn back time and not make this phone call.

"Well, you paid up for two months, and that asshole Tim was drinking in front of me, even though I told him I am in recovery. My sponsor said I should move, so I did," she says. Tim, not Greg. I make a mental note.

Damn. I blow out a frustrated breath, and she copies me like the petulant child she is.

"Don't give me any grief, Heather. I need a place to stay, and you aren't here. There is no reason why I shouldn't stay here. Kristen agrees." She pulls the phone away from her mouth and yells, "Don't you, Kristen?"

I don't hear whatever Kristen yells back, but it doesn't matter. It's done, and now I may not have a place when I go back, because the only reason my mom would move out is if she met a new man. Which, to be honest, could happen as soon as tomorrow.

"Are you still going to work at the walnut processing plant?" I ask. I rest my forehead in my hand and wait for the excuse I am sure she has.

"Listen, that was a shit job, and the foreman was always looking at my ass. Plus it was all the way out by the river, you know, and I couldn't always get a ride. Your car is a piece of shit, by the way." She says it like I am the reason she couldn't make it to her job.

"Who gave you keys to my car?" I ask. I am actually grateful it died for good before I left. I meant to call the salvage company to come pick it up, but I forgot.

"You left a set on the rack. Hey, why don't you have a dresser in your room? Did you know there is no closet in there?" she asks as I am pulling the phone away from my ear. I can't do this.

"Yeah, sure. Be right there!" I yell to the empty room, then say to my mom, "Hey, I gotta go. I'll call when I am coming back, I guess."

"Okay. Have fun in San Diego," she says, and I don't bother correcting her.

"Okay, bye, Mom." I hang up before she can say anything else. I wonder what it's like to have an adult for a parent.

I reach for the phone again and call John Fitzpatrick at the number his mom gave me.

# SIXTEEN
# VINCE


HOLLYWOOD Hospital
Third Floor


"I AM HERE to see my father, Hugh De Luca," I say at the desk. I see his door is pulled shut, and that isn't normal. Dad likes it open.

"Let me get the charge nurse, Vince. Thanks for coming down," Mary says. I lean forward, resting on my forearms on the high counter that surrounds the nurse's station. I want to hang my head and cry, and I also want to throw it back and scream. I feel that way every time I come here.

"Vince, I am Tammy. I am the charge nurse that called you earlier. I don't believe we have met yet in person." A very big woman with a warm smile is suddenly standing next to me.

I turn to shake her hand, but she pulls me into a quick hug. That can't be a good sign.

"I came as soon as I could. Is everything okay?" I ask and I hate that my voice wobbles. Would it be so bad if this was his end? He wouldn't want to be like this, stuck in bed with people having to do everything for him.

"Well, yes and no. It's complicated, which is why I asked you to come down. His doctors are on their way, and then we can use the conference room to discuss the next steps."

An hour later, I emerge from the hospital confused about what to do. The doctors are unsure why my father has become violent, but they do know he is no longer able to stay here. One of the doctors thinks it means that his end is near, but the other doctor disagrees. They all agreed he needs to be at a place that can handle his outbursts. They gave me the name of two places to check out and even handed me their brochures like I was shopping for a new car or something.

I wish I could call my mom, but she won't help. After my dad's heart attack, she stepped up a little, but when he had the stroke, she tapped out. She said she no longer had to deal with the "worse" because he ruined the "better" with all his cheating.

I wish I could tap out. I fucking hate this.

I climb into my truck and lower my head to the steering wheel to take a moment, then I head to the shop. I know what I need to do. I just need to work. I'll deal with this later. Driving past all the stores and restaurants, I realize how nothing has changed in this part of town for years. It's stuck, run-down, falling apart—just like me.

The gate is wide open to the backyard, so I pull in and park. I slam the door and spin to kick an oil can that is on the ground and nearly bean Terrence right in the head as it flies through the air. I didn't notice him when I hopped out of my truck.

"Fuck, man. Watch it!" he says, ducking. We both watch the can clank to the ground. "You okay?" he asks, holding his hands up as he approaches me like I might hit him.

"Sure. What are you doing here?" I grumble and walk toward the open bay door. Tony has some crappy music blaring, and I walk straight to the stereo and turn it off.

"Hey!" Tony says as he peeks out from under my Bug. It's up on the lift, the full oil pan by his feet. "Oh, it's you. How did it go?" he asks as Terrence walks in behind me.

"I don't want to talk about it. You all done?" I snap, and Tony sighs.

"Yeah, I did the oil change and checked the brakes. They are fine. No need to replace them. Your air filter looked like a two-pack-a-day smoker's lung, so I changed that. You should be good to go on your trip." Tony bends and grabs the tray of dirty oil and carries it to the waste barrel.

"Where you going?" Terrence asks.

"Vegas," I snap.

"Who pissed in your corn flakes?" Terrence asks.

"My dad," I say. I toss the brochures on my desk and sit in the old, creaky chair, lowering my head into my hands.

"Fuck, did he pass?" Terrence asks, and Tony has moved in front of me. I can't look up, so I just shake my head and take a deep breath before I answer.

"No, but he has started trying to hit the nurses while they are changing him. If I ever get to that point where I am lying in my own piss and hitting girls, promise you will just end me, okay?" I choke out.

"Deal, dude. As long as you promise the same," Tony says, and Terrence agrees.

"Deal," I say.

We are all quiet, and the silence is smothering me. Tony knows me very well, so he launches into a discussion about the cars we have waiting, and my mind relaxes a little thinking about the work ahead of us. I can do this. I can. I have to.

About an hour later, I am elbow-deep in a carburetor rebuild thinking about nothing but what needs to be done next on this car. I have another car waiting for a brake job, and I need to clear one of these bays so I can bring the car Iolet stole here. I want to fix it up before I give it back. I am sure she didn't know how to properly store a car, so there is going to be some damage. It will be an honor to fix it.

"Vince, are you down here?" Heather calls from the top of the stairs. I straighten up and so does Terrence. He's been helping Tony put new tires on a Mustang. He's a good guy, helping out when he can and never asking for anything in return. If you ask me, I think he is just feeling like shit about the way his cousin treated Tony. You can't control family, that's for damn sure.

"Yeah, sorry. I should have come up and told you I was back. The Bug is all done if you want to head out," I say, wiping my hands with my shop rag. I tuck it back in my pocket and walk toward the stairs as she comes down. Every time I see her I am hit with how pretty she is. She's wearing a Chico State tank top, her denim shorts, and like always, her dirty Keds with no socks. I wish I could go to her and get a hug like before, but I stop short of the bottom of the stairs.

"How did it go with your dad? Is everything okay?" she asks, and I am planning on giving a quick answer like I did with the guys, but her big, beautiful eyes draw me in.

"He's not great. I guess he has started to get violent with the nursing staff, so they have to move him. He only has use of his right arm, but he clocked a nurse on the night shift so hard it broke her nose. I am supposed to pick a place, but I can't even wrap my head around all this," I say quietly so the guys don't hear.

"Oh God, Vince. I am so sorry." She doesn't hesitate pulling me to her, dirt and grease and all, and I am in her arms again, safe. For a moment I forget everything, lost in her scent of crisp green apples. I feel her pull me impossibly closer, and I move my hands down her back and press myself against her, forgetting where we are. I feel rather than hear her sharp intake of breath, and I know she must feel my stupid cock that thought this hug was leading to something. I pull away slightly, but she pulls me back in and rubs my back. We are alone in the world in this moment, and I want it to last forever. I rest my chin on the top of her head, and my whole world settles for the first time in a long time.

When she finally pulls away to look up at me, I smile down at her, knowing everything is going to be okay. All this shit with my dad will be okay. One look from her and I know that? Is it her eyes or her smile? Those little freckles that dot her cheeks?

"Did they give you options for placement?" she asks.

I nod, then head over to my desk for the brochures. I hand them to her, and she glances at them for a moment before putting them in her purse.

"Okay, I will go check them out after I meet with John. He has a whole case file on Albert Milton that he is willing to show me," Heather says.

"What? You don't have to do that. I can go—" I start, but she cuts me off with the wave of a hand.

"I am going to go see what these places are like. I work at a senior apartment, remember? We have residents who get shipped off to care homes, and I have gone a few times with family members to help assess the places. I'll give you my opinion, then you can go see them yourself and decide. This way, you'll have another set of eyes. It's okay." She grabs my hand, gives it a quick squeeze, then drops it.

"Alright, if you have time. Wait, so you talked to that John guy?" I ask, that little tidbit she dropped suddenly sinking in.

"Oh my gosh, yeah. He is a detective with the Hollywood Police Department now and kept his files from when he was in school. He said that Albert's murder has always bothered him, and if we have any clues he is interested," Heather says, and I can see the excitement in her eyes.

"Well, maybe don't mention the car yet. I don't want the cops sniffing around all this yet. I want to help Iolet and not just turn this over to the authorities without trying to figure out what the stuff in the boxes means. She picked us for a reason," I say in a low voice. I yearn to reach out to her again, to pull her into my chest and breathe in her sweet scent. I want to feel her warm body against mine again, and my brain and my dick are currently in a war about how to accomplish that.

"I understand, and I was thinking the same thing. Okay, I am heading out. You going to be okay?" she asks. She has narrowed her eyes in this fucking adorable little squint.

"Yeah. I'll see you when you get back. Thanks, Heather. I really appreciate your help with the stuff with my dad," I say.

"Sure, I am glad I'm here to help." She dips her head, then looks back up at me with those dark, beautiful eyes, and I feel my stomach flip. She raises her hand and gives me a little wave, then turns to go, almost running face first into Tony's large chest.

"Oh! Hi! I didn't see you there. How are you today, Tony?" Heather asks. She smooths a hand over her hair, and I wonder if she is as rattled as I am.

"Yeah, you seemed kind of busy, so I thought I'd wait to say hi." Tony smirks like the idiot he is.

"Hi, you are new," Terrence says, and I step forward, trying to intercept whatever stupid pickup line he's about to spit out.

"Yeah, I am a friend of Vince's. My name is Heather. You are?" Heather asks with her hand extended.

"Charmed and in love." Terrence takes her hand and fucking bends to kiss her knuckles. I hear Tony laugh, and I can't be positive, but I think I just growled. I fucking hate that he is touching her.

"That's Terrence. He's not as big as a schmuck as that pickup line would make you believe," I say, stepping forward. I put my arm on Heather's shoulders, dropping it there like I do it all the time.

"Right, got it. My bad. Nice to meet you, Heather," Terrence says, noting the look on my face and my possessive grip on her shoulder. Thankfully Heather doesn't seem to mind. Well, at least she doesn't push me away.

"Nice to meet you too. I have a lot to do, so I'll catch you guys later," she says while reaching up to pat my hand that is gripping her.

"Okay, sure. See you soon," I say, giving her a little squeeze before I let her step away. I keep my eyes on Terrence the whole time, hoping he gets my point.

# SEVENTEEN
# HEATHER



I WAIT until I am a few blocks away to pull over and collect myself. I could have held him all day, and I am pretty sure if his friends weren't there, a lot more would have happened. I was having a hard time not pulling him down for a kiss. I fan my face with my hands, trying to cool the flames that have taken over my body. I should not get turned on by comforting him, I know that, but his body pressed against mine felt so good I forgot why I was holding him.

After I calm down and refocus on the task at hand, I pull back out into traffic and head to the police station to meet this John guy. I have so many questions, but I really should be careful with what I say. He knows that Iolet left me and Vince a few things from her movie days. I explained that I wanted to learn more about her for a celebration of life at Serenity Falls, and that led me to the library where Margaret remembered his research.

I park and walk up to the brick-covered building. With its low, flat roof and few windows, it's obviously a government facility. In the lobby, I look around for an information desk or something, but John is waiting. I know it's him because he told me on the phone I wouldn't be able to miss him. He was right. He is a tall, thin man with bright red hair and a face full of freckles that make him look a lot younger than I think he is. He's wearing suit pants and a white button-up shirt with a blue tie. He has a badge clipped to his belt on one side and a gun on the other. I take a steadying breath, reminding myself this has nothing to do with me or my mom. I am here to help and to get information. That is it.

"John Fitzpatrick?" I ask, and he smiles and nods.

"Heather Fields, I presume?" He is holding his hand out, so I walk forward and grasp it to shake.

"Thanks for coming down. You know, I didn't tell you this on the phone, but I had just pulled Albert's file last week to give it another look," he says. He has both hands tucked in his pockets in a relaxed pose. I wish I felt as calm.

"Really? That's wild. I got here two weeks ago to meet up with Vince, the other recipient of Iolet's . . ." I trail off, not sure how to describe it.

"Oh, right. You mentioned him. Vince DeLuca. He is the owner of Hugh's Auto Body, right?" he says. He starts to walk toward an office and stops to wave me along.

I follow him, wondering if I told him that or if he looked it up somehow. Crap. My stomach feels tight all of a sudden. I hope I am doing the right thing by coming here. I glance over my shoulder at the doors I walked through a moment ago, wondering if I should just leave.

John opens the door to his office and motions me in, then pulls out a chair for me to sit. He walks around to the other side of the desk and settles into his chair. I see the file sitting on his desk marked Albert Milton, and it's thick.

John pulls the file closer to him and opens it. He lifts the long, brass-colored brads at the top and slides a paper free. He hands it to me without comment.

I take it and look down to see Albert's death certificate. I wince when I see cause of death was a bullet wound to the head. There isn't really anything else to mention. He was born in Orange County and died in North Hollywood at his home. His occupation is listed as actor.

"Shot? I think Margaret mentioned that to me, and the article in the paper said that too," I say.

"Yeah, so that's what the report says, and I am not doubting he was, but I bet there was more than just the bullet hole. I think the shot to the head was the final shot, not the only wound," John explains, folding his hands in front of him.

"What makes you think that?" I slide the paper back to him.

"How is your stomach for crime scene photos?" he asks.

"I really don't know. I have never seen one, but I do clean up some pretty gross stuff where I work. I'll probably be fine," I say, and he chuckles.

"I think you can handle it. They are black-and-white photos, so the dark patches you'll see are blood. That's what got me when I first looked at this case. There is blood everywhere, more than you'd expect from just a single gunshot wound. I am betting there was a struggle or maybe even an outright brawl. I think it was not just Albert who bled, but his attacker as well." John is flipping through the left side of the file until he finds what he wants. He pulls out two pictures, and I lean forward to take a closer look.

There is a man lying on the floor, face up. He has light-colored hair, and it's a little disheveled, sticking up on the side, with a piece he probably slicked back in the style of the day hanging over his face. He has an obvious bullet hole right in the middle of his forehead, and his eyes are still open. The trickle of blood that runs out of the hole is dark like John had said it would be. There is also a dark puddle under his head.

He's wearing a dark suit, and while his jacket is open and flipped up on one side, it is not noticeable at first glance because his button-up shirt is also a dark color. I take in every detail of the picture.

The second picture was taken from further back, and it shows more of the room and all of Albert's tall frame. I see a puddle of blood under his left hip that isn't very big, and then I notice that he isn't wearing any shoes. He has on dress socks, and one of them is pulled a little so the toe area hangs down.

Crap, we were right. We have Albert's shoes.

I start to breathe a little faster, and John asks if I am okay.

"Sure, yeah. Maybe a glass of water?" I ask, hoping for a minute to myself to calm down.

"Of course." John gets up and walks out to the hall, returning quickly with a small paper cup from a watercooler.

When John is back in his chair, he leans forward and points to Albert's hands. "See the swelling here and here? I think he punched whoever killed him. His knuckle looks like it might be split here, making me wonder if he got a good head shot in. Then look here at Albert's feet. There are drops of blood that wouldn't have come from the bullet wound."

I pick up the picture and study the floor in it. Albert's carpet must have been a very light color because the blood droplets are very obvious, and they are all around where he would have been standing.

"Why is Albert not wearing any shoes? He has a suit on, yet he's just in socks," I ask, praying my voice sounds calm and normal.

"You're good at this, Heather!" John beams at me, and I blush a little. "That and the blood splatter were the two things I noticed when I got this file. Someone took his shoes, and it looks like maybe they were going to take his socks too but changed their mind. We won't ever know, because crime scenes in the thirties weren't investigated like they are now. It could have been anyone." He shrugs.

"What are you talking about?" I ask.

"Well, the police report stated that the officer was able to question all of Albert's neighbors who were in the living room when the police arrived. Apparently, the neighbors heard the gunshot and rushed over to see what happened." John shakes his head and grabs another picture from the stack of evidence.

"This is a footprint in the blood behind him, and you can see it leads to the kitchen area here. I learned from one of the detectives who was on scene that it was from a neighbor who wandered repeatedly through the house touching everything. It was like a goddamn cocktail party in there. I think that detective said he counted at least ten people who came in and out before they could remove the body." John is shaking his head again.

"Oh, man. No wonder this was never solved," I say, feeling a little relieved he didn't mention Iolet. I have those damn shoes in a box at Vince's, but why? Why on earth would she have taken them off a dead body?

John shuffles the papers, then pulls out a picture that looks very familiar. I have seen it before but from a slightly different angle. He taps the image of Iolet, who is sitting behind Frank and Ava Gardner, and says, "Iolet was on to something. The Hollywood detectives and cold case agents followed her everywhere once they realized she knew something. This is her in Vegas. I learned that shortly after this picture was taken, she and Sinatra had a conversation in a side room. She left quickly after that, and the agent wasn't able to trail her. We still don't know what that was all about, but I suspect there are mob ties to Albert's death," John says. He leans back in his chair, studying me. I think I am sweating a little.

"Mob ties?" I manage to squeak out.

"Yeah, she was from New York, and from what I learned, she left suddenly in 1935, showing up here a few months later. She auditioned and landed a lead role in a movie with Albert. It doesn't happen very often that an unknown gets paired with a superstar like him," John says.

"Margaret said they dated. I found an article that reported Albert being seen with a Broadway star on his arm. Wouldn't that explain it?" I ask.

"Maybe if she was actually a Broadway star, but I looked into that. She wasn't in anything on Broadway, or even any of the little theaters off Broadway," John says.

"Oh, right. I know she was in a lot of things out here, but I noticed she was never a lead. Margaret said Iolet was the busiest actress she knew because she was willing to take any part," I say, and John nods.

He pulls out two pages of handwritten notes. He taps the first page and says, "These are all the movies she was in. You are right. She was either a background person or she had one line. I think the most she was on camera was in *Gentlemen Prefer Blondes*. She didn't have any lines, but she was in the background in almost every crowd scene."

I make a mental note to tell Vince that. I am wondering if they can play that movie at Past Times Theater when John pulls out a picture of Marilyn Monroe wearing long pink gloves and a matching dress. He taps a small, dark head behind her and says, "Here she is. It's the only shot I am sure it is her, because in the film it's more obvious."

My eyes go straight to the long, pink gloves, and I have to force myself to look at where he is pointing.

"Wow, she sure was in a lot of films," I say. I look back at the handwritten list. "Can I see this?"

"Sure, I may have missed one or two, but I think that is all of them," John says.

"Wow." I scan the list that is way longer than the one she left us in the boxes. Those must be important, another thing I make a mental note of, wishing I could actually write this stuff down.

"The residents at Serenity Falls would fawn all over Iolet when she lived there. I guess they must have known she was semi-famous. She accomplished a lot in her life. Thanks for showing me all of this. I think I can use some of this information at her celebration of life. I won't mention the murder or mob ties or anything, but you know." I stand quickly. I suddenly feel the need to get the heck out of here.

"Wait, I was hoping to ask you a few questions," John says as he stands with me.

"Oh, right. Well, I have somewhere else to be. Something came up with a friend, and I promised I would help. I can come back maybe Monday?" I say.

John squints at me, and I know he is wondering what the heck just happened. I am wondering that too, if I am honest. This room got smaller and warmer when I saw those gloves.

"Sure, Monday will work. Thanks for coming by." He extends his hand.

I reach out and shake his hand, then turn and scurry out of the room like I am about to get arrested. As soon as I am outside, I lean against the glass doors and take in a deep breath. I don't know what to do first. Do I go back to the garage and tell Vince everything I learned, or do I go to the library and try and find more information about this Albert guy? When I reach in my purse for the keys to Vince's Bug, my hand hits the brochures, and I know what I have to do. I can't believe I almost forgot.

I pull them out when I get back in the car and look at the map Vince has tucked up in his visor. One of the care homes is only a few blocks away, so I decide to start there. As I drive, I let myself freak out a little bit. Holy shit. I have Albert's shoes and Marilyn's gloves, and the police know that Iolet met with Frank in Vegas. Vince and I are behind in this little investigation, that is for damn sure.

I park and walk into Grandview Care Home and turn around immediately. It smells like someone died in the lobby, and I can hear a patient wailing from down the hall. Nope. No way. I have never met Hugh, but I am certain Vince wouldn't want his dad here.

I map out where the other place is and head there, pulling up twenty minutes later to what looks like a home. It's in a nice neighborhood too, and for a moment I think I have the wrong place. I duck my head to look out the passenger window and see a woman in nurse's scrubs walking out the front door. She turns and locks the door behind her, then stands on her tiptoes and waves a hand at the glass arch on the door. When she turns back to me, she smiles. I climb out of the car quickly and approach her.

"Hi. I am sorry to bother you. Do you work here?" I say, motioning to the house.

"Yeah, just got off shift. Do you have a family member here?" she asks, and I immediately like her.

"No, not yet. I came to look at it," I explain.

"Oh, you'll need to make an appointment. They won't answer the door unless they know you are coming. Do you have a pen? I can give you the number."

I shake my head and pull out the brochure. "It's okay. I have this. I was just in the area so I drove over. Do you like working here?" I ask, because if the staff is happy, that says a lot.

"I love it. The people are great. My coworkers and the patients. It's a smaller facility so we can provide more personalized care. I think that is why I like it," she says, and I smile.

"That's all I needed to hear. I will tell my friend to call and make an appointment." I pause, then clarify because I don't want to get Vince's hopes up. "Do you know if there are openings, and also you take patients that have, um . . ." I stop, unsure how to go on.

"Violent tendencies? We get a lot of patients that have nowhere else to go. Is that what is going on?" she asks with a small smile.

"Yes," I say on an exhale.

"Yeah, we can handle that. There are two beds open right now, and I am sad to say when I get to work tomorrow there will probably be a third." She sighs.

"Oh, I am sorry to hear that, but is it wrong that I am also glad you have an opening?" I ask.

"Not at all. I would want my family in a place like this." She holds out her hand to me. "Hi. I am Victoria."

"Hi, Victoria. I am Heather." I take her hand and shake it.

"Nice to meet you. I hope it works out for you and your family. I have to get home before my babysitter starts charging me overtime. Have a great day." She spins on her heels and walks off.

I get back in the Bug and drive back to the shop, anxious as hell to talk to Vince about everything that happened today. I turn onto the street where the shop is and can see already that the front bay doors are pulled shut. Vince usually keeps at least one of them open when he's working. I slow to turn into the driveway and see the gate to the back lot is closed and the chain lock is in place. I glance down at my watch and see it's only three o'clock. That is weird. Thankfully, the set of keys for the Bug holds keys to everything, so I shut off the car and get out to unlock the gate.

Once I am inside the lot, I close the gate and lock it back up, hoping Vince is inside working and didn't want to be bothered. I reach for the back door and find it's locked. Well, hell's bells. He isn't here.

I let myself in, grateful he left the lights on at least. I go upstairs and open the apartment and see a note on the table.

*Needed a break from all this, went to the beach with the guys. Not sure when I will be back but we can leave early tomorrow for Vegas. See you then.*
*Vince*

WOW, okay. I drop my bag and look around. Shit. I should go check out the address that was in the glovebox since Vince isn't here. I don't want to sit around with nothing to do but think. Seeing those gloves and John confirming that Iolet was in the movie with Marilyn made me very nervous. I felt like John somehow knew I had the gloves.

I grab my bag and head back out, mildly irritated with Vince for leaving like that. He should be here so I can tell him everything and maybe try and find a reason to hug him again. Damn it. I also want to go to the beach. I have never seen the ocean in real life, and if I had been here, I could have gone.

I stomp down the stairs and out to the back lot, locking everything back up before I leave. The address isn't too far away, so that's nice. I watch the numbers as I drive and slow down when I get close, parking on the street at a meter. I walk the last block and stop in front of a bank.

I pull out the paper and check the address again. Yeah, this is the place. How strange. I look at the key and the tiny metal tab that hangs from it and notice a number. Maybe the teller will know what this is.

I walk into the bank and wait in line for a teller to open. When it's my turn, I smile at the sweet older woman behind the counter.

"How can I help you today, dear?" she asks.

"I am not sure. My friend passed away and this was in her things. She wrote the address on a piece of paper that was with this key. Do you know what this is?" I try to be vague, because it feels weird to say some woman I barely knew is driving me crazy with random clues, and this is one of them.

"Oh yes, dear. I am sorry for your loss. This is to a safety deposit box. Let me call the manager and she can take you." She turns and waves to a woman at a desk behind her.

"Laura, this young woman has her friend's key to a safety deposit box. Her friend has sadly passed, and the key was with her belongings. Can you help her?"

"Of course. Meet me at the end of the counter, dear," Laura says and walks away, so I follow, thinking it can't be this easy.

"I'll just need to see some ID or a letter from the attorney," Laura says when we get to the end. There is a low wall with a door separating us.

"Oh. Okay, I have a letter she gave me, and I can call the attorney if you let me use your phone," I say.

"What was your friend's name, dear?" Laura asks, and I swallow hard. I guess if she doesn't let me in, the attorney could help. I just want to get this over with.

"Well, her name was spelled Violet, but she went by Iolet. Her last name was Merryweather," I say, and Laura taps her chin, thinking.

"Let me check the records. One second." Laura disappears to a bookshelf and pulls out a ledger, then sits and starts flipping through the book. I watch as her finger dances along what I assume is a list of names.

"Ah-ha!" She reads something, looks up at me, then down at the book, then back up at me. She walks over to me with a puzzled look on her face.

"Your friend has two people listed as co-owners of the box, and I have to say I have never seen anything like this." Laura is scratching her hand like she is nervous. She steps forward and in a low voice says, "I am going to assume you are not Vince DeLuca?"

"No, but I know him. He and my friend were close," I say. I can feel the sweat start to trickle down my back even though I have done nothing wrong.

"I see. Well, you fit the description she gave of the second owner, but she didn't give a name. I don't know why she would have done it that way," Laura says.

"I fit the description? When did Iolet write that?" I ask, feeling like I might throw up.

"She secured this box in 1975 and has never been back," Laura says, looking me up and down.

"My friend was quite eccentric," I say, trying to remain calm. I am doing the math in my head, and I am pretty sure Vince said he mowed her lawn in 1974. How is this happening? Did she plan to find someone that would help Vince with all of this? Has she been looking for someone like me since 1975? I take a deep breath while Laura continues to stare at me.

Laura reaches down and turns the handle on the little door and opens it, inviting me in. We walk to the ledger, and she points to Iolet's line. Sure enough, under "other owners" it says, *Vince DeLuca and a tall pretty girl with long, brown hair and brown eyes.*

"Huh. I guess that describes me. I can come back with Vince if you would like. Or we can call the attorney. I have his card in my purse," I explain and reach in my bag to find the business card. Once I find it, I hand it to her, and she nods.

"I'll be right back, dear. Let me just verify this." Laura walks off, her heels clicking on the linoleum.

She is back quicker than I thought possible, and she has a smile on her face. "All sorted out, dear. This way." She hands me Mr. Daniels's business card. I take it and tuck it back into my purse as she leads me down a hallway to a locked room, and after a moment of fumbling, she lets me in. It looks like a post office in Chico with various sizes of boxes set into the wall. There is a small table in the middle of the room with two chairs. Laura leads me to a small box numbered like my key.

"I am going to give you some privacy. When you are all done, you can ring that bell, and I will come and let you out. No one else will have access to this room while you are in here, and we don't have any appointments today. Take your time, dear." Laura pats my arm, then leaves.

I lift my key and try to fit it in the lock, but my hand is shaking so bad I have to try a couple of times before I manage to get it open. There is a metal box inside that has a handle, so I pull it out and carry it to the table. I slide out a chair and sit, breathing in and out in slow, measured breaths.

When I open it, I see a note on top of a black velvet bag.

*Vince, or whatever lovely lady I found, I am so glad you are here. In this bag you will find costume jewelry that belonged to Norma Jean. She let me have it as part of our little pact. I hoped you would be able to talk to her, but they killed her. She knew what happened to Albert, and she thought I was right about who killed him. She was a kind and wonderful woman, and I know she would have helped. She believed me when no one else would. I hope you can believe me too.*

*All my love,*

*Violet*

NORMA JEAN? Who the hell is Norma Jean? I set the letter down and reach for the bag, and as soon as I open it, I understand. This jewelry belonged to Marilyn Monroe. I saw this necklace just this afternoon in the picture at the police station. I run my fingers along the beautiful piece of jewelry, grateful she told me in the letter that the items were fake. Otherwise I would have had a heart attack for sure. Now that I think about it, I remember I read somewhere that Marilyn's real name was Norma.

Holy shit. I grab the letter again and smile at the first line. She always planned on finding a girl to help Vince with all this. I kind of love her for that. I also realize that she had just met Vince a year before she did this. She was putting her trust in a fourteen-year-old boy, but why?

# EIGHTEEN
# VINCE


HOLLYWOOD, California
Hugh's Auto Body


MY HEAD IS BEING HELD by two large, angry gorilla hands. That is the only thing that makes sense as I attempt to open my eyes. My eyelids easily weigh a hundred pounds each. I give up for a moment and try and get my bearings. I am on my side and in a bed. My head is resting on someone's very soft shoulder. That's all I know without opening my eyes. Why do I smell apples?

Fuck.

My eyes snap open painfully and I see the gentle slope of Heather's breast right next to my face. My rock-hard dick is pressed into her hip. I have one leg over her thighs, and my arm is across her stomach, trapping her. What the fuck is happening? I pinch my eyes closed again and try and remember last night. I remember getting dinner at the crab place by where we like to surf. I remember the beach, and maybe volleyball. There was definitely a bonfire and lots of beer. I have a vague memory of singing.

"Good morning, Mr. Sinatra," a sweet voice says.

I groan and move my arm and leg off her. She scoots away just enough to roll toward me.

"Why am I in here?" I croak. My mouth is so dry, like someone stuffed cotton balls in it while I slept. I think my teeth are wearing tiny sweaters.

"I am not really sure. You came home around midnight singing and happy and I *thought* you passed out on the couch." She giggles and reaches over my shoulder, skimming her fingers up to my hair. She tugs a little then says, "But I woke up a few minutes ago because something very hard was poking me in the hip."

"Oh my God." I roll to my stomach, trapping my stupid cock against the mattress. "I am so sorry," I mumble into the pillow. Fuck, I miss my bed. Was it always this comfortable?

"It's okay. I am going to take a shower, then make us some breakfast. I filled the Bug's gas tank yesterday, and I solved our clothing problem for Vegas," she says, entirely too chipper for my current state.

I groan into the pillow. I must have fallen asleep again, because I wake up to the wonderful smell of bacon and a warm, soft hand on my chest. I am not wearing a shirt, and I can feel the heat of her skin against my beating heart.

"Vince, breakfast is ready. Think you can make it to the kitchen?" She is rubbing her thumb across my chest, and for a second I want to pretend to still be asleep so she will keep doing it. I move my leg a little, and then I feel my dick twitch against the sheet. Yep, still hard and apparently naked.

Jesus.

"Yeah. I, um, seem to have taken off all my clothes," I say, draping one arm over my eyes. I move my other hand to my crotch to try and contain the tenting I know is happening. I can't look at her right now. This is so embarrassing.

"Yes, you did. They are in the living room. Would you like me to bring them to you?" she says sweetly.

"No. Just leave me here to die of embarrassment, please," I mumble.

"Sure thing, Vince," she says and walks off laughing.

When I know she is gone, I glance down and move my hand I see I am indeed tenting the very thin white sheet that covers me. Stupid morning wood. There is no way she didn't notice. I grab it and give it a few tugs, then roll out of bed and head into the shower to finish the job.

When I emerge dressed and deflated, I walk straight to the coffeepot without looking at her. I pour myself a cup and take a sip before turning around. I wish I could splash some alcohol in this to give me a little more courage to face her, but since I can't, I just take another gulp and turn. She is cutting up her pancakes and humming a tune that sounds familiar. I squint at her and try to place the song but come up short.

"What are you humming?" I grumble.

"Oh, sorry. You just kept singing it last night, and now it's stuck in my head." She snickers and takes a bite of her pancakes.

"I sang here?" I ask, moving to the table. I sit in front of a full plate of bacon, eggs, and pancakes because this woman is an angel.

"Oh yes, and you do have a lovely voice, Vince, just like Iolet said in her note to you." She winks at me, and all I can do is hang my head.

I finally get the courage to look up at her, and while she still has a big grin on her face, her eyes are soft and kind, giving me the boost I need. "It seems I have a lot to apologize for. First of all, I am sorry I climbed into bed with you." I pause and then add, "Naked. That was unacceptable. I'm sorry."

"It's okay, Vince. I didn't notice you were there until this morning. I feel bad that you have slept on the couch these past two weeks. Your drunk self knew where you would be comfortable," she says with a chuckle. I watch as she wipes the last bit of her pancake through the syrup and places it in her mouth. It shouldn't turn me on to watch her eat, right? Damn it.

"Well, I hope drunk me didn't do anything inappropriate," I say. She is licking the syrup off her lips now and I stifle a groan.

"You didn't." She smiles, then goes back to humming that tune. She picks up her plate and carries it to the sink, continuously humming. She even does a little twirl and then shoots me a look over her shoulder.

"Okay, Heather, what's that song?" I ask while rubbing my temples.

"I am not sure of the name of it, but I bet it is a Sinatra song, because you said, and I quote, 'Blue eyes ain't got nothing on me' before you launched into your rendition." She beams at me, and if she wasn't so damn cute, I might be mad at her for acting so smug.

She starts to hum again, and I have a flash of a memory of me out here in the living room stripping out of my clothes while singing "Strangers in the Night." Just as it comes to me, Heather looks over her shoulder and sings, the next line of the song then wiggles her eyebrows.

"Oh my God." I moan and push my plate away.

"No, Vince, you need to eat! I'll stop. I'm sorry." She smiles and sits next to me, placing her hand on my arm. "I just couldn't resist teasing you. If it helps, I think after your little song you fell asleep out here. I don't know if you crawled into bed after you used the bathroom or what, but it is really okay. This is your home. You should sleep in your bed. When we get back from Vegas, we are trading, and I am sleeping on the couch."

I don't feel like arguing, but no way in hell is that happening. I nod and work on finishing my breakfast.

An hour later and somehow we are on the road headed to Vegas. I say somehow because we had what could only be described as our first fight. We worked it out, and true to all fights I had with my mom over the years, I lost. Women will outsmart me most of the time when it comes to a debate; I am not ashamed of this. I love a smart woman, and Heather is a fucking genius.

It was a simple argument. I did not want to drive. She also did not want to drive. Guess who is driving?

Me.

"Just till we get away from these crazy freeways, then I'll take over," she said, but now that we are almost to Barstow, I realize she hasn't offered to take over.

"I am pulling over to get more gas before we hit the desert. Want to drive? I kind of have a headache," I say.

"Oh, sure. I am sorry. I was enjoying this book I got at the library. I can totally drive now," she says.

"What are you reading?" I ask

"It's called *Kent Price, Man on a Mission*, by an author named Patrick Smith. It's pretty good. Kent is like ex-military and he solves all these crimes. I guess there are a few in this series. One of the staff recommended it when I was at the library the other day," she explains.

"That sounds good. When you are done can I read it?" I ask as I exit the freeway and head to the Shell station.

"Sure! You like to read?" she asks.

"Oh yeah. I always have a book going," I say, and I can tell that surprises her.

"I did not peg you as a book nerd, Vince. I think we need to play a little get-to-know-you game the rest of the trip," Heather says.

"Deal, but first, bathroom, snacks, and gasoline. In that order," I say, pulling up to the pump.

Heather jumps out and takes the pump, saying, "You go ahead. I will get the gas."

"Thanks." I do a quick jog to the cashier and drop some money, telling him to fill it up on pump three, then hightail it to the bathroom. I am feeling surprisingly good considering I drank an ocean's worth of beer last night. Fucking Gio showing up and my dad getting worse, it was just too much. I am glad I already had plans to leave town for the weekend because I remember everyone saying they were going to party with Gio tonight. Of course he found a way to stick around when he was getting attention for being drafted. Since I left town, I don't look like a prick for not being there to celebrate someone else living my fucking dream.

I mean, it was my dream. Is it still? I don't know. I enjoy playing with the city league. Those guys are good for my ego. When I first started playing for them, I told myself it was to stay conditioned. After the first year, I told myself it was to keep the guys happy since they were finally winning. After that I had to admit it was the only thing keeping me sane. I like fixing cars, but it was always my backup plan. It wasn't supposed to be my life. Not until after I pitched in the World Series, you know? Then I would buy my own little shop and only work on classic cars.

I know I am doing that now, but I missed that middle step where I got to play professional ball. After I am done in the bathroom, I grab some snacks from the limited selection and head to the register to pay. Heather comes in, and I watch as the clerk checks her out. She has on a pair of jean shorts and a pink T-shirt that hugs her curves. She's wearing sandals today, and I see her cute pink toenails. I can tell she doesn't notice me or the guy at the register staring at her. She's like that—totally oblivious to men checking her out.

"Oh! Hey, I need to use the bathroom too. Is that okay?" she says when she finally sees me at the register.

"Sure, of course." I hold out my hand for the keys. She has pulled the Bug away from the pump and is parked right out front. That's really fucking courteous of her, and I find myself nodding in silent approval.

"Anything else?" the clerk asks, and I glance back at the hall where Heather disappeared.

"You have any condoms?" I ask, trying to seem casual. The clerk looks back at the hallway and winks at me.

"Sure do. One box or two?" he asks with a big grin, and I immediately regret everything.

"Uh, one is fine." I want to say, "And hurry it up," but I don't, because I am cool and buy condoms all the time. At least that is what I want this guy to think.

He drops the box in the bag of snacks and tells me the total. I pay quickly, then walk out to the car before she can see what I bought. I grab my duffle bag and unzip it, shoving the box of condoms in the bottom. I am zipping it up when she comes up behind me.

"Get everything you need?" she says, and I jump, smacking my head on the stupid trunk lid.

I rub at what I am sure will be a bump very soon. "Yeah, I got some snacks. They didn't have a lot to choose from so I have Slim Jims, Cracker Jack, and some of those mini doughnuts."

"Chocolate or the powdered sugar kind?" Heather asks excitedly.

"Powdered sugar of course. That's not chocolate, Heather. I swear it's wax," I say, and she laughs. I feel my stomach flip, and I smile at her like a complete goofball.

"Did you get drinks?" she asks, and I groan and shake my head.

"I'll go get some. Coke okay?" she asks.

"Sure. Thanks." I watch her walk back in, then turn and close the lid on the trunk, twisting the lock shut. I walk to the passenger seat and climb in, just in case she tries to get out of driving.

NINETEEN

HEATHER



I WALK to the cooler and grab two Cokes, pausing for a moment to talk myself into what I am about to do. I have never in my life bought condoms, but what if things happen this weekend? I'm on the pill but I want to be extra careful, plus there are things that guys can give you if you don't use protection. My friend Chris was on antibiotics for two weeks after a one-night stand. No thank you.

I take a deep breath and spin toward the register, walking with all the confidence of a woman who knows what she wants. What she wants is what was pressed against her hip this morning. Holy hell. It took all my strength not to reach down and investigate what exactly he was dealing with. When I came in to tell him breakfast was ready, it was almost comical the way the sheet pulled away from his hips. Impressive too. Yep. I am buying condoms. I can do this.

"Is that all you need?" the clerk asks, and I glance out at the car and swallow hard.

"No, I will also be taking a box of condoms," I say, but I choke on the word "condoms," and he has to ask me what I said.

"Condoms. I want condoms please. One box. Of condoms," I say to the counter, nice and loud, like I am announcing to people next door that I hope to have sex at some point in my future.

I don't look at the clerk because I can hear him trying not to laugh. I just wait for the total, then shove the box in my purse and carry the Cokes out to the car. My face is hot, and I know there are beads of sweat forming on my upper lip.

I climb in the driver's side, shoving my purse down on the floorboards behind my seat. Then, like in that Edgar Alan Poe story "The Tell-Tale Heart," I swear the damn box of condoms starts to thump. Okay, that might just be my heart. I need to calm down. I take a deep breath and hand Vince one of the Cokes. He takes it and tucks it between his legs, drawing my eyes to his crotch.

"Trojan, Trojan, Trojan," my purse thumps from under my seat.

Holy mother of God.

I swallow and turn back to face the store. The clerk is standing in the open doorway, and he waves at us like we are old friends. He is cracking up. Damn it. I wave back, then look at Vince, who is beet red and waving too.

I shift the car into reverse and get the hell out of there like I just robbed the place. Thankfully, Vince also seems relieved to be on our way and doesn't question my hasty departure.

We drive in silence for a few minutes, and the silence is making me uncomfortable, so I push the tape into the stereo. The last few chords of a song plays, and then "Strangers in the Night" starts, and Vince laughs and shakes his head. I start to feel a little more relaxed. Then he joins in with Frank and sings along. My heart starts beating faster again. He has a beautiful, deep, rumbly voice that I can feel all the way down to the tips of my toes.

"I am sorry about climbing in bed with you, Heather," Vince says when the song fades away.

"I told you it's okay, Vince. Like I said, I really think you must have gotten up to use the bathroom, then just went where you were used to sleeping," I explain. I wonder if that is all there was to it since this is the second time he's apologized.

"I think I went where I wanted to be," he says, but then he looks out his window and grows quiet.

"Are you feeling better? Can I tell you what I learned yesterday?" I ask after a few more uncomfortable moments.

"Yes!" he says a little too loudly.

I jump, and then holding my hand to my chest, I say, "Okay, great. So first let me tell you, I know which place you should pick for your dad. No contest. One smelled like death and the other was in a nice neighborhood and is like a house. I talked with one of the nurses there and she loves her job. That is all you need to know as far as I am concerned. I didn't see the inside because you have to make an appointment, but they have two, possibly three spots open."

"Oh wow. I forgot you were going to do that. Thank you so much. I guess I got overwhelmed by hearing that my dad was getting violent, and I kind of shut down," Vince explains. He shifts uncomfortably in his seat.

"I understand that. It is hard when you stop being the kid and have to act like the parent," I say, knowing exactly what that is like. I have been an adult since the ripe old age of nine when my mom first fell off the wagon. Her sobriety wagon had three wheels and a broken axle, and it was filled with vodka.

"I will call and make an appointment when we get back. Would you be willing to go with me?" he asks. There's a hint of vulnerability in his voice.

"Of course I will go. I was hoping you'd ask." I reach over to pat his leg, and he traps my hand with his, interlacing our fingers.

"So tell me what else you did yesterday." He leans his head back onto the seat but keeps his head turned toward me.

"I met with that John guy and saw crime scene pictures of Albert's murder," I say, trying to keep my eyes on the road and my focus on driving, not on how good my hand feels in his.

"Are you kidding? That's nuts! Were they awful?" He has turned a little in the small seat so he can face me. I notice him shift the Coke bottle a little and end up staring a little too long at his package. Damn, is that the outline of his dick? Is he not wearing underwear? My hand is so close to it. What would he do if—

"Heather!" he says, and I snap my eyes up to his, then realize I should be watching the road. My eyes dart to the road in time to see I am about to drift off into the desert. That tumbleweed wouldn't have stood a chance.

"Crap, sorry," I say, straightening out the wheel as my face turns what must be a deep burgundy.

"Want me to open your Coke for you?" he asks, reaching for my soda that is tucked between the seats.

"Um, yes, sure. That would be great. I am really thirsty all of a sudden," I say. My mouth is like the desert we are passing, and I feel hot all over.

He drops my hand, and I quickly place it on the steering wheel. This is better since I was totally tempted to keep inching toward that bulge I saw. What is wrong with me? Who does that? Just randomly gropes a guy while driving?

He hands me the open Coke bottle, and I take a big gulp, then say, "Okay, sorry. The crime scene photo wasn't so bad. It was black-and-white so the blood just looked like dark spots, you know?"

"Sure, that makes sense," he says.

"There was something that really stood out in the picture that showed his whole body. You aren't going to believe this part, Vince," I say.

"Let me guess. He wasn't wearing shoes?" Vince says, and I gasp like I am really surprised he figured it out.

He laughs and says, "Yeah, so why would she have taken them and kept them all these years?"

"I have no idea, and it's driving me crazy, Vince." I then proceed to tell him about the rest of the meeting and what led me bolt out of there.

"The address that was in the glove with the key was to a bank. It was to a safety deposit box," I tell him, enjoying how invested he is in this conversation. I realize how much I love having all his attention. I love that I get to spend the whole weekend with him away from his obligations and whatever has been making him so grumpy.

"No shit? Did you go to the bank?" he asks, and I nod then tell him all about that.

"So Iolet was friends with Marilyn Monroe, and she thinks the mob killed both her and Albert? It's wild that the police had that same picture of Iolet behind Frank and Eva," Vince says, then freezes in his seat and puts one hand on his door and one on my leg.

"What?" I ask, taking my foot off the gas pedal a bit.

"No, don't slow down," he hisses, then he turns slowly and looks out the back window. "Okay, we are good. No one is following us."

"Why would anyone follow us?" I glance at my side mirror and in the rearview, seeing absolutely no one behind me for miles.

Vince settles lower in his seat and shrugs his shoulders. "No idea, but I bet that was the 'danger' Iolet was talking about. The mob is nothing to mess with."

"Well, I went to see Henry at the theater, and he said—" I start, but Vince cuts me off.

"Man, you were busy yesterday. I am sorry I wasn't there to help." He looks down at his hand that is still resting on my leg. I wasn't going to say anything since I was enjoying it. I am getting the impression he had no idea he hadn't moved it since he yanks it away like he touched fire.

"It's okay. I had fun. I hope you did too." I pause, then ask, "Vince, is everything okay?"

"Not really. I mean it is, I guess. Yesterday just sucked. I had that meeting about my dad, and then a guy I played ball with in high school came to brag that he got picked up by the fucking Dodgers," Vince says.

"What? Wow, that's really cool. Isn't that really hard to do?" I ask.

"Not for Gio. He got a full-ride scholarship to college and played up there for a few years, and now he's going to the majors." Vince's voice is heavy with sadness.

"Up where?" I ask.

"Chico State, if you can believe that. Want to hear something even more interesting than that?" he asks, and I nod.

"I got the same offer. The scouts that picked up Gio for the Chico State team also offered me a spot. We were supposed to go together, play ball, get our degrees, get picked up . . ." He trails off, and I have to force myself to relax my grip on the steering wheel. I knew something else had happened yesterday. I wish I had pushed it and asked more questions, but I didn't feel like it was my place.

"What happened, Vince? Why didn't you go?" I ask, even though I am pretty sure I know the reason.

"The day the offer came, I went home to tell my mom, and while we were in the kitchen talking about how fucking awesome it all was, the hospital called to tell us my dad had been brought in unresponsive. He had a massive heart attack at the shop and one of his customers found him. They didn't know how long he was down." He pauses, so I reach over and place my hand on his. This time it's different. I need him to know I am here. I wait until he takes my hand in his and let my breath out slowly.

"Anyway, he was bad off, but he surprised everyone and made it through the night, then the next night and the next. The doctors started talking about rehab and how he could maybe even go back to work. Mom was at the hospital every day with me, and as weird as it sounds, it was the first time since they divorced that I felt like we were a family again," Vince says. He is rubbing my hand with his thumb, and when he stops talking, he wraps his other hand around mine so I am completely engulfed in his grip.

I glance over at him and see the same flat expression he wears so often. I squeeze his hand but stay quiet, willing him to continue. After a moment he does.

"It was about two weeks after the major heart attack, and he was in physical therapy. He was laughing and joking around with the staff, and they said his words stopped making sense. It was like someone hit a gibberish button on him. Paul, his therapist, said my dad looked at him and said some weird shit, then just dropped like a rock. He had a massive stroke." Vince falls silent. He relaxes his grip on my hand, but I don't let go.

"Oh God. Vince, I am so sorry," I say. This time I do look at him and see pain where the vacant gaze once resided.

"That was four years ago. They didn't expect him to survive, and I am a shit son because I wish all the time that he hadn't," he says softly.

"You are not a shit son for feeling that way." I squeeze his hand again and say, "I wished my mom would drink herself to death so the state would come and put me in foster care. I started having that fun little fantasy when I was nine."

"Fuck, that is awful," Vince says, and I shrug.

"Awful that I thought that, or that I was nine years old and taking care of her drunk ass every day?" I ask.

"Both. I hate that you went through that." He rests his hand over mine again, sandwiching my hand between both of his. It is my new favorite thing. I wish this stupid car was an automatic so I never had to move my hand again.

"Right back at ya. So how did your mom take the stroke?" I ask.

"Not great. She decided God was punishing Dad for being a cheater and she refused to go see him anymore. I was mad at first, but then I kind of saw her side of things. She told me that when she stood before her friends, family, and God and my dad promised to be faithful, she took that as truth. I guess he started seeing other women shortly after I was born. Mom didn't find out until I was about ten," Vince says.

"Good lord. How did he get away with it for so long? Was he taking women to the apartment you live in now?" I ask, then immediately regret saying it.

"No, thank fuck. That was actually how she caught him. He had an apartment about halfway between the shop and our home in Palm Springs. His apartment complex in Riverside had a small fire, and my idiot father had put Mom as an emergency contact."

"Oh no!" I say and steal another glance at Vince. He seems more relaxed at least now.

"Yeah, Mom pretended like she knew and got a lot of information about Dad's little home away from home. She waited until things settled down, then had me stay at my aunt's house. She went to his apartment to confront him," he says.

"Holy shit! That must have been intense!" I say.

"I am seriously surprised my father's heart didn't give out right then and there. I guess he was with one of his girlfriends, and my mom walked right in after picking up her key at the office. Brenda the apartment manager was super helpful that way," Vince explains.

"Oh no!" I squeak out.

"Yeah, no one wants to see their husband buried balls deep in another woman. He's lucky Mom didn't carry a gun." Vince chuckles a little, like he is telling a story about someone else's family. I think about how I learned to joke about my mom's alcoholism with my friends. I remember what that feels like, and I catch a smile that is lingering on his lips.

"Oh gross. No, that would be so awful!" I say.

"Yeah, well for most women that would have been it, but my mom is a good Catholic who doesn't believe in divorce, so she tried to make it work," Vince says.

"That's admirable, I guess," I say, squinting a little, scrunching my nose up.

"What? You wouldn't have given him another chance?" he asks.

"No. I don't have the energy for that. I mean, if you love me, you do. I can't fathom wanting to be with someone who didn't think I was enough," I explain.

"Right. I feel the same way," he says with a sigh.

"So how long did they try and work on it?" I ask.

"Well, that I am not exactly sure. I know I was ten when he got caught, and I was fourteen when the divorce was final. He moved out when I was about twelve, then moved back in. It was a lot of back-and-forth BS," he says.

"That's awful. I am sure that was hard on you," I say.

"Yeah. It really was. The summer I mowed Iolet's lawn my dad wanted me to come stay with him at the shop. Iolet kind of saved me from having to go. I feel bad that I forgot about that until the attorney showed up," Vince says. He gives my hand a squeeze, then lets me go, reaching for the Coke bottle nestled between his legs. He twists off the top and takes a drink, then bends forward and pulls the paper sack at his feet up into his lap.

"Slim Jim or doughnut?" he asks.

"Doughnut for sure," I respond. I am grateful for the snack break, if I am honest. That was a lot of information. God, this poor guy. I get why he went out and drank like that last night, but I wonder if he makes a habit of hiding in the bottle when things get tough. That would be a deal-breaker for me.

He tears the plastic wrapper open, and then I see a small, perfectly powdered doughnut in front of my mouth.

"Here," he says softly.

I start to move my hand from the wheel to take it from him and he pulls it away.

He says, "Hands on the wheel, Heather." His voice is deep and commanding, and my stomach flips, then bottoms out.

I swallow, nod, then open my mouth and wait, my mind instantly flooded with thoughts of what it would be like to be waiting for something else to touch my lips.

He moves the doughnut to my mouth and stops short. I dart my tongue out and lick the side, enjoying the sweet sugar.

"Sneaky, aren't you?" he rasps.

My eyes are glued to the road. I know if I were to look at him right now, I wouldn't be able to look away. I let my eyes move to the rearview mirror and the side mirror. No one is behind us, and we haven't passed a car in at least a half hour, but I know if our eyes lock, I am rolling this stupid car.

The doughnut touches my lips and I wait, expecting him to pull it away again. When he doesn't, I open my mouth slowly and moan softly as he pushes it in a little at a time. I slide my tongue down to pull the doughnut into my mouth and end up licking his finger.

I shoot a quick glance at him as he pulls his hand away. He has his eyes closed, and he is shifting in his seat. I chew the doughnut and take a drink of my Coke, hoping to lower my temperature a bit. I squeeze my legs together, trying to ease the pressure I feel building. God, I am so glad I bought those condoms.

TWENTY

VINCE

SOMEWHERE BETWEEN HOLLYWOOD and Vegas

JESUS, Mary, and Joesph. This girl is going to be the death of me. I almost came in my jeans when she licked my finger. I am so glad I bought those condoms. I am definitely making a move tonight. I can't ignore the pull to her any longer.

When she said Iolet was looking for a beautiful girl with long brown hair to help me with all of this, I said a silent thank you to that nutty lady. Why she decided to be my matchmaker after meeting me when I was only fourteen is something I may never understand. But I am so grateful she picked Heather.

We drive along chatting about everything from our childhood, to books we loved, to places we want to visit someday. I still can't believe Heather is twenty-two and had never been outside of Chico.

She makes a comment about all the places she wants to go when all this is over, and I shut down that conversation fast. I don't want to think about a time when she isn't here with me.

When we are about a half hour outside of Vegas, I have her pull into a shopping center that has a Taco Bell and a gas station. Once we get a real meal and fill the tank, I offer to drive so she doesn't have to navigate the traffic in this crazy place. People are so focused on the flashing lights and signs around them, they aren't paying attention to the road.

I pull onto Fremont Street and glance over at Heather to see her reaction. Her eyes are twinkling with delight, and her lips are turned up into the cutest fucking smile.

"What do you think?" I ask.

"It's amazing, Vince! Is our hotel really on this street?" She turns to me and places her hand on my arm. Another zing of electricity zips right to my dick.

"Yeah, it is right up here," I say, following the signs to the valet parking entrance. I am pulling out all the stops, and I don't care how much it costs. I have a sudden need to impress her, to show her I am worth her time. The more I learned about her on the drive here, the surer I became that I need to let her know how I feel. Or better yet, show her.

I pull into the casino and hop out, racing around to open her door. The bellhop comes with a cart and helps us with our luggage, and it is only then I notice the two garment bags in the back seat.

"These too," I say, handing them to the man, who hangs them on the cart. I look over at Heather, then nod to the bags with a questioning expression.

"I told you I solved our clothing problem for tonight," Heather says with a wink.

"I trust you," I say, then grab her hand. Everyone in this place is going to know she is with me. I toss my keys to the valet, then we follow the bellhop to the front desk. I feel like a million bucks with her hand tucked in mine.

"Can we go explore a little before the show?" Heather asks as we head down the hall to our room.

"Sure, whatever you want to do is fine with me," I say. I'd rather explore every part of her in the hotel room, but there will be time for that later.

It doesn't hit me until I open the door to let the bellhop push the cart in that there is only one bed. I should have asked for a double. I mean, I don't plan on letting her sleep anywhere but with me, however I am realizing I should have provided her with the option.

I watch as Heather steps into the room. She looks around, and a smile lights up her face. She looks at me and says, "Vince, this is so nice!"

My stomach flips, and I smile back at her. "I am glad you like it. I wasn't sure what the rooms looked like here. I have only ever been in the casino."

"Oh, it's amazing. I have never stayed in a hotel, so this will be fun!" she gushes, and I want to grab her and pull her into my arms. My lips are literally aching to touch hers.

"Cool, yeah. Cool," I say, because I am a fucking idiot.

I hear a man clear his throat and look over at the door where the bellhop is now standing with his empty cart.

"Anything else, sir?" he asks, and I shake my head and dig out my wallet, fumbling for a dollar to give him.

"Thanks, sorry about that," I say, and he smiles and gives me a little wink like he knows how nervous I am.

Heather grabs the garment bags from the bed and takes them to the closet.

"Where did you get those?" I ask, still smiling like an idiot because God, she is cute. I am trying not to focus on the fact that I am alone with her in this room.

"I went to see Henry at Past Times. We have that key to the costume closet, remember? I got you a very nice suit and a dress for me," she says doing a cute little tip with her head.

"You are amazing. Thank you." I step a little closer to her and her eyes go wide. Her smile fades, but her chest is rising a little faster. I let my eyes wander all over her, and when they make their way back up to her face, I see she has powdered sugar from the doughnut on her cheek. Before I can think, I move closer to her to brush it off with my hand, but when I touch her cheek, she closes her eyes and leans into my palm. I trace my thumb over her soft, sweet face, and she steps into me and opens her eyes. Her tongue peeks out of her mouth, rolling across her bottom lip, and I watch like it's the most fascinating thing I have ever seen. I look into her eyes, searching for approval for what I am about to do, and those beautiful brown eyes look almost black now. Her eyes are darting from mine to my mouth, and I place my other hand on her hip and pull her in closer.

Fuck, she is so soft. I let my hand slide from her hip to her back, and I lower my head just a bit so our lips are almost touching. I don't know what I am waiting for. I know she wants this. I know I want it, but I don't think I can stop if I kiss her now. My brain isn't listening to my body anymore, so that thought floats away as I step even closer, pressing her against me.

I slide the hand that was on her face to the back of her head, and she tilts her face toward me. I bend and let my lips graze hers with the softest of touches. She lets out the sexiest little whimper, so I do it again and again with a little more pressure each time. She tastes like sugar and heaven, and her lips part, inviting me in. All my restraint is gone, and I grab her as our kisses become more frantic. I spin her and pull her with me as I step backward toward the bed. When my leg hits something solid, I assume I have reached the king-sized bed, and I lean back, taking her with me.

It is not the bed.

I fall, expecting a mattress to cushion us as we are a tangle of lips and tongues and hands roaming, seeking. The bench that I ran into is just wide enough to catch my ass, fooling me long enough for me to lean back and pull her to the floor in a heap.

It probably wouldn't have been too bad if we hadn't been locked in the most passionate kiss of my life. I feel my jaw snap shut as we make impact with the floor just as I go to nibble on her lower lip. It's never good to taste blood when you are kissing someone. Never.

"Oh shit! I am sorry, Heather. Are you okay?" I roll us so we are on our sides. I brush the hair away from her face and see a bit of blood in the corner of her mouth.

"I'm okay. Are you okay?" she asks a little breathlessly, then she starts to laugh one of those silent, shoulder-shaking church laughs. The kind of laugh when you know you aren't allowed to make noise, like you are one slap to the back of the head away from being grounded. Tears are streaming down her face, and she is shaking so hard I can feel it. I start to laugh too, gathering her in my arms as we lie on the floor in a heap of shaking limbs and watery eyes.

She pulls herself together before I do and presses her forehead to mine as she catches her breath. Her hands are clutching my shirt, and she has draped a leg over mine.

"I have never in my life had a kiss like that," she says softly.

"I know, I am so sorry. I thought I hit the bed with my legs, and —" I start, but she puts her fingers on my lips and shakes her head.

"No, before that. Before we fell." She swallows hard after saying that, and I know what she is thinking because I am thinking it too. That kiss was all it took for me to fall.

"You are a really good kisser," she says, then touches the part of her lip where I accidentally bit her. It's a little swollen, but the bleeding has stopped.

"So are you," I say and press my mouth to hers gently. I stop myself before this goes any further. I don't want to maul her here on the floor between the bench and the air conditioner.

I prop myself up and see the bed behind her and laugh again. "Oh, look. There's the bed," I say, and she turns her head and looks at it with me.

"I bet it will be really comfortable later. Want to go check out some sights?" she says.

"Yeah." I get up, then help her, pulling her up and into me. I wrap my arms around her and sigh at how good she feels in my arms.

"We better get out of here before I try something again," I whisper into her ear. I feel her shudder against me, and she hugs me tighter.

"Me too. There is time for all this later." She surprises me by snaking her hand in between us to grab my very hard cock that is pressing against my shorts. I growl and thrust into her hand.

"You better stop that or we will never leave," I say into her ear, then give her lobe a little nip with my teeth. That makes her giggle and twist her head away.

"Okay, okay," she says as she steps back and holds her hands up in surrender. She runs her hands over her hair, trying to fix the pieces that fell out of her braid. Her skin is flushed in the most beautiful way, and her eyes are twinkling.

"Do you just want to walk down Fremont Street, or do you want to drop a few quarters in the machines?" I ask. I try to discreetly adjust myself in my shorts so I don't scare the old ladies out on the gaming floor.

"Can we do both? I don't like the idea of losing money, but I really want to try the slots," Heather says with a hopeful smile.

I dig around in my duffle bag, pulling out two rolls of quarters. I wink at her like a cheese ball as I hand her one. "Tell you what. Once these are gone, we will walk around. I always gamble like this. It's fun if you give yourself a limit," I say.

"Okay, I will follow your lead," Heather says, placing a quick kiss on my lips. She steps back before I can grab her and pull her into a deeper kiss like I want.

"You are making it hard to leave the room, Heather," I say, but she just laughs turns toward the door. I move quickly, placing my left hand on the door just as she is about to open it, then trap her with my right hand on the other side of her. She turns slowly in my arms and smiles up at me.

She stands up on her toes and plants another kiss on my lips but keeps her hands at her side.

"Impressive self-control, Heather," I say, and she winks at me.

"I've been practicing since I met you, Vince," she whispers in my ear. My knees buckle, and my hand slides off the door.

She's quick and takes the opportunity to pull it open and step into the hall, glancing over her shoulder at me with a wicked little smile.

All I can do is place my hand over my heart to try and keep it where it belongs. This girl is going to steal it if I am not careful. If I am honest, she already has.

As we walk down the hall, the clanging of change hitting the metal trays becomes louder. As we step into the smoke-filled room, I grab her hand to lead her to my favorite slots.

"This way. I know where they put the loose slot machines," I say, weaving through what must be a whole busload from a senior center.

Heather stops to pick up a man's cane that slipped from his hand.

"Here you go, sir," she says smiling brightly at the old guy.

"Well, thank you, my dear. Aren't you sweet. Glenda, did you see that? She picked up my cane, and she didn't even yell at me for not using the damn strap! I told you it was possible!" he says, turning from us to yell at his wife.

"Carl, give me my bucket, and you go play keno. That way if you drop your cane, the keno girls will bend over like you want. I got better things to do," Glenda snaps, reaching for the bucket of quarters that Carl is holding.

Heather just wiggles her fingers at them and reaches for my hand again. I pull her along until we are by the bathrooms and a main path through the casino. There are two slot machines right next to each other here, and they are the Double Diamond kind I like.

I pull out her chair and sit next to her, explaining about the max bet and letting her decide how she wants to play. My mom always played one quarter at a time to draw out the fun, but when she hit a jackpot, it wasn't as high. I play all three quarters and hope for the best. The jackpot on these isn't super high, and they hit often because people walking by see you win, then want to play.

Heather puts three quarters in and pulls the lever. She hits two cherries and a diamond and wins a small amount. The look on her face is so fucking cute; you would think she just won a million dollars.

"Nice job!" I say, then turn and start dropping my quarters.

We play for quite a while, long enough to get the cocktail waitress to come by. I order us two beers and tip her when she brings them back quickly. Heather has inserted all her quarters now and is playing on the credits. I am down to my last two pulls if I do the full bet, so I switch to single quarter bet and pull my last six tries. I lose every single pull.

I stand and step behind her to watch and look down at her credits.

"Holy shit, Heather, that's like two hundred dollars!" I say.

"I know. I hit a few small pots and then I just got a big one. Should I cash out?" she asks

"Up to you. You can do whatever you want." I lean in and give her a quick kiss on her cheek.

"I'll remember you said that, Vince, so you better be careful." She winks at me and my legs turn to Jello. Fuck, this girl is too much.

"One more pull, then no matter what, we will go." She looks up at me and smiles.

"Deal," I say and watch as she loses seventy-five cents.

"Okay! How do I get the money?" she asks.

"Push that button that says 'cash out,' and be ready. It's going to be loud," I say with a laugh.

She pushes the button, then we wait as over 800 quarters fall into the tray. She starts laughing as they fall and tips her head up to me for a kiss. At least I think that is what she wanted. It is what she got, that's for damn sure.

Her haul fills her cup and mine, and we head to the cashier to get some lighter currency. We hand over our buckets to the cashier and wait while the machine counts out the quarters.

"Two hundred and ten dollars and twenty-five cents," the cashier says, counting out the bills into Heather's hand.

"Thank you! That was a lot of fun," Heather tells her.

"I am glad you had a good time, honey. Come back anytime, and good luck," the cashier says, and Heather beams at her like it wasn't a canned line.

"Here," she says, thrusting the cash at me. "That was so fun. Thanks for letting me play."

"Fuck no. That's your money, Heather. You won it, not me," I say, stepping away from her.

"Vince! No, you can't do that. I can't take your money. You paid for the room and for the show." She pulls my hand toward her, places the money in my palm, and closes my hand around it, then brings my hand to her lips and places soft kisses all along my knuckles. Chills run up my arm and collide with the fire that is growing in my chest.

I remember thinking earlier that I would do anything for this girl, and I can tell how important this is to her. I reach for my wallet and put the cash away, then pull her in for a real kiss. I have both my hands on either side of her face, and I am kissing her like we are alone and I have all night. She isn't complaining and seems to be stepping closer for more.

"Excuse me, do you know where the buffet is?" a tiny, shaky voice to my left says.

I pop my lips off Heather's and look down at a woman who has to be a hundred years old.

"Um, I don't know," I say to her, but she isn't looking at me. She is looking up at Heather.

"One second. Let me find out," Heather says and scurries back to the cashier.

The old lady blinks up at me and smiles with someone else's teeth. No way she was born with those choppers. I smile at her and look over the top of her head to see if I can spot Heather in the crowd. No such luck, and now the woman is staring at me.

"Have any luck with the slots today?" I ask dumbly, shoving my hands into my pockets.

"Slots? Who the hell plays slots? Blackjack is where all the action is, young man," she says, pointing a bony finger at me.

"Oh, right. Sure." I take a step back because this little lady is kind of scary.

"Okay, I know where the buffet is. Would you like me to tell you or take you?" Heather asks.

The woman slips her arm into Heather's and says, "Take me, please."

So we head off, and by the time we get to the buffet, there are about ten more old people following us. The lady that interrupted the second-best kiss of my life kept waving to her friends and yelling, "Come on. We are going to the buffet." It was like a conga line with walkers. I really have never seen anything like it.

"How did she know?" I whisper to Heather as we finally make it to the restaurant.

"How did she know what?" Heather asks.

"That you would help her?" I ask, a little baffled.

She just shrugs and starts directing traffic of what can only be described as a jumbo shrimp migration. No wonder these people can't find anything. One guy has to stop and lean way back to see where he is going since he is shaped like a tiny question mark. What the fuck do I need to do so my back stays straight? Whatever it is, sign me up now.

Once everyone is in the line for the cashier, Heather smiles at me and says, "Ready?"

"Sure." I glance at my watch. We have about an hour and a half before we have to be back to the room to get ready for dinner and the show. I lead her out the double doors and onto Fremont Street. It's hot today, and going from the cool casino to the heat outside is a bit of a shock, but at least the air is clean out here.

TWENTY-ONE

HEATHER


LAS VEGAS, Nevada
Fremont Street


I SIGH and push the hair out of my eyes. These flashing lights and neon signs are getting old pretty quick, and I think I've lost five pounds because I am sweating up a storm. I tell Vince I am getting a headache from the heat, and he doesn't seem disappointed at all. In fact, he immediately turns us to head back to our hotel.

"I'd like to take a shower before the show if that's okay," I say as we walk back toward the Gold Nugget, the hotel where we're staying.

"God, a cool shower sounds amazing. Let's do that," he says, waggling his eyebrows at me.

"You really want the first time I see you to be in a cold shower?" I ask and nod at his crotch.

"Uh, no. Right, bad idea," he says with a laugh.

Vince holds the door open for me when we reach the hotel. I step in and enjoy the cool air for about three seconds before the cigarette smoke wraps around my soul.

"God, I hate cigarettes. You ever smoke, Heather?" Vince asks.

"No. I think it's so gross. My mom had a boyfriend that would come around every now and then, and he was a chain-smoker. I remember grabbing my stuffed animals and shoving them deep into my closet so they wouldn't stink when he was at the house. I know my mom hated it too because she would open all the windows when he left. Even if it was freezing. They didn't last long, thankfully."

"You drink," he says when we get to the elevator.

"What?" I ask, confused by the turn in the conversation.

"Well, you said your mom is an alcoholic, but you drink. I would think you would hate alcohol," he says.

"Well, when I was little, I swore I would never touch the stuff, but when my twenty-first birthday rolled around, the cooks at Serenity Falls wanted to take me out and celebrate. I didn't feel like explaining, so I had a beer," I say with a shrug.

I see a cloud cross his face, and I cock my head questioningly, but he brushes it off with a wave of his hand.

"Anyway, the next day I realized I didn't care if I ever had a drink again. I don't have the pull my mom has. She *needs* it, you know?" I say.

"Yeah, I get that. I could never have a drink again and I would be fine. After the vat of beer I drank last night, it might be a good idea to lay off it for a while," he says.

I laugh as the elevator opens to our floor. It was a relief to hear him say that. I could not deal with a guy who was a heavy drinker. I follow him down the hall, mesmerized by the wild print on the carpet. It was like that in the casino area too. It's almost nauseating with its swirls of reds, blues, and gold.

"Here we are. You can take a shower first." He holds the door open for me, and I step inside and turn to him.

"Why are you in the hall still, Vince?" I ask.

He looks at me dead in the eye and says, "I can't be in there while you shower. I am going to go for a walk."

"That bad?" I ask, a smile taking over my lips.

"Yeah, it's that bad," he says, and he adjusts himself in his shorts.

"Okay, give me ten minutes." I lean out the door, grab him by the shirt, and pull him in for a quick kiss. Then I close the door as he tips his head back and sighs.

I love that I have that kind of effect on him. I rush into the bathroom, pulling my shorts and T-shirt off as I go. He doesn't come back until I am fully showered and dressed. I am leaning over the sink, putting on what little makeup I wear, when I hear the door.

My stomach flips and drops to my knees, which have turned to Jello. I have never in my life worn a dress like this, and I am nervous to see what he thinks. I straighten and look in the mirror, smoothing the fabric of the tight-fitting pink dress. It comes up high in the front, with a straight line across my collarbone. It has cap sleeves and no back, and it cinches tight at my waist, flaring out in a full skirt that hits just below my knees. It is the most beautiful thing I have ever seen. The print is like waves of light and dark pink, and there are two small bows just above the end of the zipper in the back. Whoever this dress was made for was exactly the same size as me.

I take in a deep breath and step out into the room. Vince removing the suit I picked out for him from the garment bag, so he doesn't see me right away. I watch as he runs his hand over the fabric of the grey suit jacket and see the approval in his eyes. I wonder if he recognizes it. When Henry told me what movie it was from, I knew I had to pick it for Vince.

He turns towards me, his fingers still on the lapel of the suit, and I am pleased to see the emotions that flood his face.

"Heather, holy shit," he says, his hand dropping to his side.

"Do I look okay?" I ask, hating that my voice comes out a little strained.

"You are stunning. You are perfection wrapped in satin, or whatever the fuck that material is. Turn around," he says with a commanding, deep, gravelly voice.

I spin slowly and hear the sharp intake of his breath when he sees my bare back. I hear him step toward me and try and move but he is quick, and his hands are on me in seconds, spinning me around.

His chest is rising and falling rapidly, like he walked miles, not a few steps to reach me, and as he raises his hand to brush the hair away from my face, I see his hand is trembling.

He grips my shoulders, and I sense it is more to steady himself than anything else.

"Beautiful," he rasps, then places his lips on mine gently. It feels like heaven as his soft full lips move over mine. He's measured and controlled though, and he is still holding me by the shoulders. I realize he is keeping me at arm's length when I try to step into him.

"No, we will never leave the room," he says after breaking the kiss. He gives me a little squeeze, then grabs the suit and heads into the bathroom to take a shower.

I walk over to sit on the bed and wait but decide against it since I don't want to wrinkle the dress. I stand in front of the window instead and pull the heavy drapes back. It's still light out, but the sun is fading, and I assume it has only dropped a degree or two. I am glad we just have to go downstairs and not back out into that furnace.

The shower shuts off, and my nerves ratchet up again, knowing I'll get to see him in that sharp, stylish suit. I imagine this is what it felt like for the girls that went to prom. I worked that night, not that anyone asked me anyway. I wouldn't have been able to get a dress and shoes or have my hair done, so it really was for the best.

Shit, my shoes! I dart over to the garment bag and dig out the simple black pumps. They have a low heel, making it easy to walk while still looking sexy as hell. Henry said this dress had matching shoes at some point, but Iolet must not have saved them. I wish I could thank that nutty lady right now.

Vince steps out of the bathroom and I literally gulp. I know my mouth is hanging open because he smiles and runs his hand through his hair. Damn, he is a ten, maybe an eleven.

He spins around and puts his hands in his pockets, striking a pose that I will remember until the day I die.

"I clean up pretty good, huh?" Vince says with a wicked smile, and it takes all my strength to stay where I am.

"Yeah, you sure do, DeLuca. You look really good," I say, the last part coming out in a whoosh as I lose my breath.

"This suit is fucking awesome, Heather. Thanks for going by the theater and getting us these. It makes this so much more special. It's like prom or something," he says with a smirk.

I bark out a laugh. "I thought the same thing."

"I just need to grab the ring. Hang on." Vince steps over to his bag, where he digs around until he pulls out a small box. He opens it, then slides the ring onto his pinky.

Seeing it makes me remember the copy of the picture, and I grab it from my purse. "Here. It's just a photocopy, but I think if he doesn't remember Iolet, you can show him this," I say, handing him the picture.

He takes the folded picture and tucks it in the inside pocket of the suit. I wonder if he'd figure it out if I call him Fred. Holly calls Paul Fred in the movie *Breakfast at Tiffany's* because she said he reminded her of her foster brother. Henry promised to show me the film when we get back, and the thought of watching another movie with Vince makes me happy.

"Are you ready to see 'Ol' Blue Eyes' sing?" I ask him.

"I can't believe this is real. I am so fucking excited," Vince says as he steps forward. I can smell his heavenly cologne, and I want to bury my face in his neck. He holds out both hands, so I give him mine and step forward.

"Let's get out of this room before I tear that dress off of you," he says. He is looking directly in my eyes, and my breath catches in my throat.

"You'd miss seeing Frank for me?" I ask in barely a whisper. Our eyes are locked, and he's rubbing his thumb over my right hand.

"Good thing I don't have to choose," he says with a wink.

I laugh and squeeze his hands before tugging him to the door. "Let's go."

# TWENTY-TWO
# VINCE



I AM the luckiest person in the whole world. I have the most beautiful woman on my arm, and I am about to see my idol.

I don't think my feet are touching the ground, and if Heather wasn't holding my hand, I am sure I would float off like a Macy's parade balloon. When we get to the Theater Ballroom and are escorted to our table (up front, thank you very much), I don't know whether to laugh or cry when I see who we are sharing a table with.

The six other chairs at our table are occupied by the herd of elderly people Heather helped earlier. I pull out her chair and she sits, immediately grabbing her napkin to cover her smile.

I slide in next to her and nod at the old man on my right. He doesn't see it, of course, because he is folded in half over his plate. A woman to his right, who must be his wife, leans over and yells next to the poor guy's ear, "It's that nice couple that helped us find the buffet, Charles. Look to your left!"

With considerable effort, Charles turns and gives me a smile, straightening to a full upright position. He holds up a shrimp tail like he's holding the winning catch in the World Series.

"Found the little sucker. I told you I didn't fling it in your hair, Betty." He laughs a deep, hearty laugh, and I lean forward enough to see her cracking a smile.

"You're lucky you didn't. If I get Frank's attention tonight, it better not be because a damn shrimp tail is stuck in my hair," she says with a little giggle.

"I am Charles, and this beauty next to me made me the happiest man in the world fifty-eight years ago. Her name is Betty. Next to her is her maid of honor, Hilda. She isn't a very honorable person, but at least she can't hear anymore, so I can say that as often as I like." Charles elbows me to make sure I know he's being funny.

"Next to her is husband number four. He has no idea where the hell he is, but that's okay. He bought us all drinks earlier. Now on the other side of your lovely date is my best man, George. He's a real good guy, but I guarantee he is already making a move on your girl."

I whip my head to my left and see a guy who is older than time with his shriveled lips all over Heather's hand. Before I can say anything, Charles continues, "And next to him is a saint of a woman who has put up with him for the past fifty years. Her name is Katherine, but she wants people to call her Kat."

I smile when I notice she has cat earrings hanging from her stretched out earlobes.

"So this is your anniversary, Charles?" I ask, glancing back around at the table.

"Yep. We said if we made it to fifty-five years married, we would treat our friends to a trip of a lifetime. That came and went. Poor Betty fell and broke her hip a week before our trip to Hawaii. So here we are instead!" Charles reaches over and grabs his wife's hand, giving it a little squeeze.

"Nice to meet all of you. I am Vince, and this is Heather," I say. I steal a glance at her, and she is discreetly wiping her hand on the skirt of the tablecloth. George must be a drooler. She tries to keep her expression neutral but fails miserably as I laugh.

"Hi," Heather says with a little wave of her now dry hand.

A server comes by with another round of cocktail shrimp and takes our drink orders. The group returns to their own conversations, leaving Heather and me to take in the rest of the room. I see an area that might be a dance floor, and I hope to God it is. I can't picture a more perfect thing than dancing with Heather while Frank sings "Fly Me to the Moon."

After a few more rounds of drinks and dinner, the lights finally dim, and Frank comes out like the king he is. He doesn't walk, he glides, and I watch as he stops at the table next to ours and makes small talk. I can't hear what they are saying, but everyone is smiling and laughing. Suddenly the music starts, and without missing a beat, he launches into "Luck be a Lady." My smile is stretched across my face and my foot is tapping. I reach over without looking and find Heather's hand.

We listen to the Chairman of the Board belt out one hit after another. I leave my body when he sings "Fly Me to the Moon." I am a little embarrassed to admit that I seem to be competing with the elderly ladies at the table for the biggest fan award. I swear Frank made eye contact with me and I gasped. I fucking gasped. I would like to say no one heard, but Heather reached over and patted my leg, so that little hope crashed.

Our idea to talk to him after the show seems ridiculous now, as his performance is winding down. I lean over to Heather and love that she immediately leans into me. She knows I need her close.

"I don't know how we are going to get his attention after this. I am sure they won't just let us talk to him," I whisper to her. Those deep brown eyes of hers are focused on my lips, and I feel my stomach do a little dip.

"I know. I was thinking the same thing. Maybe we can push Betty down and he will rush over to help?" Heather suggests. I am pretty sure she is joking, but I shake my head no just in case.

She gives a little shrug and a smirk, then says, "I'll just go talk to that guy." She points toward to an older man wearing all black at the side of the stage area. He has a thick gold chain around his neck, and his hands are as thick as baseball mitts. I am instantly reminded of the guys my dad used to hang out with at the shop.

"Want me to go with you?" I ask, and she shakes her head. Before I know it, she is walking across the room to him. His position changes from arms folded across his chest and a wide leg stance to a more relaxed one. She rests her hand on his chest and whispers in his ear, then turns and points to our table.

He squints, then nods and smiles. Then I watch as Heather plants a little kiss on his cheek. She spins and saunters back to our table, hips swaying with each step, and the man is watching her every move. He lifts his big hand and touches the spot on his cheek where her lips were moments before. I realize this may be my last night on this earth, because if he lays a hand on her I will fight him. I will lose, but I will fight him.

She sits back down and leans forward to whisper in my ear, but I turn my head and claim her lips and her. I kiss her like I just got back from war and she is my long-lost love. I kiss her like she has my air, my heart, and my soul. I don't even realize I've moved my hand up to her face until I pull away and trail my fingers down her cheek.

"Wow," Heather breathes, her chest rising and falling rapidly.

I blink at her, unsure what to say after that unexpected display. Charles leans over and saves me by saying to Heather, "I think you were gone a little too long, dear. Next time maybe take him with you." He winks at her, and she blushes.

Frank is finishing up his last song, and people are clapping and waving at him. As he walks to the side to get a drink, the big man Heather talked to waves him over and whispers in his ear. Frank glances at our table and nods his head. He walks back to the center of the stage, picks up the microphone, and says, "I have just been told we have a very special anniversary at this table. Charles and Betty have been married fifty-eight years!"

Betty clutches her chest and smiles brighter than a summer sun, and Charles is straightening his suit jacket. Frank steps closer and asks them a few questions. I am so nervous that I am only one person away from him that I start to sweat, and my throat grows painfully dry.

I reach for my water glass and am downing it in a few gulps when I hear Frank say, "Well, aren't you an attractive young couple. Are these your grandparents?"

I swallow and look at him. My mouth opens and closes with no sound emerging. Heather leans forward and smiles at him.

"No, sir. We just met them tonight. We kind of crashed their party. Everyone here was in their wedding all those years ago. Isn't that amazing?" Heather gushes, and I watch as Frank's gaze moves to me, my face, my suit, and my hand that is holding the glass of water. He squints at the ring on my finger, and it's like time stands still. I expect him to say something, but he doesn't. He just gives a polite nod to us and wishes Betty and Charles a happy anniversary before waving and walking off.

"Well, shoot. I was hoping he would stay a little bit longer. I was going to ask him if he remembered Iolet," Heather says close to my ear. People are talking and standing from their tables to leave, and it has gotten quite a bit louder in here.

"It's okay. Maybe we can catch that bouncer guy you talked to earlier," I suggest.

"Mario? Yeah, that's a good idea!" Heather stands up and looks around, trying to spot him, so I join her. The area by the door where he stood is empty except for a few people taking pictures of where Frank Sinatra was singing.

"It's okay. It was a long shot anyway, right?" I take her hand and pull her toward the door, dodging couples who are also trying to leave. I notice a small bar off to the side and pull Heather that way, hoping to wait out the crowd. We climb onto the barstools, and I lean over and plant a small kiss on Heather's cheek.

"What can I get you?" I ask close to her ear. I love that she shivers and leans into me.

"Can I get a glass of red wine?" she asks.

I raise my hand and smile at the bartender, and he nods and heads our way. "What can I get you crazy kids? I think you are my first customers under the age of fifty all night!" he says with a chuckle.

I glance around at the people who are still leaving and realize we *are* the youngest people here. I shrug and say, "I have an old soul, I guess. I love Sinatra. Heard he was playing here and had to come."

"I respect that." He leans forward and places his hands on the bar, waiting.

"We will take two glasses of red wine. Let's do a cabernet. Anything from the Napa Valley is fine," I say.

"Coming right up." He returns quickly with two very full glasses of red.

"To a lovely lady and a wonderful evening," I say, holding up my glass to her.

"To a handsome man and the best night of my life," Heather replies.

"The best part hasn't happened yet, Heather," I say, taking a sip of the wine.

She does the same, and her face turns a lovely shade of pink. Heather sets the glass down and traces her finger along the top of the glass. She is looking down but glances up at me through her impossibly long lashes and asks, "What was your favorite song tonight?"

I lean back in my chair and sigh. "Probably 'Fly Me to the Moon.' My only regret is no one got up to dance."

"Oh? Do you like to dance, Vince?" Heather says it like a challenge.

At least that is how I take it. I stand up from the barstool and hold out my hand for her. She cocks her head at me questioningly, so I wiggle my fingers and say, "Yes, come on."

She takes my hand, and I spin her out and pull her back in, wrapping my hand across her beautifully bare back. My fingers dig into her soft skin as I tug her into me. We begin to sway, and I hum in her ear, then start to sing "Fly me to the Moon" close to her ear.

She pulls back enough for me to see her face as I sing the song about longing for her, I spin her out, and she twirls that full skirt, looking like a goddess. Just as I pull her back in, I notice the guy she spoke to by the door walk into the room and look around. When he spots us, he makes eye contact with me and walks straight toward us. It's a little intimidating since the guy is built like a brick house. I stop and clear my throat, nodding my chin toward him so Heather knows why I stopped dancing with her.

She spins around, and I can't see her face, but I can only assume she is smiling at him because the large man just about tripped.

"Hi! I was hoping to see you again," Heather says, then steps away from me and right into his path, holding out her hand.

He takes it, and I swear her whole hand and wrist disappears. "I was looking for you both. I didn't realize you were still in here," he says.

"Oh yeah. We decided to have a drink here while the crowd thinned out, and then Vince wanted to dance." Heather looks over her shoulder at me.

I wave like a fucking moron.

"The Chairman of the Board would like to speak with you," the man says, staring at me.

"Me?" I ask and look over my shoulder because I am sure there is someone behind me.

"Yes, you. That's his ring," he says, pointing a finger at me.

I have an overwhelming desire to turn around and run because, holy crap, this guy is scary, but I don't. Instead I nod and say, "Yes, I believe it did belong to Mr. Sinatra."

"We can explain why we have it," Heather says, stepping between us.

"Follow me," the giant man grunts and turns, walking off. I pull out my wallet and leave some cash on the bar for the wine we didn't get to finish and hurry to catch up to Heather and the brute.

## TWENTY-THREE
## HEATHER

LAS VEGAS, Nevada
Gold Nugget

TWO HOURS later as we walk back to our hotel room, Vince hasn't said a word. His silence began when we shook Frank's hand as we left and has continued as we were escorted back to the main gaming floor.

Vince digs the room key out of his pocket, and I wait, watching him fumble a few times before getting it. He steps aside, pushing the door open with his hand, so I step inside and flip the switch on the wall. The whole room lights up in a cheery glow. I pull off one shoe, then the other, and set them by the table.

"I just met Frank Sinatra," Vince says to the room. I don't know if he realizes I am here. His eyes are glossed over, and his upper lip is twitching a little. He's loosened his tie, making him look even sexier than he did when we left. If that is possible.

"You did. You sat and had a drink with him too." I step in front of him cautiously.

"Did that happen? Heather, I want you to pinch me. No, punch me. I won't feel a pinch." Vince squares his body to mine like he's preparing to take a gut punch.

I laugh and step closer to him, placing my hands on his face. I wait for him to look me in the eyes, then I step in and kiss him softly on his lips.

"That isn't going to work. That makes me think I am still having the best dream of my life. There is no way this is real, Heather," he says, shaking his head. His hands have moved to my waist, and he pulls me closer.

"Why are you so calm?" he breathes and closes his eyes briefly.

"Well, for one, I have had two glasses of wine," I say, stepping into him a little more. "And I didn't just meet *my* idol." I place my hands on his chest, running them over the front of the suit jacket.

"We need to talk about this. I can't . . . I don't, I feel . . ." Vince stumbles over not just his words but his feet. I step out of the way, and he makes his way to the small table and sits in one of the chairs.

I pull out the other one and sit across from him, folding my hands on the table. I wait while he takes a few deep breaths, then slowly lowers his forehead to the table.

"Are you okay, Vince?" I ask. I am trying not to laugh, because I think he is in actual distress, but damn, this is funny to watch. It's like someone caught part of their sweater on a nail and it is slowly coming undone.

"I don't know where to start," he says with his head still on the table.

"Well, how about we start with the fact that Iolet didn't steal the ring. That seems like a positive thing, right?"

"Yeah, no, that was great, and the fact that he let me keep it was even better." He sits up and twirls the ring on his finger, staring at it as it spins.

"And the fact that he agreed with Iolet that Albert was murdered by the mob or whatever you want to call them—that was good, right?" I say again, trying to snap him out of whatever stupor he is in.

"Listen, I never doubted Iolet. I am sure Albert got whacked for some reason other than a regular robbery. That's not it, Heather," Vince says.

"What's wrong then?" I lean forward a little. I wish his hands were on the table so I could grab them and hold them.

"Now we have to figure out why the mob wanted him dead and what all these clues mean. I thought our biggest problem was fixing up the car," Vince says, lowering his head to rest on the table again.

"Right, yeah, it did just get more complicated. I better call my roommate and let her know I won't be home anytime soon," I say with a sigh. I don't mention that she isn't going to care since my mom lives there now. I don't want him to know I don't really have a home to return to when this is over.

Vince perks up, lifting his head. He looks at me, then around the room like someone else might have said that.

"You'd stay?" he asks.

"Well, yeah, I said I would see this through. I am not just going to leave because it became an actual mystery. I might have to get a job and an apartment—"

He cuts me off. "No. Nope, you are staying with me," Vince says, and I have to admit I love the possessive tone.

"Okay, but you can't keep sleeping on the couch, Vince. I feel terrible about that," I say, again wishing I could touch him in some way. Without warning he stands up and comes toward me like a man starving and I am a piece of steak. He lunges, grabbing my arms and pulling me up.

"I won't be sleeping on the couch, and neither will you," he says in a gruff voice that surprises me. I nod and blink, unsure about this new aggressive Vince.

"I want you in my bed, Heather. I am tired of acting like it's no big deal that you are sleeping in my bed without me. I am tired of walking past you in the morning and seeing you in that fucking crop top. You sleep on your back. Did you know that? With your hair spilling over my pillow, and this arm right here," he says, trailing his finger up my left arm, "is usually up over your head. Do you know what happens to that little shirt you wear when you have your arm over your head, Heather?"

I shake my head, unable to speak. He has moved closer to me now, and the hand that slid down my arm is making its way to the bare skin of my back. God, I love this dress so much. His touch is lighting a fire deep in my belly, and my legs are more than wobbly.

"Your shirt pulls up, and I see the swell of your breast. Your very perfect breast. Do you know what that has done to me?" He steps so close that we now share the same air.

"What?" I ask in a breathless whisper.

"It makes me crazy. It makes me want to climb in bed and lift that flimsy cotton shirt off your chest, slowly so that I don't wake you," he says.

"You don't want to wake me?" I ask. My heart is going to jump out of my chest, I just know it.

"No, not yet. I want to see you first," he says as he runs his nose up my neck to my ear. He nibbles on the lobe of my ear, and I whimper.

"I would wake you up like this," he says, then carefully traces his thumbs over my nipples.

"That would do it," I huff out. Jesus, my legs are pudding. What is he doing to me?

"Do you like that, Heather?" he asks. I nod.

"I do. I like it very much," I say.

Vince runs a finger up my arm, slipping it under the cap sleeve of the dress. He tugs it forward, then moves to the other side and does the same.

"I want this off, Heather. I need to see you. If you don't want this, you need to stop me now. Once I touch you, once my lips are on you, there will be no stopping. Do you understand me?" Vince says.

I swallow hard, willing myself to speak, but all I am capable of is a nod.

"Words, Heather. I want to hear you say it," Vince says as he pulls at the front of the dress again.

"I want this. I want you," I say, leaning into him, desperate for his lips.

We fall into each other, hands roaming, lips frantic. He has pulled the front of my dress down, exposing me to the cool air of the hotel room. The cold air mixed with the hot skin of his hands is exquisite. I moan as he holds each breast in his hand, and when he dips down and pulls my nipple into his mouth, I grab the back of his head to keep him there. This is all I have wanted for the past week—to be cherished by him.

God, I knew by how good he kissed that his mouth was magical, but this is unexpected. Can you have an orgasm just from a guy sucking on your tits, because I am about to lose all control.

Vince pulls away, leaving me wanting more, and my body follows him instinctively. He pulls his tie free and undoes the buttons of his shirt. He's still wearing the suit jacket, and the contrast of the white shirt next to his tan muscular body is doing things to me. Not like I needed any more help. I am a torch.

He slides the suit jacket off and tosses it on the small table, his eyes never leaving me. They roam over my body, my face, lingering on my lips. I feel beautiful for the first time, because I feel like someone is actually seeing me. He's taking his time, enjoying exploring me. I can see reverence in his eyes, along with a longing that I have never seen before. I take in a sharp breath, as Vince's fingers dig into my hips. He is steering me backwards, and I look over my shoulder to make sure we are actually heading to the bed. I don't want to end up on the floor again.

Vince realizes what I am doing and he laughs, breaking the tension a little. I love that I get to see all these different sides of him, the passion that is dancing across his face, the need.

My legs hit the bed, and I reach back and place my hand down, easing us onto the large king-sized bed. God, to be this close to him, to have his hands all over me is so intoxicating. I arch into him and grumble in frustration at all the material of my skirt.

"Roll over. Let me help you," Vince says in my ear, then he eases himself to his knees, straddling me.

I turn under him, and as soon as I am on my stomach I feel him working the hook above the zipper of my dress. It doesn't take him long to get it undone, and I sigh when he pulls the fabric apart, baring me.

"Beautiful," he says as he trails his finger down my spine and to the top curve of my ass. He does that a few more times, causing goose bumps to erupt on my skin, then he places his hands flat on my back and slides them down until he holds my ass in his hands. He starts squeezing and rubbing, and I realize it has been far too long since I have been touched. I moan and glance behind me to see his eyes locked on my face. I turn again so I am face up, and he slides my dress off, then tosses it on the floor.

Climbing back over me, he straddles my thighs and traces his finger along the top of my underwear. I wish it was something delicate and fancy and not a plain pair of cotton briefs from Kmart. He doesn't seem to mind though.

"I like the black," he whispers. His fingers dip lower, and I lift my hips so he can slide them off.

He tosses them to the floor to join my dress, and I sigh at the feeling of being laid bare in front of him. No more pretending I am not attracted to him, no more averting my gaze so he doesn't catch me staring. I am drinking him in now, with full license to stare.

"You are so handsome," I say, trailing my fingers down his chest to that delicious trail of hair that leads into his slacks. I like how his stomach muscles quiver under my touch and how his eyes flutter shut. I grab his belt and smile up at him.

"One of us has too many clothes on, Vince," I say.

"Not yet. I need to do this first." He starts to kiss my chest, moving his lips to each nipple, then lower, kissing along my stomach, covering my body with his mouth like he needs to. I arch and moan as he gets closer to the top of my pubic bone. I expect him to dive in, but he doesn't. He teases me and drops lower to my thighs, spreading them with his big, strong hands and kissing a path down to my knee. My knee, which is apparently very fond of being kissed. Who knew?

Finally, he crawls his way back up and places his mouth over me, working me into a frenzy quicker than I thought possible. This has never really been my thing, to be honest. I always get in my own way and worry about things when a guy is down there. I almost stopped Vince. I am glad I didn't. The things he is doing with his tongue are not like anything I have experienced before. He is devouring me, and the feeling of being consumed by him pushes me over the edge to the most mind-blowing orgasm I have ever experienced. I grab his hair and grind shamelessly on his face, seeking more. He stays with me, coaxing all I have from me until I am limp and happy. He pulls away and grabs his wallet from his pocket, pulling free a condom. He undoes his belt and slacks. He scoots off the bed and stands, letting his pants drop to the floor. My mouth goes dry seeing him in his white boxers, all tan and toned and ready to take me. I sit up and pull him to me for a kiss, then help him remove the last barrier between us.

With his boxers on the floor, I hold out my hand for the condom, and the smile Vince gives me, dirty and full of lust, will stay with me until the day I die.

# TWENTY-FOUR
## VINCE

LAS VEGAS, Nevada
Gold Nugget

JESUS. She is going to put the condom on me. I might come just from that. I am so amped up right now, I have to take a few breaths to calm my racing heart. The sight of her tearing open that foil packet then reaching for me is almost too much. Before she slides the condom on, she dips her head and licks across the head of my cock.

"Fuck," I growl and grab at her, trying to stop her. It's no use; it's like once she had a taste, she can't stop. I know how that is. I just experienced that myself.

I close my eyes as she slides that beautiful mouth further down my shaft and I battle to keep my composure. My hips are jerking and thrusting as if they have a mind of their own, and I look down to see if she is okay, only to find her looking up at me with those big, beautiful brown eyes. I thread my fingers through her hair and let her have her way with me. She is licking and sucking and humming over my cock.

I don't want to come like this. I mean I do. I want to come like this, and inside her, and on her. I want it all, and I want it right now.

Just as I am about to explode, she pulls off me with a pop and smiles. She slides the condom down the length of me, then tips her head and asks, "How do you want me, Vince?"

I growl because my brain can't form words right now. I grab her and kiss her like she is all I need to survive, because in this moment, that is what it feels like.

"On your back to start. I want to see your face when I sink into you for the first time," I say, knowing that I will want there to be more times—later tonight, tomorrow, next week. I will never get enough.

She smiles and scoots up, pulling the covers back and climbing in bed alongside me. Her tan skin is offset by the white sheets, and the sight of her hair spilling over the pillow fulfills every dream I have had of her. How is that I only just met her? It feels like she has always been here, waiting for me. I crawl to her and lower myself over her. I find her lips with mine and moan into her mouth when I feel her hand guiding me. She wraps her legs around me, and for a moment I hover at her entrance, waiting and praying for the strength to last. I push in a little, then pull back, and she uses her hand to guide me through her wet slick folds. She arches and moans and transports me back to the entrance to heaven. Without any restraint, I slam into her, loving the gasp that escapes her lips.

"Oh fuck, Vince. Yes!" she says, and the fact that this girl is a dirty talker in bed short-circuits my brain. "Come on. You know you want to fuck me hard and fast. Do it, Vince. I can take it. Don't be gentle," she says huskily in my ear.

I lose control. I lift her hips and thrust in and up, grunting like a madman, feeling her contracting around me as she comes again. It's too much. Watching her face as she falls apart triggers my own release, and we fall together into that euphoria where nothing else matters. Where there are no murders to solve, or violent fathers, or alcoholic mothers, or lost dreams. This right here is the new dream, my new reality, and it crashes around me as I spill into her again and again. I have never come so hard in my life. I collapse onto her, trying to not crush her. She isn't having it though, and she pulls me closer, my chest pressed to hers, skin on skin. Both of our hearts pound and stutter until they sync. I know she feels it too because she makes a sweet sound and kisses my shoulder. She isn't letting go, and I am not fighting it. There is nowhere I want to be, nowhere I want to go that doesn't include this girl. This beautiful, sexy, dirty-mouthed girl.

"That was incredible, Vince," Heather says. She is trailing her fingers up and down my back, and I am fucking melting.

"It was." I lift myself up enough to see her face and kiss her softly on the lips. I finally go soft, and I slip out of her and get up to use the bathroom, disposing of the condom. I catch a glimpse of myself in the mirror, and I don't recognize the guy I see. Who is that happy bastard? I haven't seen him in years.

I bring a warm, wet washcloth out and hand it to her, mesmerized by the flushed look on her face. She hasn't covered up or even moved since I went into the bathroom. She looks like a fallen angel, my angel. I wait while she cleans up, then I take the washcloth from her and toss it in the sink in the bathroom.

"My God, you are so beautiful, Heather," I say when I turn back around.

She is propped up on her elbows, tits on full display. Her ankles are crossed, and she is raking her eyes over me like I didn't just rock her world and she is ready for more, and soon. Her lips part, and then she smiles a big, beautiful smile that lights up not just her face but mine.

"Thank you. I think you are pretty handsome yourself. I guess we can talk about that now, huh?" she says with a little giggle.

I cross the room and climb in bed next to her, pulling the covers over us. She rolls to face me. My beard scruff has made her neck red, and it makes me unreasonably happy. I reach out and touch the area, letting my fingers explore the slope of her neck and shoulder.

"I thought Iolet had sent me an angel when I saw you walk out of the airport," I tell her, my voice quiet.

"I thought the same thing. I can't tell you how worried I was that you'd be some creepy guy," she says with a laugh.

"I do worry about your judgment that you still got on that plane, Heather, but I am glad you did," I say.

"Me too," she agrees, and some emotion crosses her face, but it disappears quickly.

I arch a brow in question and she ignores it, pushing me to my back. She climbs on top of me, straddling me just above my cock. She places her hands on my chest and leans forward to kiss me, and it's everything. Soft, sweet, and slow. I just had her, yet I feel my cock stirring to life again. It twitches and taps her on the ass, making her laugh.

"Well, hello," she coos at me, grinding her hips in little circles. She sits up and pulls her fingers through her hair, twisting it up and somehow tying it in a knot on top of her head.

I reach up and cup her breasts, enjoying the view of her on top of me. I knead each breast, then run my thumbs over her very tight nipples.

"Fuck, I love how rough your hands are, Vince. If you don't have any more condoms, I bought some. Or we could go without if you're clean. I know I am, and I am on the pill," she says. She is still making those little circles with her hips, and her ass keeps bumping into my cock, which is fully awake now.

I grab her hips and hold her still. "You bought condoms? When?"

"At that gas station when I went back in for drinks," she says with a devilish grin.

I laugh and shake my head. "That's really funny. I bought a box from that guy too. No wonder he came out to wave at us."

She puts her hands over her face and laughs hard enough to make her whole body shake, which is oddly arousing since she is sitting on top of me.

"That does make sense now. I thought he was just amused that a girl was buying them," Heather says. She starts circling her hips again, and I grip her to slide her down a little. She sits up and moves back to straddle my thighs, then she wraps her hand around my hard-ened length, and I groan.

"So what will it be, Vince? You want me to grab a condom, or are we okay like this?" She is looking at me like a challenge has been laid down.

"I haven't been with anyone in over a year. I assume I am clean, but it's up to you," I say, and before I can wonder what her choice will be, she is sliding down on me. She arches her back as she raises up, so just the tip of my cock is at her entrance. She pauses then slams down, setting a pace that will surely be the death of me.

---

TWO ROUNDS later we both stumble into the bathroom to clean up and brush our teeth. Standing here next to her brushing my teeth, wearing only my underwear, feels oddly normal. She has nothing on but the little black cotton underwear, and she is as comfortable as she was in that beautiful dress. I noticed that about her when I finally made my move. She isn't shy, and she goes for what she wants, what will make her feel good. I have never been with a girl like her. I have only been with two other women, and neither of them lit me up like Heather. The first girl I ever had sex with was a virgin too, and it was awkward and bumpy and over really fast. We never went out again, and she moved away without even saying goodbye. The second girl I dated for a while. When I told Heather that it had been over a year since I'd been with someone, I lied a little. It's been more like two years.

Jennifer and I were together for a year and a half and probably only had sex ten or twenty times. She just wasn't into it, and I always felt like I was bothering her. That was hard on my ego.

Tonight? I feel like a superhero. Heather couldn't get enough of me, and her dirty mouth asking for what she wanted was a surprising twist. It was exciting, and I never had to wonder if she was enjoying herself. I bet our neighbors know she was enjoying herself. Fuck, that was so hot.

We crawl back into bed, and I am asleep before I can wonder if Heather wants to snuggle.

I wake up with a foot in my ass and another tucked between my legs. It takes me a minute to place where I am and whose body is tangled with mine, but then the memories of last night flood my mind, and I feel my heart expand a little. I haven't woken up happy like this, well, ever.

I lift my leg and carefully scoot away so Heather can sleep longer. I duck into the bathroom and take care of business, then brush my teeth and start the shower. I didn't check the time, but it feels early still. We have to check out by eleven, and if we can get on the road right away, we won't hit too much traffic. Once we get to Victorville the traffic will slow us down a lot, but that can't be helped. I know I am not stopping to get gas at the same station as last time. I don't want to see that guy looking at Heather like he knows the shit she has done, even if it was with me.

I take my time in the shower, enjoying the hot water and a shower big enough to actually wash myself. That phone booth of a shower at my apartment is awful. Eventually I turn off the water and dry off, and in no time I'm dressed. I walk over to the bed in our darkened room and lean down to kiss Heather, finding only a pillow and a bunched up blanket. My heart drops into my stomach for a second, and I glance around the room to see her dress and my suit are laid out neatly.

I am just about to put on my shoes and head downstairs to look for her when there is a knock on the door. I yank the door open to find Heather holding a tray of food. She has a brown paper bag in her teeth as well. I wonder briefly how she knocked but decide it's more important to help her out, so I grab the tray and push the door open with my ass so she can step in.

"Thanks. I didn't think that through when I went down for breakfast. I would have been in a world of hurt if you were still in the shower, or worse, if you had left!" Heather says. She opens the bag and dumps out silverware and little salt and pepper packets. The tray has two plates of food piled high and, God bless her, coffee.

"This is amazing, but you didn't have to do this!" I say, then add quickly, "Thank you so much."

"Sure. I thought it would be easier to eat in here so we could talk freely. I mean I also really had to use the bathroom, and you were in there." She shrugs.

"Heather, we did things to each other last night that should make you comfortable enough to pee while I am in the shower," I say. She gives me a look that I can't read at first, then it hits me.

"Oh! Right, well sure. That makes sense," I stammer.

"Yeah, I don't ever want that kind of a relationship with you, Vince," she says and then snaps her mouth shut and looks down.

I know it was the relationship word that freaked her out, so I reach for her hand and give it a squeeze. "I agree. Let's never do that." I wink. Her shoulder relaxes again, and we both dig in to the delicious food.

We get back to the shop at around six, even though we left Vegas at ten. Heather wanted to see a cactus up close, and apparently she has always wanted to chase a tumbleweed. I had to pull over several times before she was able to actually run after one that was moving. I leaned against my car with my arms folded as she chased the huge ball across the desert. She didn't believe me that they were sharp, so we had another detour to a store to get a Band-Aid for her finger.

Once we are upstairs and our stuff is put away, Heather starts putting together some dinner. "I think if I am going to stay here, you need to let me pay rent or something," she says as she works.

"No," I say simply.

"Vince, listen, you have to let me pay my own way. I have never been, nor will I ever be a charity case!" Heather says, her voice rising a little.

"Heather, first of all, if you are going to start using words like 'nor' then I am gaining to revoke your cool girl card," I say. She rolls her eyes at me, but I continue. "I don't pay rent. This place is owned outright by my father. He owns the land, the shop, the equipment. All the operating costs are covered by the repairs I do, and whatever is left over is my income. Dad was smart with his money. He wasn't smart with the rest of his life, but that part he got right. I can't accept money from you."

I can see the defeat in her eyes but also something else. Concern? Pity? I don't know, but I don't like it one bit. I stand up quickly and start helping her chop vegetables.

"What are we having?" I ask

"Stir-fry, I guess. How about this: I will clean and cook," she suggests while pointing a knife at me.

"No. You aren't my maid or my chef," I say, exasperated with this discussion.

"Well, what am I then? I don't want you to resent me, Vince. I don't want to be a burden," Heather says. That last part came out just above a whisper.

I set down my knife, then take hers, placing it on the counter. Even though she is cute as hell, I don't like having a knife pointed at me. I grab her hands and give them a squeeze.

"Who made you feel that way? Tell me their name so I can go and punch them," I say, looking her dead in the eye.

That earns me a small smile and one shoulder shrug. "I just want you to know I can pull my own weight. I don't need anyone to take care of me." She puffs her chest out a little, but I see that same flicker as before dance across her eyes.

Hurt.

I know it like I know my own name. I have that emotion on speed dial. Mine tends to burst out like anger, but yeah, I recognize it. I step closer to her and drop her hands so I can wrap my arms around her. I pull her in and hold her to me. It takes a minute before she relaxes into me, and when she does, I feel like I did when I'd win a ball game. I start rubbing her back with one hand, and she takes a deep, ragged breath. She tries to pull back, but I don't let her. I just hold her tighter and wonder who back home does this for her? Does she have anyone that she can count on? My life hasn't been perfect, but before Dad's heart attack and stroke, there was nothing he wouldn't do for me. And my mom? Forget about it. She would walk across flaming glass if I needed a tissue.

We stay like that for a little while longer, and when I feel like I have made my point, I relax my grip a little, and she steps back. She looks up at me with those eyes of hers, that capture my soul. "Thank you, Vince," she says.

"Sure. Let's not worry about any of that right now. If six months from now we are still working on this Iolet bullshit, we can talk about a trade or something then," I say.

"Sounds fair." She tips up her face to me and I kiss her softly. It is so easy to get lost in her. Would that be such a bad place to be lost? My heart says no.

TWENTY-FIVE
HEATHER

HOLLYWOOD, California
Hugh's Auto Body

I PULL AWAY before we get carried away again. God, his lips are going to be the death of me, but what a way to go.

I let him finish with the vegetables, and I grab the last of the chicken from the fridge. I am going to get groceries tomorrow. I don't think he can argue with that. We fall into a rhythm, and before too long there is a nice dinner on the table.

"Vince, we need to figure out our next step. Mr. Sinatra said he thinks Albert's killer is still around. I imagine he's at least in his seventies now, but he might have dangerous friends. Iolet wanted us to find the man who killed Albert and her dreams. We owe that to her," I say, stabbing a piece of chicken with my fork.

"Well, I need to look into who owns the car. Once Frank said he gave Iolet the ring, I started to wonder if maybe she didn't steal the car. Maybe we aren't supposed to give it back to anyone. Maybe it's just a clue."

"Oh crap, you might be right. So we have a car, a ring, a pair of men's shoes, and costume jewelry that Marilyn Monroe wore," I say.

"And a chicken foot," Vince says around a bite of food.

"What?" I ask.

He finishes chewing, swallows, then says, "A dried chicken foot. That was in my box too."

"Are you fucking kidding me? A chicken foot? What the hell, Vince?" My voice tips up a few octaves.

"Yeah. See, I didn't want to tell you, and I was right. It is freaking you out." He points his fork at me, then he scoops up more chicken and vegetables like he didn't just mention the weirdest thing ever.

"Why on earth would she put a chicken foot with the other things? Was there a chicken foot in one of the movies? Is it from *The Maltese Falcon*? Could that be it?" I rattle off the questions without giving him a chance to answer.

Vince wipes his mouth with his napkin and leans back in his chair. He rubs at his jawline and squints off in the distance.

"No, I don't think so. We should ask Henry what movie a chicken foot might be in. Maybe it's not on the list. I think the movies on the list she gave us are important, but I don't think we have props from all those, you know? They might be separate."

I groan and lean back in my chair. "Okay, so we have a dried chicken foot. Is that like finding a horse head on your pillow? That's a mob thing, right? What's a chicken foot?" I ask.

Vince scrunches his nose and shakes his head. "No, I am pretty sure it doesn't mean anything like the horse head thing."

"Damn." I look down at my now empty plate, grateful I didn't know about the foot while I still had chicken on my plate.

"I want to talk to Henry about that, and maybe we show him our list to see if it means anything to him?" Vince says.

I remember the pages of movies that the detective had and mention it to Vince. "So, since she was literally in over a hundred movies and shows, I think the ones she wrote down for us mean something. That has to be it."

I walk over to Vince's phone and phonebook, grab the notepad and pen, then return to the table.

"Okay, I am going to write all these down on one page. She said it will make sense when the boxes are together. Right?"

"True. I guess it's worth a try," Vince says with a shrug.

I write down each movie and stare at the paper. Maybe it's just a coincidence and how I wrote them, but GTB is staring me right in the face. I spin the paper to Vince and point.

"Look. This is just the order I chose to write them, but *Gone with the Wind, The Maltese Falcon, Breakfast at Tiffany's.* GTB. Maybe that's what she was referring to with those initials she wrote on the note with the key."

"That could be. What if the first letters all spell something?" Vince says, grabbing the paper off the table. He squints and bites his lip, turning the paper to see the words at a different angle.

"I don't think that can be it. There aren't enough vowels, and it gets worse if you add the first letters of the physical items." I lower my head to the table and sigh.

"Maybe we just let this go for now and get some sleep. My brain isn't working at all," Vince says. He stands and clears our plates while I continue to rest my forehead on the table. He's right. I know he is, but I am a stubborn girl. I always have been.

I can sense him step behind me before he puts his hand on my back. I smile like a fool into the table when he trails his hand up and down my back.

"Come on. I am excited about sleeping in my bed again," Vince says.

"Okay. Do you have a side of the bed?" I ask as I let him lead me into the bedroom.

"I like the side next to you," he says.

"Vince, everyone has a side of the bed. Well, except me because I have only ever had a twin bed. Actually, come to think about it, this past week is the longest I have ever slept in a big bed," I say. It comes out sounding more pathetic than I meant it to, but thankfully Vince has walked into the bathroom, so he missed it.

---

THE NEXT MORNING I walk out to find Vince on the phone with the care home. I study his face as he talks to the manager, but I can't tell if it's good news or not. I walk quietly to the couch and sit, waiting for him to finish.

"Well, sure, I can understand that. I don't know if he would care as long as the other guy doesn't. No, he's bedridden. Right. Okay, sure. Ten?" Vince says and looks to me for approval. I give him a thumbs-up, and he smiles.

"Yeah, we can come by at ten. Thank you so much. Right. See you then." Vince hangs up and walks over to me.

"So they don't have a single bedroom available. I guess the openings were filled, but there is a double bedroom, and she says the guy in there is super cool. You can go with me at ten?" he asks.

"Yes! I am sure it will be a good fit. I mean from what I saw at least." I have the urge to keep talking because I am nervous suddenly, but Vince steps in and places his hands on my shoulders.

"It will be fine. I am sure." He bends and gives me a quick kiss.

After breakfast and a shower, Vince heads down to do some work in the shop while I go over the box items and lists again. I really think GTB stands for "get the bastard," not "give them back." What is special about those other films on the list though? My head is swimming trying to figure it out, and I start to wonder why on earth Iolet couldn't just tell us what she knew. How hard would it have been to say, "So-and-so murdered Albert, please alert the authorities"?

"Almost time for us to head over. You ready?" Vince says and I jump.

"Shit, sorry. I didn't hear you come in. I was trying to figure this out," I say, waving at my notes.

"Yeah. When I was doing an oil change I was thinking what if she was just nuts? I mean what if it doesn't mean anything and she was just crazy? Like the costume jewelry. She knew we couldn't talk to Marilyn but that was included in the stuff anyway," Vince says.

I blink a few times to clear my own thoughts and consider what he just said. That could be it. I mean all the stuff she said the day I met her in her room was pretty crazy.

"I kind of assumed she had dementia or something, but what if that is how she always was? Then the things we are assuming are clues could just be things?" I say, and Vince nods.

"Yeah, I say we get the car, fix it, and return it to the studio. Someone there might know why she had it. Or should we mention it to that detective guy?" he asks.

"No, let's not do that. At least not yet." I stand to grab my purse. "I am ready. Let's go find your dad a new home."

"You are the best," Vince says. He gives me a quick little kiss on my cheek, and we head out.

Vince is quiet on the drive over, and I have to fight the urge to fill the silence. He probably wants to think and not hear me ramble on and on.

"It's right here," I say as he turns onto the street.

"Thanks," Vince says with a sigh. He pulls to the curb and stops but doesn't kill the engine.

"You okay, Vince?" I ask quietly.

After he takes a big deep breath, he says, "Yeah. I just hate this. I can't believe this has been going on for so long." He winces a little, and I put my hand on his arm.

"It's okay to feel that way. This is hard. Can I tell you something?" I say.

"Sure." He shuts the car off and leans back in his seat, hands still resting on the steering wheel.

"You asked why I drink when we were in Vegas, and I didn't tell you the whole story," I explain.

He raises an eyebrow at me but remains quiet, so I continue.

"I missed out on a lot of things because of my mom's drinking. I had to grow up and be the adult way too early in my life. I didn't get to do things other teenagers took for granted. I didn't get to go to prom or celebrate my graduation. I haven't had a birthday present since I was about eight years old," I say, more words coming than I planned, but I want him to understand.

"That sucks, Heather. I'm sorry," Vince says.

"I know. Thanks. It does suck. So that's the thing. All the guys at Serenity Falls would talk about going out and partying and how fun it was, and I realized that was one more thing my mom took from me. One more thing other people got to have that I never would. That's why I went out and had a drink with them on my birthday. Well, I think a part of me wanted to know if I was like her too, you know?"

Vince nods but doesn't say anything, so I keep going.

"The next day when I woke up, I didn't care if I ever had a drink again. I had fun, felt a little tipsy, maybe a little reckless the night before, but it didn't change me. My mom said to me once that the first time she had a drink she knew she had found her best friend. She craved the buzz, the numbness, and I just don't." I cock my head at him and ask, "Does this make sense?"

"Yeah, I get it. I don't know what that has to do with me, but I appreciate you telling me," Vince says with a small smile.

"Well, I am telling you because I want you to know that until my twenty-first birthday, I was living for her and me. I was making decisions in my life that would accommodate her if she fell hard. I never let myself relax because I was in charge. After that night, I slowly started to see my life as my own. I would call her and check in, but I stopped giving her money every month." Vince's lips turn into two thin lines. I know that look. It's the look of frustration of someone who has nothing left to give but still finds scraps to hand over to their parent.

"It's okay to start allowing yourself to feel disappointed, Vince. It's okay to put yourself before him. It's the first step on your journey out of this. He doesn't know you feel this way. He doesn't need to know. But when your heart is feeling something that your brain is trying to ignore, you end up miserable," I say.

"Right. I know. I do. I let myself feel these things, thinking the end is in sight, that he can't live like this forever, but then he just keeps . . ." His voice trails off.

"Vince, what if you step back more once he's settled here. How often do you see him at the place he lives now?" I ask.

"I go a few times every week," he says. He blows out a breath and tips his head back, staring at the roof of his Bug. He brushes away a smudge on the headliner.

"Maybe start by going once a week and see if that helps," I suggest. I bite my lower lip, hoping he doesn't get angry at my suggestion.

"I can do that?" he asks.

"Does he know what day it is?" I ask.

"I don't think so. Sometimes he doesn't even wake up when I am there. He is all backwards and is awake at night, but I can't bring myself to go late at night," Vince says, his voice strained.

"Well, then I think it would be okay if you started stretching out the time between the visits." I open my door and climb out. I lean in the window and wait for him to look over at me. I give him my best smile, and my heart melts a little when he smiles back.

He climbs out, locks up the car, walks straight to me, and grabs my hand. "Thanks for coming, and for what you said. I needed to hear that. Let's see what this place is like. Maybe I can step back. Maybe," he says as he squeezes my hand.

We spend a good hour talking with the case manager before we are taken back to the room that Hugh would share. Vince seems really impressed with this place, and I am so relieved. It's incredible.

We walk down the hallway, and Janice taps lightly on the door-frame before peeking her head in and speaking to the man in the room in a soft, sweet voice.

"Mr. Chin? We are here. Is it okay to come in?" she asks.

A thin, tiny voice creaks out a yes, so we all step in. I look around the room and smile. It's nice and spacious with two hospital beds next to a big window that overlooks the backyard. I glance over at Vince to see what he thinks, but he stands frozen in the doorway.

"Mr. Chin, these are the people I was telling you about. This is Heather and that is—"

"Vince, how are you doing, young man?" Mr. Chin says.

"I am good, sir. How are you doing?" Vince says as he steps cautiously toward Mr. Chin's bed.

"Dying a little more each day," he says, and he attempts a smile. He is a tall, thin man with a full head of hair. His skin is smoother than the skin of any of the residents at Serenity Falls, and I wonder how old he is.

"You two know each other?" Janice asks.

"Mr. Chin lived in my neighborhood over in Palm Springs," Vince says. He relaxes his shoulders a little, and his smile is small but genuine.

"You here for a grandparent?" Mr. Chin asks, and Vince shakes his head.

"No, sir. My father. He had a heart attack, and then a major stroke. He's not able to care for himself anymore."

"Hugh? That big strapping man? I don't know if I can believe that." Mr. Chin falls into a coughing fit. Janice grabs a glass of water off his nightstand and holds it out for him. Once he is able to stop coughing, he reaches for it gratefully and takes a sip.

"He changed a flat for me once and I don't think he even used a jack. He just lifted the car right up with his bare hands," Mr. Chin says with a chuckle.

"Now that can't be true!" Janice laughs, and so does Vince.

"I swear." Mr. Chin makes a cross over his heart, then says, "I would be honored to share a room with him. Janice, make it happen. It's my dying wish." Mr. Chin waves his long, thin fingers like the matter is settled.

"You say that about everything, Mr. Chin. Last night you said the extra chocolate pudding was your dying wish. It starts to lose some impact, you know?" Janice says with a wink.

"Call me George, please. I can't leave this earth with everyone calling me mister." He strains to pull himself up a little further in the bed. I notice he is wearing very nice silk pajamas. The sleeves are long, but it is obvious how thin he is under the fabric. He is a very handsome man, and I can picture him being well-dressed as a younger man.

"Does your family still live in that house on Lantern Street, Vince?" George asks.

"You have a very good memory. Yes, my mom still lives there. She just retired from being a teacher at the high school," Vince says.

"Right. I think she had just gotten the job when she and your father moved in. You must be what, twenty-five?" he asks.

Vince shakes his head and laughs. "I am twenty-four. I'll be twenty-five in a few months."

"Well, time really does march on," George says, and his eyes flutter shut. His chest rises and falls in a steady, even manner.

Janice smiles and nods toward the door, indicating that we should follow her. Once we are out in the hall, she turns to Vince and me and asks, "What do you think?"

"I think my dad would be lucky to be here, especially with someone he knew as a roommate." Vince's whole demeanor is relaxed.

"Wonderful. Let's take care of the paperwork and we can initiate the transfer, hopefully by tomorrow," Janice says.

# TWENTY-SIX
# VINCE



FUCKING FINALLY. I feel like I am finally catching a break. That place was incredible. Having Mr. Chin as a roommate will be so good for my dad, maybe give him a little more joy. I know my parents liked George. I remember him coming over a few times for dinner when I was little. He stood out to me because I had never known anyone that tall. I always wanted to ask him how tall he was, and I am embarrassed to say that question almost slipped out as we talked today.

I need to call my mom and tell her what is going on. I have been dreading it, but now? Now I can say Dad is moving in with an old friend. I am sure that will make her happy, even if she will pretend she doesn't care. I don't talk to her as often as I should, I know that. Hell, I haven't been out to the house in months. I just can't seem to make it a priority, and after visiting Dad, driving out to see my mom feels like one more chore.

I'm quiet as I drive back to the shop, thinking about all that just happened, I run through all the things I can remember about Mr.

Chin which, as it turns out, isn't much. I have no idea what he did for work or how long he lived in our neighborhood. Fuck, is the fact that he was a tall, thin man the only fact I know about him?

I wish I knew how much my dad understands or can remember. I wish I could ask him questions and actually get an answer. This past year it seems like he's just a shell, but I don't know if it's because I have let go of my hope, or if he has been that way since the stroke. I saw something in his eyes when I talked to him before—recognition, frustration? I can't be sure, of course, but it felt that way. Now? He doesn't know I am there when I actually catch him awake. Maybe Heather is right. Maybe it's time for me to pull back a little.

My stomach tightens at that thought. I am the last one who still visits him. After his heart attack, everyone came around—his friends, our family, and hell, even a few of his customers. After the stroke, the number of people started to dwindle until I was the only one who still visited. It's a lot of pressure to be someone's only tie to the past, their only support. What happens if I stop too? I feel a lump grow in my throat, making it hard to swallow. I try and take a breath, but it feels like someone strapped a metal band around my lungs and is tightening it very slowly. I grip the steering wheel, like if I can bend it, all my problems will disappear.

"Vince, what's wrong?" Heather asks. It sounds like she is very far away, and I realize the road in front of me has gotten very long and narrow.

"Vince, pull over here." I feel her hand on my arm, then on the wheel, easing us to the side of the street. Together we steer into a gas station parking lot and I kill the engine. My left hand still has a death grip on the wheel, while my right is resting on the gear knob. The small, smooth knob that my dad helped me find when we first bought this VW. It wasn't even running, and the whole back seat was missing. We worked on it together until it was something I could be proud to drive. The porcelain feels oddly cool in my hand.

"Hey, Vince. Look at me." I hear her, but it's almost impossible to respond.

"Vince, you are scaring me," she says.

I try to answer her. God, why does my chest feel so tight? I lean forward and rest my head on the steering wheel, pinching my eyes shut. Off in the distance I can hear a car door open and shut, and I rock gently with the movement, no longer in control of my own body.

I feel her hands on my shoulders, then the seat moving back. She is climbing onto my lap and wrapping her arms around me. Her warm lips are on my face and her fingers are wiping away wetness that is on my cheeks. Am I crying?

"Hey, it's okay. I am here. It's okay. Yeah, I know, I know," she is saying as she holds my face. I see her now, like someone turned on the defrost and the windshield is clearing. She presses her forehead to mine and continues to speak softly to me. We sit like that for a while. I honestly don't know how long it is before I can move, and then I just bury my face in her neck and wrap my arms around her, pulling her closer.

"It's going to be okay, Vince. I am here. Can you take a few deep breaths for me? Yeah, like that. Slowly now. Yeah, good." Her voice is an anchor. No, that's not right. Anchors pull you down, and she is lifting me up.

"Lifeline," I manage.

"What?" she asks.

"Thanks for being my lifeline," I say in a gravelly voice. I move my hands to rub her back and hit her folded leg. I pull back and see that she has one leg bent up under my armpit and the other hanging out of the open door of my Bug. I barely fit in this seat by myself, and she has somehow wedged herself in here with me.

Just as I am about to say something about that very thing, she leans back and hits the horn on the steering wheel.

"Shit! Sorry. Oh, fuck. Oh no. Cramp. Oh my God. Vince! Help. My leg is cramping," she whimpers.

"Which one?" I ask.

"The left one that is shoved up in your armpit. My foot is stuck between the seat and the e-brake!" she says frantically.

I glance down and see the problem. I reach over to the side of the seat and lower the back, then push her at the same time. Her back hits the horn again, but this time she just laughs as she pulls her leg over me, sitting with both legs out the door.

"Oh, that is better. Thank you so much," she says, twirling her ankle. "Calf cramps are the absolute worst."

"So is whatever the fuck I just went through. Sorry about that," I say, pushing my hand through my hair.

She gets off my lap and steps out the driver's side door, then turns, waiting. I pull the seat back up and climb out and into her open arms, feeling a little unsteady but a thousand times better than a few minutes ago.

"Do you get panic attacks often?" Heather asks.

"I don't know what that is, so I am going to say no. That has never happened to me before," I say.

"Oh. Yeah, those are when your whole world turns into a tunnel and your chest feels tight and your vision gets all wacky. I would hear a high-pitched noise like a whine. It was annoying, but in a way it helped because I could tell when the attack was passing because the noise would fade. Now that I think about it, I might have been screaming. I mean that is always a possibility," she says with a little shrug.

I blink at her a few times before I realize she is smiling at me, trying to make me feel better with a lame joke.

"Right. Next time I will try that. The screaming, I mean. Wait, I don't want there to be a next time. How do I do that?" I ask. My voice sounds a little more panicked than I want.

"Well, that's the thing about panic attacks. You don't really get a choice. There are things you can do to prevent them, but sometimes your brain is just going to say 'Nah, we need to freak out right now. Check back later if you want normal thoughts,'" she says. It sounds like she really understands, and she isn't looking at me with judgment or even pity.

"Listen, I haven't had one since I started talking to a counselor.

My English teacher in high school witnessed my first one. My mom had just gone on a wild bender and came home with not one but two gross biker dudes. Thank God I had a lock on my bedroom door. By the time I got up to go to school, they were all passed out, but I had to step over a guy to leave my room," Heather says.

"What? Did he try and get in?" I say, my stomach roiling at the thought.

"Probably. I went to school like nothing had happened, but by third period I felt like my chest was on fire. I got through math okay, but the next period was English, and we were going over *Flowers for Algernon*," she explains.

"Oh, that book gutted me." I wince.

"Me too! Mrs. Haney was going on and on about the symbolism, and all I could think about was how poor Charley had it all then lost it, and I was never going to have it all. I lost everything without ever having it, you know?" she says with a pointed look.

"I do," I manage to say quietly.

"Well, the whole room started to shrink, and my chest felt tight, and there was a buzzing noise in my ears. It was awful. I finally calmed down enough to follow my teacher to the nurse. That night my mom got arrested for DUI," Heather says. She lets out a big sigh and continues, "My second panic attack alone in our apartment was worse, but I got through it somehow. A week later Mrs. Haney set me up with counseling appointments that I never had to pay for. I still don't understand how she did that, but I will be forever grateful. I learned how to talk about what had been going on in my life with someone. That wasn't normal for me. My mom sure as hell didn't care about me," Heather says.

I step forward and wrap my arms around her, pulling her into a hug that I wish could erase her shitty childhood.

"My problems seem pretty lame compared to what you went through, Heather. Thanks for helping me," I say. I shake my whole body like a dog getting out of the water so I can clear the cobwebs and the weird feeling I still have in my chest. It's not painful or anything, but I have never felt like this. I look down into Heather's eyes and smile when I see her looking up at me.

"It's not lame. Who has been here for you? Tony? Does he know how hard all of this has been on you?" she demands.

"No. Maybe. I don't know. He went through his own shit, being left at the altar and all. He didn't need to hear me whine about my problems," I explain.

"Vince, what happens when you overinflate a tire?" She has her arms crossed in front of her chest now, and I know if I looked down, I would see her tapping her little foot.

"Um, the tire blows," I say, fighting a smile that betrays my mood. She is just so damn cute.

"Right, so if you don't learn to let off some of the pressure, what is going to happen to you?" she asks with a nod of her head. She would make a good teacher, or an attorney, or hell, a nurse. She could do anything. I wonder what her dream job is?

"I'll explode," I say.

"Right. You had your first one just now. Let's keep talking about this stuff. That is like your pressure release valve. You have to let it out," Heather says. She reaches for my hand and gives it a squeeze.

"I'll drive us back to the shop and we can talk some more. Come on." She walks around me and climbs into the driver's seat before I can protest. I have a feeling it's going to be a long night.

---

THE NEXT MORNING she is up and out the door early with plans to meet the detective and go to the library again. It wasn't as bad as I thought to sit around and talk about things. I shared things with her that I have never talked about, and she gave me more information about what her life was like. I wonder if I would have met her if I had gone to Chico.

I head downstairs, ready to tackle my day. I have an actual pep in my step. I haven't felt that way since I was in high school. Tony and I finish up with the cars in the shop and even one that was in the back lot waiting for a brake job. I guess without a black cloud hanging over my head I can actually be productive. Who knew?

"Want to head to the beach since we got done early?" Tony asks.

"No, I need to pick up a car. It's in storage. Want to help me?" I ask.

"Sure. You want to have the tow guy meet us there or is it drivable?" he asks.

"I'm going to put it on the flatbed. It has sat for a long time. It was that lady Iolet's car. It was part of her estate," I say, hoping that he doesn't ask any more questions.

"Cool, sure, I can help with that," Tony says. He grabs the keys for the flatbed from my desk. I almost sold the stupid thing more than once since taking over the shop for my dad since I only use it once or twice a year, but man, am I glad I have it now.

We drive over to the storage unit while Tony talks about all the funny shit that happened the night they all went out with Gio. It sounds like Gio was a bumbling idiot when he saw Michael in his wheelchair. Becky gave him a bunch of shit about being a terrible friend, and Monica hit on him. Gio thought he was the luckiest guy in the world and ended up leaving the bar with her, so I guess that is a perfect ending.

We pull around to the back of the storage lot, and I park the flatbed so we can get the car onto it. I pull up the door and marvel again at Iolet. This is a fucking cool car, and I can't wait to fix it up. Heather is going to talk to the detective today about it and see if he can find out who it belongs to without telling him we have it. She said she has an idea and to trust her.

After everything we talked about last night, I do trust her. Fuck, we didn't even have sex last night; we just cuddled. I have never slept better in my whole life. Her body wrapped around me like a blanket, feeling her heartbeat against my chest, was like a powerful drug.

I open the driver's side door to put the car in neutral so we can push it out. The tires are flat, so it's a bitch to get it to roll even a few inches, but Tony is one strong bastard, so eventually we get it out enough to get behind it to push.

"What's that?" Tony asks as we walk around the back of the car.

Shit. What the hell *is* that? Iolet, what have you done?

"I, um, I'm not sure." I look down at the large lump covered in the thick, grey blankets that moving companies use. I lift one corner then start to laugh.

"What is it?" Tony asks, lifting the other side of the blanket. He stares and scratches his head. "Why is there half of a bathtub in here?"

"I guess it belonged to Iolet," I say, grateful he's never watched old movies. Anyone who has seen *Breakfast at Tiffany's* would know right away what this is. Holly's couch. Iolet stole Holly's couch. Jesus. How did that tiny lady get this off set and here?

"Do we bring it too?" Tony asks.

"Yeah, I mean I guess we should." I lift one side and test the weight. I think we can lift it together.

I pull the blanket all the way off and see the cushions and pillows are still on it. I put them in the cab of the truck, then come back to the shed and work with Tony to get the car all the way out and onto the flatbed. Next, we manage with great difficulty to move the cast-iron half tub. I cover both with a tarp and strap them down good.

Heather is not going to believe this.

# TWENTY-SEVEN
## HEATHER

HOLLYWOOD, California

MY LEG IS BOUNCING, and I know I look nervous, possibly guilty, but I can't stop it.

"Heather! Great to see you again. I was worried you wouldn't come back," Detective Fitzpatrick says as he walks out to the lobby to meet me. I stand and cross the short distance to meet him.

"Oh, right. No, I was definitely coming back. I just had some things to take care of. Vince's father needed to be moved to a new facility, and I was helping sort all that out." I wave my hand like I am part of the family or something.

"Right. Hugh DeLuca. Yeah, that stroke was a real doozie," John says as he turns to walk back to his office down the hall. I follow him, wondering why he seems to know so much about Vince and his family.

"Did you know him? I mean before the stroke?" I ask. John holds the door of his office open for me and I step inside. My stomach is doing cartwheels, and I have to place my hand on my chest to settle myself. I sit and take a deep breath.

"Well, no. I know of him. The DeLuca family has been on my radar for a while. Something I would have explained the other day if you had been able to stick around," John says. He has moved behind his desk and is sitting now, hands folded. His blue eyes are boring into my soul. I swallow hard and force a smile.

"A car mechanic caught your attention? There must be a reason for that. Was Hugh running a chop shop or something?" I say with a nervous laugh.

"No, nothing like that. I think Hugh was just caught up with the wrong people. I personally think the day he had his heart attack he was paid a visit by someone who threatened him," John says.

This has taken a very different turn. I came to ask him about the movies and the *Casablanca* car. My story was that I needed to find out who owned it so I could get a picture of it for Iolet's celebration of life. Now I am trying to digest the news that Vince's father was possibly involved in something illegal.

John pulls a file off the shelf behind him and places it in front of me. It's not the same one I saw the other day. This one is labeled "Hugh's Auto Body." My heart rate speeds up, threatening to leave my chest.

He opens it and rifles through the pages until he finds the one he is looking for. He slides it free of the stack and hands it to me.

It's a list of movies, some that are on the list Iolet gave us, some I have never heard of. I blink a few times before looking up at him.

"What is this?" I ask.

"Hugh's Auto Body, and the shop owners before Hugh, worked on cars for those movies. The studio used Hugh a lot to fix problems with their cars or to add things to cars they were using in the movies. I think that connection to the film industry is how he got involved," John says cryptically.

"Involved in what?" I ask, licking my lips nervously.

"The mob. Well, the Italian group of men that were trying to run drugs through Hollywood. I don't know if they were true mob men. They seemed kind of incompetent to me," he says with a shrug.

"So wait, you think Hugh was helping them?" I ask.

"No, I think they wanted him to help, and who knows if he was about to finally cave. Like I said, we know he was visited the day of his heart attack by one of the members of this group. His brother Carlos had already turned them down, but Hugh kept letting them come around. I think he was considering it."

"Considering what exactly? I am sorry. I am really confused," I say.

"Well, we think they were buying the cars from the movie sets, taking them to a local shop to be fitted with secret compartments, then using the cars to transport drugs. The Batmobile in the 1966 movie was at Hugh's shop. I think they wanted him to use it as a mule. I mean, think about it. Hiding drugs in such a famous car would make it easy to move about, even across the border. Everyone, including law enforcement, would be enamored with seeing it in real life. No one would think to search it," John explains.

"So you suspect the cars on this list were used to smuggle drugs?" I ask, glancing back at the list with *Casablanca* near the top.

"Yes, some of these cars went missing. The 1940 Buick from *Casablanca* is one of the last ones that was never located. We think it was their test car to see if they could get away with moving drugs across the border. I think they had packed it with drugs and were planning on taking it on a tour to deliver the goods. It went missing the night the movie wrapped. It could have about fifty pounds of cocaine tucked away in the door panels," John says, leaning back. He stares at me, then gives me a reassuring smile and says, "That wasn't done by Hugh's shop, by the way. It was a guy out in Ventura. We learned about it in weird way, to be honest. An elderly gentleman got pulled over for driving too slow on the freeway, and when the officer contacted him, he started talking about this car drug smuggling scheme he got involved with in the forties."

"Do you think Iolet knew about this? How is she involved?" I manage to ask. I feel like I am going to throw up.

"That I am not sure of. We questioned her of course, but it was like trying to nail Jell-O to a wall. She was all over the place, and most of the time I don't know if she really understood what we were asking," John says.

"Yeah, I had that experience with her too. When did you speak with her?" I ask. I can't remember anything about Iolet having official visitors at Serenity Falls, but I guess I could have missed that.

"Off and on over the years. She came back on our radar when a detective realized she was in all those movies on the list. At first they thought maybe she was a part of the smuggling ring, but that got ruled out pretty quickly," John says.

"Yeah, I can't see her being a drug dealer," I say.

"I think she was looking for whoever murdered Albert, and those two things started to cross paths. She knew some pretty influential stars: Frank Sinatra, Marilyn Monroe, even James Stewart. That is what drew me to Albert's case, what kept it in my mind all these years. Background actresses don't usually gain favor with the stars. Iolet was well-known and well loved by some pretty big names. I still haven't figured that out, but I don't think she was involved with the drugs. I think she wanted revenge for her friend," John says.

"Do you think it goes back that far? Was Albert involved in drug smuggling?" I lean forward, absolutely riveted by this new development.

"It's possible that is why he was killed. Drugs are a huge money-maker, and the loyalties among those who sell are fickle to say the least. One little misstep and things can turn," John says.

"I should tell you Vince and I saw Frank Sinatra this past weekend. He was playing at the Gold Nugget in Vegas, so we went to see his show," I say. I need to get some of this out. We haven't done anything wrong, and now I realize Iolet hasn't either. She just wanted to find Albert's murderer.

"Wow, that must have been fun. Was it a good show?" John asks with a smile. He leans back in his chair relaxed, like we are old friends. I like him. He feels like someone I can trust.

"Well, Iolet gave us Frank's ring, and we wanted to see if we could find out why," I explain.

"And did you?" he asks with the raise of his eyebrows.

"Sort of. Frank knew Albert, and he agreed there was a mob connection there. He thinks Albert was killed by the mob, so maybe it was about the drugs," I say.

"Interesting." John opens the file again and roots through it. He pulls out a paper and takes down a few notes.

"I'll see if we can get a guy in Vegas to talk to Mr. Sinatra about this. We didn't have a reason to speak with him before. I mean Iolet going to see him wasn't anything law enforcement should care about, right?" He chuckles a little, then continues, "But now that I know why she was there, we can talk to him. Did he have any idea who shot Albert?"

"No. He didn't, and he didn't say anything about drugs, so I don't know if he knows about that," I say, nervous now that I have somehow betrayed Mr. Sinatra by telling the police about our conversation.

"Yeah, that doesn't surprise me." John sighs and leans forward again. "I sure wish I could have spoken with Iolet before she passed. I hate that I missed that opportunity."

"I am not sure she would have been much help. Her memory was kind of a mess. She said some really weird things to me when I met her," I offer.

"Right. Well, like I said, we had a hard time getting any information out of her even in her younger years. I don't think what you saw was age related. I think that is just who she was," John says with a little smile.

I laugh at that. "So what would happen if you found the *Casablanca* car? Would that help?" I try to sound casual, but I see the flicker of interest in his eye.

"Well, that depends. I don't know if we could get prints or

anything that would be of use forty years later, but it would be nice to at least try," John says.

"Okay. Well, is there anything else?" I ask.

"Not really, unless you have more to tell me about Iolet?" John looks at me hopefully.

"I didn't really know her that well, to be honest, and it is the same for Vince. We don't really know why she chose us to plan her celebration of life," I say.

"Well, if anything at all comes to mind, you have my number," John says.

I stand and smile at him, reaching out to shake his hand. "I will for sure call if anything comes up. Thanks for meeting with me again. Sorry if I wasn't any help," I say.

"These cold cases aren't a high priority to anyone but me, Heather. I appreciate your interest. It would be nice to move Albert's file to the solved pile, but I am not holding my breath," John says.

I smile at him again and turn to leave, pausing for a moment when I remember one of the things I wanted to ask him. "John, wouldn't Albert's murderer be in his late seventies or eighties now?" I ask.

"Yes, if he was the same age as Iolet, there is a very real chance he has passed away. That's why I say that I am probably the only one who cares about this case. I want to find out if Albert's murder and the movie cars are related like I think they are. I can't get past that, and I need to know if I am right," John says.

"I guess it's a good thing you became a detective then. I hope you get your answers," I say, giving him a wave as I leave.

I had planned on going to the library today too, so I drive over and park in the back like last time. Maybe I can find out more about Albert and who he knew. I wonder if any of the cars from his movies went missing.

After a few hours, coming up with nothing more than a headache, I make my way to the front desk to check in with Margaret.

"Is Margaret in today?" I ask the young girl at the desk.

"Yes, she is helping someone right now. Can I do something for you?" She pushes her hair back from her face and smiles.

"I was actually wondering if you guys are hiring, or if you take applications." The words fly out of my mouth before I let myself think.

"I think so. I am doing internship hours for a class at my high school, but I know they need help. Hang on." She holds up a finger, then she bends down and pulls a drawer open. I can't see over the counter, but I hear the scrape of the hanging files. She pops back up with a smile. "Here it is! I knew I had seen an application." She hands it to me just as the phone rings.

"Thanks," I say quickly so she can answer the phone.

I leave with a strange feeling in my gut. I would love to work at a library—at this library. I would love to stay here in Hollywood. There really isn't anything for me in Chico. I would miss Boyd and a few other residents, but I feel free here. To be honest, once I climbed on the airplane in Sacramento, I started to feel the rope around me loosening. When I landed here, I started to realize I don't have to go back. That thought has been slowly making its way to the front of my brain since I got in Vince's truck at the airport. I would have never said anything to him though. *Nice to meet you. Can I live here forever?* That seems a little desperate and sad. When Vince asked if I would stay, my heart soared. The fact that he wants me here makes me feel so damn good. No one has cared about me like that, ever.

I get in Vince's Bug and drive to the grocery store. I am determined to get groceries since he won't let me pay for anything else. I run through the things I know how to cook and gather other items Vince might like, including beer and wine. When I get to the register to pay, I swallow when she tells me the total. I remind myself that I don't have any bills right now and I can afford this as I write out the check. I can find a job here and eventually get my own place. I don't want Vince to feel responsible for me, and I don't know if living together while we date is such a great idea. It feels wonderful right now, but I worry I will outstay my welcome.

I pull onto the street with the shop just as a huge flatbed truck is turning into the back lot of Hugh's Auto Body. The whole back part of the truck is covered with a tarp and straps, but I know what is under there. I need to stop Vince before he does anything with that crime scene of a car.

TWENTY-EIGHT

VINCE

HOLLYWOOD, California
Hugh's Auto Body


TONY GETS OUT and guides me so the rear of the flatbed is close to the back bay doors. I park and hop out of the truck and just about land right on top of Heather.

"Jesus! I didn't see you there. Sorry," I say as I grab her by the shoulders. She looks at me, then glances quickly over to where Tony is standing.

"Did you touch anything inside the car?" she whispers frantically, looking back over at Tony again.

"No, not really. We opened the doors to push it out but didn't get in it or anything. Why?" I glance at Tony, who has ducked down to tie his shoe.

"I can't explain out here. I don't want him to hear. Just don't go rooting around in the car. It's a crime scene," Heather whispers. She's being kind of dramatic.

"A crime scene?" I ask, my eyebrows shooting up to my hairline.

"Maybe. Probably. I don't know. Just don't touch anything if you can help it," she says. Then she steps back and waves at Tony.

"Hey, Heather! How are you?" Tony asks.

"I'm good, real good. Yep, awesome actually. You? Are you good, Tony?" Heather asks in a voice a few octaves higher than I have ever heard her speak.

"Real good. Wait till you see what weird shit we found at the storage unit." He then turns to me and asks, "Want me to lower the bed of the truck?"

"Can you get the roller dolly? If we can put that on it, we won't have to lift it twice." Tony nods then heads into the shop.

"What is that?" Heather asks. She is pointing to the back of the flatbed where we strapped down Holly's couch.

"Another prop from a movie. It was behind the car, so we didn't see it when we were there. I might make you watch the movie before I let you see it," I say with a wink.

She opens her mouth to answer but Tony comes out pushing the flat roller dolly. Instead, she just smiles.

"Did he tell you about the weird half tub?" Tony asks.

"Not yet. Half of a tub?" she asks.

"I'll explain later," I say, fighting a smile. She is going to love that movie.

Tony, Heather, and I manage to get the tub and the car into the shop. Heather still seems super nervous about Tony being here, so I tell him he can head out for the day.

"Okay, man, but I can't wait to work on that car. That thing is pretty badass. We could drop it down, you know, like those low-rider cars. Maybe add some hydraulics?" Tony runs his hand over the hood.

"Fuck no. This is a classic car. I am not ruining it like that. Get out of here," I snap, but he just laughs.

"I knew that would piss you off. Okay, see you tomorrow. Good seeing you again, Heather," Tony says with a wave.

We watch him leave, then even though it's not my usual closing time, I follow him and pull the gate shut and lock it. Heather's nervousness has me amped up. I walk back into the shop and pull the back bay door closed and push the pin through the bottom. When I turn around, Heather is standing by the car, staring at it while biting her lip.

"So what did you find out?" I ask.

She starts to explain, but I can hear the upstairs line ringing and glance over to the stairs, wondering if I can make it in time. I expected to hear from that facility today, but they didn't call this morning.

"You want to get that? I can follow you up," Heather says, but I shake my head.

"Nah. They will leave a message."

"Okay, so as I was saying, the police know this car went missing, and they have been looking—" Heather is cut off by the shop phone ringing. I hold up a finger and step over to the desk to answer.

"Hugh's. Can I help you?" I say into the phone. Then I listen as the woman from Peaceful Care Home gives me details my father's transfer. I like her. She is a no-nonsense, get-things-done kind of person.

"So it went well?" I ask, then follow up with, "Should I come see him tonight? Oh, right. I understand. Tomorrow or the next day works for me. I will wait for your call. Thanks again, Mrs. Rivers. I am so grateful," I say. After a quick goodbye, I turn to find Heather standing right behind me. She opens her arms, and I step into them, relaxing immediately in her embrace.

"Sounds like it was a good day for your dad," she says into my neck before placing a sweet kiss over the same spot. Her lips travel up my neck and to my cheek, finally finding my mouth. I kiss her back, diving in because even though I was busy today getting shit done, I missed her. I missed this—feeling her against me. Her warmth, her sweet scent is like a damn drug.

She pulls back a little with a little peck and says, "Sorry. I didn't mean to maul you. I just missed you, your lips." She looks down, and I realize she is nervous I don't feel the same way.

I pull her back in, kissing her deeply. I rest my ass on the desk and spread my legs a bit, and she steps in between my thighs, her hands dropping to my chest as we kiss.

"It was a long day. I missed you too," I say close to her lips. I am about to resume when her head snaps back and her eyes get big.

"I seriously need to tell you about the car, Vince. Can we go upstairs?" she asks.

"Yeah, sure." I push her back a little so I can stand up.

"Let me grab the groceries out of the car, then we can head up," she says. She walks out to the back lot to my Bug and opens the trunk.

"Holy crap, Heather! We having a party or something?" I ask, seeing all the bags of food.

"No, but since you won't let me pay rent, I decided to get some food for us." She looks over her shoulder at me.

No one has done this for me, ever. I mean, fuck, when I moved in, my mom brought me a sheet cake that said congratulations on it, like it was a celebration instead of an obligation. That was the only time she did anything like that. It feels good to have someone taking care of me, thinking about me and what I might need. My chest feels warm, and I know I have a dopey smile on my face as I reach in and grab a few bags.

"This is awesome. Seriously, thank you so much," I say as we head upstairs to my place.

As we put the food away, Heather fills me in on everything the detective told her. I shake my head in disbelief at the drug thing, but something is needling my memory.

"Did he mention my Uncle Carlos at all?" I ask.

"Yeah, he did, so I wasn't sure if I should tell you this part. Do you want to sit down?" she asks.

"Well, that is never good," I say.

"I don't think it's terrible. I just, well, it's weird. Did you know that law enforcement has been watching your shop?" Heather asks.

"What? What the fuck? No, I didn't know that. Jesus, why?" I ask, sinking into the chair next to her.

"Your dad turned down the requests to build secret panels in the cars for years, so did Carlos. That's something you should know first off," she says.

"Okay, yeah. I have a vague memory of my dad and uncle arguing about something when my grandpa owned this place. My uncle was pressuring my dad to promise he wouldn't . . ." I trail off, the memory forming a more solid footing in my mind.

"Wouldn't what?" she asks.

I shake my head to clear the fog, but it doesn't help. "That I don't know. I assume now they were talking about transporting the drugs. But hell, I don't know."

"Well, Hugh has been approached many times over the years because of his work on so many movie cars," Heather explains.

"I don't remember my dad or uncle ever bragging about working on movie cars. That is so weird to me. But I was busy with school and baseball, then when my parents split, I kind of avoided my dad and this place. I guess I wouldn't have known." I rub my face with my hands. I get the phone and hand it to Heather.

"Call the detective and tell him we have the car," I say.

"Really? Are you sure?" she asks.

"I don't want anything to do with it if there's drugs involved. I thought we'd fix it up and return it to the studio. But now? I want it the fuck out of here," I say, blowing out a breath.

"I am so glad you said that. I feel the same way, Vince," Heather says. She pulls her purse open and rummages around until she finds the card with John Fitzpatrick's number.

I listen as she explains everything to him, nodding every time she looks at me for confirmation that she is doing the right thing. She doesn't tell him about the other movie props we have so, when she hangs up, I raise an eyebrow at her.

"I thought you were going to tell him everything," I say

"He and I talked about Iolet's connection to this. He believes she was looking for Albert's murderer, but the drug smuggling kept crossing paths with her little investigation."

"I guess that makes sense. So we don't mention the tub or the bell or the chicken foot?" I ask.

She groans and covers her face. "I forgot about the chicken foot. Get it. I need to see it, or it will give me nightmares"

"Are you sure?" I tease.

"Yes. Do we know what movie it's from?" she asks.

"No. I was going to ask Henry if he had any idea. I want you to see *Breakfast at Tiffany's* so you can appreciate how fucking cool it is that we have Holly's couch. Let's eat something, then head over," I say as get the box. I lift the lid and grab the foot, bringing it to her. I set it down gently in front of her while she peeks out through her fingers.

"Gross. Is that a feather stuck to it?" she asks, pointing to the shriveled thing.

"Huh. Yeah, that's a feather. I didn't notice that before." I pick the foot up. I examine the bottom and see glue stuck to the base where the feather is hanging.

"This was attached to something. Look at all the glue," I say. Heather leans over and looks at it but doesn't touch it again.

"I hope Henry knows," I say with a sigh. I place the foot gently in the box. When I turn around, Heather is at the sink washing her hands, so I join her.

While she makes dinner, I call Past Times and see if Henry is there and if he is willing to play *Breakfast at Tiffany's* for us, then I take a shower. My head is spinning with everything Heather told me, and I wish I could talk to my dad about it. I will ask my mom, but I doubt she will know anything useful. I am sure she and my father didn't discuss anything about the shop. I know she was mad when he closed the location in Palm Springs and started devoting all his time here. My grandfather had passed, and he and Uncle Carlos were sharing the responsibility, but Carlos wasn't a mechanic, and he hired someone that my dad didn't like. That's all I remember. My uncle and my aunt moved away last summer, and I don't know their new address or phone number. One more thing to ask my mom, I guess.

I pull on a clean pair of shorts and a black T-shirt and walk out to the main room. The smell of garlic and butter washes over me, making my mouth water. I didn't even realize I was hungry.

"Smells great, Heather. What did you make?" I step behind her, circle my arms around her waist, and pull her back into me. Her hair is pulled back over her other shoulder, so I take advantage of her exposed neck and kiss her over and over.

"Vince, stop. You're giving me chills," she says as she scrunches her shoulder up, trying to fend me off.

"Is that tomato soup?" I ask, leaning over her shoulder.

"Yeah. I dressed it up with some garlic and pepper and mushrooms. There are grilled cheeses sandwiches too. It is the only thing I could think to make that is fast."

"Smells amazing. Thanks for doing that." I turn to put the dishes out but see she has already set the table too.

"Careful, Heather. I could get used to this kind of treatment," I say, pulling out my chair.

"I could too. This is so nice. I never felt like I could cook at my apartment back in Chico. My roommate, Kristen, was kind of a bitch. She was super picky about her cookware and made all kinds of comments the few times I did make us something. I am not going to miss her at all," Heather says. She sets a bowl of soup in front of me that looks like something you'd get at a restaurant. There is a dollop of sour cream and dried oregano sprinkled across the top. The grilled cheese she sets down next to it is a work of art.

"I used sourdough bread. I hope that's okay. It adds a lot of flavor," Heather says, sitting next to me.

"You can never leave me," I say, mostly joking but my heart is telling me I am not kidding. This girl is it for me.

A FEW HOURS later when we climb back up the stairs to the apartment, I take a deep breath and walk back over to the box.

"*Gone with the Wind*," I say, shaking my head. "I wouldn't have guessed the chicken foot was from that movie in a million years, and it was on her list!"

"Well, it was pretty clever of her to pull the foot off the hat. I think Henry was right. It was about the foot, not the hat. Do you think that has anything to do with the shoes?" she asks. We both sit on the couch and turn toward each other.

"No, that doesn't make sense. Chickens don't wear shoes," I say, and she swats at my arm, laughing.

"I mean maybe she wanted us to focus on feet," Heather says.

"No, I don't think that's it. The shoes have blood on them, right? That blood probably belongs to the murderer. Iolet knew that, so she kept them, but she must have known who killed him. She kept the shoes as proof, not as a clue," I say. I thought about that the whole time as we watched *Breakfast at Tiffany's*.

"I agree. Should we give the shoes to Detective Fitzpatrick tomorrow when he comes for the car?" she asks.

"Yeah, I think we should. We don't have any reason to keep them, and I don't want to keep something that might help the cops," I say.

"Right. I want to give them the jewelry then too. Not the ring from Frank—that is yours—but the stuff that was in the safe deposit box. I can't talk to Marilyn, and I am sure the studio would want it all back. John can make sure it gets to where it belongs," Heather says.

"So if we are giving everything to him, are we done? Is that it? I feel like we let Iolet down. We aren't any closer to finding Albert's killer than before," I say.

"No, we have the bell, the chicken foot, and the bathtub." Heather gets up and grabs her purse off the counter, bringing it back over to the couch. She pulls out a notebook and some papers, riffling through the stack. A piece slips out and falls to the floor, so I pick it up.

"Why do you have a job application?" I ask

"It's for the library. I thought I'd apply there and a few other places," she says. She looks at me nervously.

"That would be awesome. You know I want you to stay. Are you sure though?" I ask.

"I am. I wanted to stay the minute I climbed into your truck at the airport," she says. She is plucking at the rip in her shorts.

"Really? I had that much of an effect on you?" I ask. I have a big smile on my face, and I am not even going to try and hide how happy I feel.

"Calm down over there," she laughs. "You definitely had my attention from the beginning, but that wasn't it. It felt like I could finally breathe," she says.

"People don't usually say that kind of thing when they land in LA. We aren't known for our fresh air, Heather." I wink at her, and she laughs.

"Right. No, that's not what I mean. I felt like I left the weight I carried around for years back in Chico. Like I shed a hundred pounds."

"Because of your mom?" I ask, and she nods.

"Yeah, I don't feel the urge to check on her all the time here. I am twelve hours away, so even if she needs something, it's not like I can help. I feel free for the first time in my life," she says.

The words stab at my heart. I want that for her, I do, but I know that feeling all too well. I feel like I have a chain around me tethering me to this place, this job.

TWENTY-NINE

# HEATHER

HOLLYWOOD, California
Hugh's Auto Body

THE NEXT MORNING when the police arrive with their flatbed to get the car, Vince is waiting at the gate. Detective Fitzpatrick was both relieved and disappointed when I told him Iolet stole the car. That probably means it wasn't involved in moving drugs, but they plan to search it just in case.

I feel bad for Vince. I don't think he slept very well last night. He was tossing and turning, and at one point he got up and went out to the living room. I am sure he is freaked out that I plan on moving here permanently. I tried to assure him I would get my own place, but that seemed to just make him more stressed out.

I wish I knew what I could do to help him. I cleaned the apartment from top to bottom because when I am nervous, I clean, but also, it's one of the few things I have to offer right now. I filled out the application for the library, and I used Vince's typewriter to type up a cover letter. When I'm at the library today I am going to check the local paper for rentals. I bet if I was in my own place, Vince would feel better about all this. He doesn't need one more thing to feel responsible for while he is dealing with all this stuff with his dad.

The phone rings, and I check where Vince is before I answer. He is still outside talking to the police, so I grab the phone.

"Hello? No, I am sorry, he is busy at the moment. Can I take a message?"

The lady on the phone says, "This is Rachel from Peaceful Rest Home. Can you have Vince call or come by today? It's important."

"Is his dad okay?" I ask.

"I'm not at liberty to discuss that unless you are family," she says.

"No, I am just a friend." I feel a rock in my stomach as I say those words. We haven't talked about what we are to each other yet, and his reaction to my job application makes me wonder.

"Well, please have him call," she says, and I nod, even though she can't see me.

"I'll make sure he knows right away. Thanks for calling," I say, then hang up the phone and head downstairs to find him.

The flatbed is gone, but Vince is still talking to John, so I walk up quietly. I am relieved to hear Vince laugh.

"No, don't get that car. They have a shit engine. What you want is a Mustang. You can't go wrong there, any year," Vince says.

John smiles and nods at me, causing Vince to turn. His face softens and he smiles. "Hey, I didn't see you come down. Everything okay?" he asks. His relaxed tone makes me wish I didn't have to tell him about the phone call, but I do.

"Hi. Sorry to interrupt, but your dad's new place called and they want you to call or stop by soon. They said it was important." I am trying not to sound alarmed because it could be something as simple as they need more clothes for him, but the lady sounded worried on the phone.

"Right, thanks. I will go call now unless you need anything else from me, John?" Vince says, turning back to the detective.

"No, we are all done. Thanks for calling us. You did the right thing." John reaches out his hand to Vince and they shake. Vince nods and smiles at me, then heads back into the shop to call the facility.

"Thanks to you too, Heather. I know the studio will be happy to get the costume jewelry back. A less scrupulous person would have kept that," he says but immediately shakes his head. "That is not who you are. I could tell that the minute I met you."

"Well, it's not mine. I think Iolet wanted us to talk to Marilyn, but since we can't, there is no reason to keep it, right?" I say.

"I'll make sure it gets where it needs to be. Call us if you have anything else that needs to be returned." He reaches for my hand, so I give it to him and he squeezes it instead of shaking it like he did with Vince.

"Thanks, John. I will," I say. I watch him leave and turn to the shop just as Vince is coming out. He looks worried, and he has his keys.

"I need to go. I have to go see my dad. They think he . . ." His voice trails off, and he swallows, then looks away.

"Can I come?" I ask. I don't know if he wants me there, but I have to at least ask.

"Would you? I don't know what to expect, and I don't want to . . ." He stops again, so I pull him into me. He melts against me and takes a ragged breath.

"I want to go. I want to be there for you. Come on." I push him back a little and look into his eyes. "It's going to be okay," I say.

He nods and grabs my hand, pulling me to his truck. He is quiet on the whole drive over, so I still don't know why they called and asked him to come. I'll find out soon enough, I'm sure.

As we walk into the facility, I am struck again by how much it feels like a home instead of a hospital. There isn't that sharp smell of disinfectant, even though the place is spotless. We walk down the small hallway to Hugh's room and step inside.

Hugh lies on the bed with only a sheet covering him. There are no IVs or wires attached to him, and it looks like he is sleeping peacefully. I glance over to the other bed and see Mr. Chin sitting up reading a book. He closes it when he sees us and tries to scoot up a little.

I step over to his bed and ask, "Can I help you sit up, or do you want me to get the nurse?"

"No, maybe just fluff my pillow?" he asks in a soft voice.

I reach behind him and do the best I can then smile at him.

"Better, thanks. The doctor will be in soon, I am sure." He nods over to Hugh and Vince, who is now sitting on the bed holding his dad's hand. My throat constricts, and I feel a sting at the back of my eyes.

"I can ask them to take me out to the main room if you want some privacy," Mr. Chin says loud enough for Vince to hear.

"No, that's okay, Mr. Chin. You can stay," Vince says.

The nurse who helped us transfer Hugh comes in with the doctor. She introduces him, and he reaches for Vince's hand and shakes it.

"Hello. Thanks for coming down so quickly. I have to be at the hospital soon for rounds, but I wanted to fill you in on what has been going on," the doctor says. Vince drops his dad's hand and stands up, ready to face whatever news is about to come his way.

"I think your father has had another stroke," he says, then goes on to explain how Hugh was awake and responsive when he arrived, but at the midnight check, the nurses noticed a change.

"Do you have to move him back to the hospital?" Vince asks, and the doctor shakes his head.

"No, I don't think there is anything to be done. I just want you to know that he probably doesn't have much more time. I could send him for tests to isolate the location of the stroke, but it wouldn't change our treatment plan. However, if that is what you want, I can arrange it," the doctor says kindly.

"No. If he's trying to check out, then I don't want to add stress to whatever time he has left. He can just be here until"—Vince swallows—"he passes?"

"Yes. We will make sure he isn't in any pain. His vitals are pretty weak, so I suspect it will be sometime today. I'll be surprised if he is still with us tomorrow. I am sorry." The doctor puts his hand on Vince's shoulder, and Vince stiffens at the touch.

"It's fine. I don't think he would want to be trapped in his body like he has been. This is for the best. Can I have a minute alone with him?"

Without another word, the nurse steps out of the room and comes back with a wheelchair and another nurse to help Mr. Chin up. Vince turns his back to all of us, so I follow the nurses out. The doctor says something to Vince, but I can't hear him. I walk behind Mr. Chin as they wheel him out to the main room where a few other residents in wheelchairs are sitting in front of the TV. *The Price Is Right* is on, but no one seems to be watching. I sit in a chair next to Mr. Chin and smile at him.

"He will pass soon," he says. His eyes are closed, and he looks so frail. I don't know if he has always been thin, but his tall frame accentuates it. It makes my heart hurt.

"Yeah, it seems that way. I am glad Hugh is here. This place is so nice. Have you been here long?" I ask, hoping for a distraction.

"Five years. They said I had six months to live, but I keep on going." Mr. Chin chuckles. "I am ready to go, but I guess God doesn't want me yet."

"I don't think that is true, Mr. Chin." I reach for his hand. He startles a little when I wrap my hand over his, and I almost pull back. A small smile creeps across his features, and he sighs.

"You don't know my heart, dear, and God does. I think this is my hell." He says the last part so softly I almost don't hear him.

"Are they not treating you well?" I look around at the room again for signs of neglect but find nothing but a cozy loving place.

"No, dear, that is not it. They treat me better than I deserve. I'm sorry. Seeing Hugh again just brought back some of my demons," Mr. Chin says.

I am about to ask him what he is talking about when he closes his eyes and slumps a little. I would be worried if I hadn't seen him do that in his bed. I sigh and lean back in the chair and wait.

The doctor leaves, and a nurse comes and takes one of the patients back to their room. *The Price Is Right* has ended, and *General Hospital* comes on. At Serenity Falls, this show was a big topic of discussion. I have never gotten into soap operas, even though my mom watched them. I think she preferred *All My Children* though.

Mr. Chin snaps awake and looks around, confused, so I reach for his hand again. This time he doesn't flinch. Instead he turns his palm up so I can hold his hand. It's warm and thin, his skin softer than anything I have ever felt. I notice two fingers are calloused at the top, and I cock my head, wondering what caused that.

"What did you do for work, Mr. Chin?" I ask, rubbing my finger over the thickened portion of his fingers.

"I was a costume designer," he says. His eyes brighten at the statement, so I press on.

"That must have been fun. Did you make costumes for the theater or film industry?" I ask.

"Both. I emigrated here with my parents as a child. My father was in film editing. My mother was a seamstress and taught me everything she knew. She mostly repaired and mended clothes, but she showed me how to create. She was a good woman. I have been sewing since I was about seven years old." He chuckles and rubs his thumb over the rough patches on his fingers.

"I lost feeling in the tips of those fingers by the time I was in high school. Worth it though. I had a lot of fun." Mr. Chin smiles, and I am struck by how handsome he is, and what he must've looked like as a young man.

"I bet you made the ladies swoon," I say with a wink. "A handsome man who could make them a beautiful dress? That is every girl's dream."

He shrugs and looks down. "Wasn't really interested in all that," he says, shifting in his chair a little.

"Never married?" I ask. I am not sure why I am being so nosey, except I am desperate for a distraction. Vince has been in there for a long time.

"No, dear. I couldn't marry who I wanted to, so we just lived together." He winks.

Realization dawns slowly, and I am hit with sadness for him.

"How long has your partner been gone?" I ask.

"Ten years. He was my second love. My first—" he starts, but I look up and see Vince walking towards us.

I stand and wait for him to speak, but he is silent. He shoves his hands in his jeans and walks around so he is in front of Mr. Chin. I expect him to tell Mr. Chin we are leaving, but he sits in the empty chair on the other side of him. I sink into my chair again, wishing I could take away his pain.

"Hey, Mr. Chin. Thanks for letting me have some time alone with my dad. I am all done if you want help back to your room," Vince says.

"That would be nice," he says.

Vince unlocks the wheelchair and turns it so he can push Mr. Chin back to his room. I walk silently behind them, wishing I knew what to say. A nurse spots us and follows along, helping Mr. Chin back into his bed. I glance over at Hugh, but he looks the same. Peaceful and quiet, resting.

"I was just telling your girlfriend about Michael. Do you remember him?" Mr. Chin asks.

Vince tilts his head and rubs his hand over his jaw. "Your roommate? Short, blond guy?"

Mr. Chin smiles. "Yes, that was him." His eyes twinkle. "Michael built sets for the movies. Do you remember the stage in our backyard, Vince?"

"Holy shit, yes! You guys had the coolest yard. Heather, they would put on a show on the Fourth of July every year. Well, the few years you were there," Vince says, then pauses and narrows his eyes at Mr. Chin. "Did Iolet Merryweather ever perform there?"

"Now that's a name I haven't heard in years. No, Iolet never would have. She hated me. In fact, she is the reason Michael and I moved out of the neighborhood. That crazy lady wouldn't leave me alone," Mr. Chin says.

"Why did she hate you?" I ask, stepping closer to him.

"We loved the same man," he says with a shrug. I look up at Vince, and his eyes go wide. He didn't really think Michael was just Mr. Chin's roommate, did he?

"Oh well, that would be awkward I guess," I say.

"Didn't matter. When the man we both loved was murdered, the competition was over, but she wouldn't let it go. Crazy old bat thought I killed Albert," Mr. Chin says, shaking his head.

"What?" Vince says as he steps closer.

"What did you say? Did you say Albert?" I ask. I look up at Vince and see my shock reflected on his face.

"You two look like you have seen a ghost. Everything okay?" Mr. Chin asks.

"We both knew Iolet." I add, "Not well, like we weren't close or anything. She passed recently. I met Iolet in Chico. She lived at a senior apartment where I worked, and Vince mowed her lawn when he was fourteen."

"What a small world." Mr. Chin shakes his head and continues. "I wish she was still alive so you could tell her it wasn't me. I would never have killed Albert. I loved him too much."

"Did he love you?" I ask, not caring if that is a rude question.

"He did, but his family wasn't ready to accept our unconventional relationship. They put pressure on him to marry, and that is when he sent for Iolet. He thought they could be married on paper only, and he and I could continue to be together," Mr. Chin says.

"She lived in New York. How did Albert know her?" Vince asks.

"Their families were connected. Iolet's father was a banker, just like Albert's. Old money and all that, so he thought it was the perfect ruse. They had met a few times on vacations, so Albert felt like he could trust her. I don't think she understood her role, though. She thought that he really loved her," Mr. Chin says. His voice is growing soft, and his eyes flutter shut.

Vince looks over at me, then back at his dad's bed. He nods to the door and takes a step back. I follow him out into the hall, where we both let out a breath.

"Oh my God, Vince," I say, grabbing his arm.

"This is so fucking crazy," he says.

"What should we do? Do we tell John?" I ask, but Vince shakes his head.

"No. Let's go get lunch and let Mr. Chin rest. I bet he has more information. I think we need to get the chicken foot and the bell and ask him if he knows anything about them.

"Okay, yeah, that sounds like a plan. Let's get out of here."

# THIRTY
# VINCE




I MADE excuses after lunch yesterday because I don't want to go back to see Mr. Chin or watch my dad slowly die. I just can't fucking take it. I know I've been a quiet, surly bastard since we left Peaceful Rest Home yesterday, but I can't help it. I feel so guilty for hoping he will just let go. I sat on the edge of his bed yesterday and poured my heart out to his lifeless body. I told him I was tired and I missed having him around.

I started out saying all the nice things I knew he wanted to hear. I stood up, ready to go back out to let them know I was done, but the pinch in my chest stopped me. I spun back around and unleashed years of anger on my defenseless father. I told him it was his fault I didn't get to follow my dream. I told him about Gio getting drafted and how it should have been me.

I told him I was ashamed of him for cheating on Mom all those years, and that if I was ever lucky enough to have a good woman love me, I would never treat her that way. I told him that Mom was better off without him and that I would be too.

Now the twist of guilt is balanced equally with the relief I feel for having said what was on my mind for years. I wish I had said it sooner, when he was conscious. I wish I had said all this after his heart attack, but I know I never would have. I thought there was still a chance back then. I thought he would die and I could show up in Chico and start college, then maybe play ball the next year. Four years later and here I am. Stuck.

I drop the wrench I am using and twist so it doesn't hit me in the face. "Fuck," I grumble as I pat the ground, trying to find the damn thing.

"Having trouble under there?" Tony asks. He kicks my boot, so I slide out on the roller and look up at him.

"No, just finished. You done with the tires?" I bark.

"Yep. Want to hit the beach?" Tony holds his hand out for me to grab, but I roll to my side away from him and push up.

"No. I have paperwork to catch up on. You can go," I snap.

"Listen, I am not sure who crapped on your cracker, but it wasn't me, so fuck off, okay?" Tony says. He throws a shop rag, hitting me in the head. Any other day I would have laughed it off and apologized, but today I can't. I ignore his comment and walk to my desk. I don't look up when he grumbles something under his breath or when he walks out. When I hear him drive his Toyota pickup out of the back lot, I hang my head.

I pick up the rag Tony tossed at me and set it on the oil rack. I close my eyes tightly. Why was I such an asshole to Tony? He has never done anything but support me. I shake my head, trying to push the guilt away, and grab a stack of papers.

We finished the last two cars for the week unless something new comes in today. I have a few things booked for next week, but not much. I had cleared my schedule to work on the *Casablanca* car, and now I don't have to do that. *Have to*, yeah right. I was looking forward to working on that car. That is bothering me too. I wanted the distraction of spending some time under the hood of that beauty.

I take the opportunity of an empty shop to finish organizing what I started the day Gio came. I check my inventory of oil and gaskets and air filters. I like to keep a few stock parts on hand, but most of the time I have to order things and pick them up. Some of the parts stores have started delivering, but it always costs more.

Staring at the row of neatly stacked 40-weight oil cans, it hits me how little I care about this place. I tried when Dad had the heart attack. I threw myself into it, cleaning the shop and trying to make it something I could be proud of, but that feeling never surfaced. Instead I just felt resentful.

I shove the shelf and a can tips a little, so I shake it again, yelling this time. The whole thing rattles, and a few cans fall, the sound of them hitting the cement oddly pleasing. I kick the can by my foot and yank at the metal shelving unit, toppling the whole thing. I lean back and yell, my fists balling up at my side. I wish I could punch something, but man, that felt good. I kick one of the cans and spin to watch it sail across the empty bay, but it's not empty, and I watch in horror as Heather jumps, narrowly missing the can that was rocketing toward her.

"Feel better?" she asks, turning to watch the can finish its journey to the back wall.

"Yeah, actually I do." I say it as more of a challenge than I intended.

"Good." She walks to the stairs, leaving me alone with the mess I made. When she reaches the top of the stairs, I expect her to turn back, but she just pushes the door open and goes in.

I let my head fall back and I groan. Damn it. It's like my conversation with my dad yesterday opened this ugly gash. I can't seem to get my anger in check. It's spilling out of me like a leaky oil pan. I walk around and pick up all the cans that are rolling across the shop. That really wasn't a productive thing to do, but damn, it did feel good. I wonder if she saw the whole thing. I have no idea how long she was standing there.

When all the cans are stacked back on the shelf, I walk out to the lot and pull the back gate shut, securing the lock. It's only four o'clock, but I need to be done for the day. Maybe I should have gone with Tony to the beach. Maybe I should go now. I glance over at my truck. My swim trunks are stuffed behind the seat. I could just leave, meet up with the guys, and have some beer.

The blinds in the living room of my apartment tilt, and I know it was Heather adjusting them. The sun beats on the back of the building, making it a fucking sauna up there. I shake my head and walk back inside, knowing I'll feel worse if I go.

I glance at the phone on my desk one last time before heading upstairs. Maybe the care home called there and didn't try my work number. I know that's not the case, but I still hope there is a message telling me it's over. That he has passed. I blow out a breath before walking in. Heather is sitting on the couch cross-legged with a bowl of popcorn and a book in her lap. Her hair is piled up on her head, a black clip holding it in place. Her slender neck and beautiful shoulders are on display. I didn't notice before that she is wearing a tight, black tank top with her jean shorts. I haven't seen that one yet. I wonder if she went shopping today.

I shove my hands in my pocket and step toward her, wishing I hadn't been such an ass yesterday and today. I want to hold her against me, feel her heart beating against mine. She doesn't look up from her book as she turns the page. She picks out a piece of popcorn and brings it to her lips but pauses, her mouth half open. She freezes and shakes her head, then laughs and slips the popcorn between her lips.

"Good book?" I ask. My voice sounds a little hoarse, probably due to the tantrum I threw downstairs.

She holds up a finger and continues to read, so I wait. She turns the page and finishes the chapter, then bends forward and plucks the bookmark off the coffee table in front of her. Once she secures it and closes the book, she finally turns to me and says, "It's a really good book. It's that *Kent Price, Man on a Mission* book I was telling you about by Patrick Smith. I can't wait to read the next one, and I am not even finished with this one!"

She doesn't seem mad at me, but I can't wrap my head around that, so I step tentatively toward her. My hands still in my pockets, I rock on my heels and just stare at her.

"Did you finish up down there?" she asks, giving me that beautiful smile I am addicted to.

"Yeah. Hey, was there a message on the machine up here?" I ask, clearing my throat.

"No, sorry. I take it they didn't call the shop either?" she asks. She sets the bowl of popcorn on the table and turns to face me. There is enough room to sit next to her, but I stay where I am.

"No. I really thought I'd hear from them today, you know?" My voice comes out soft and a little shaky. Damn it.

"I know. I bet—" Heather starts but stops as the phone rings. We both look at the phone, then at each other.

"Want me to get it?" she asks, pushing off the couch, but I shake my head and step toward the phone. I take a deep breath, like that will fortify me for what I know is coming.

"Hello? Yeah, this is Vince. I see. Okay. When?" rub my hand down my face. I place it on my heart, hoping I can keep it in place, because it feels like it is trying to jump out and run away. The room is getting dim, and the doctor's voice sounds like he's on one of those toy phones, or like a tin can and string phone. I reach for the table because, fuck, do I need something to hang on to, but instead of the hard surface I expect, I am wrapped in Heather's arms. She is holding me and holding me up. I rest my chin on the top of her head and try and listen to what the doctor is saying.

"Do I have to decide right now? Okay, the one over on Palm is fine. Yeah, I have to talk to my mom. I think he wanted to be buried." When I say that, Heather squeezes me, holding me even tighter.

"No, I don't need to see him. I said my goodbyes. Okay, thank you, Doctor." I let the phone slip from my hand. Heather and I both stand there as it clatters to the floor, neither of us moving to pick it up. Heather's hands are moving up and down my back, but I can barely feel it. My chest is tight again, and I try to remember what she said about panic attacks. She is taking deep, slow breaths and blowing them out, so I copy her. It takes a little while, but the constricting band around my heart is loosening. I don't even realize that she has guided me to the couch until the back of my legs hit the edge of it and she gently pushes me to sit.

Just like last time, she crawls onto my lap and straddles me, holding my face with her hands. She kisses my forehead, my wet cheeks, and my neck, working slowly, tenderly covering every inch of me. When she reaches my lips, I grab on to the lifeline she is offering, letting her pull me back up.

I have never kissed anyone like this. It isn't a romantic, leading-to-something kiss. It's purposeful and important, like our lips are mapping the way for me to find her. She is telling me she is here, that she is with me, supporting me. My breathing slows, and we both relax into the couch.

She pulls back a little and says, "I am here." Then she nestles herself into the crook of my neck, planting sweet, open-mouth kisses where she rests.

I thought she would say she was sorry or ask what she could do. Isn't that what people say at times like this? That's what they said when my dad had the heart attack and again when he had his first big stroke. I didn't realize how much I hated those words until they were replaced with "I am here." That's all I need to hear. It would have been amazing to hear that from anyone four years ago.

"Thank you," I croak. She starts to move but I pull her closer.

"A little longer please. I need to hold you," I say, and she snuggles in.

"I am not going anywhere, Vince," she whispers into my neck. My heart expands back to its normal size, then pushes past that to envelop this amazing gift on my lap. How could Iolet have known this is what I needed? That *she* is what I needed? How did she know I wouldn't be married or something? A little laugh escapes me, and I feel Heather smile against my skin. She doesn't say anything, just squeezes me and snuggles in even closer.

We sit like that for a long time. I don't know for sure, but I think I fall asleep for a bit. She never moves, never lets her grip on me loosen. My eyes feel like sandpaper as I blink a few times. The room is dark, and my stomach rumbles.

"Hungry?" she asks quietly.

"I guess so. What time is it?" I ask. I feel her move her head slightly to see the clock on the wall by my TV, something I could have done for myself, I realize.

"It's almost seven thirty. I can make you something or go pick up anything you want. Taco Bell? A sandwich from Sammy's?" she asks. I give her a squeeze and reluctantly move her to the couch next to me. I instantly miss her weight on me and grab her again, moving her back to my lap. She laughs but snuggles right back where she was.

"We don't have to move, Vince. I can be here or wherever you need me. It's your call." Her words slice open my heart. I struggle to breathe again, and she pulls back to look at me, concern etched on her face.

"What? What did I say? I'm sorry. It's okay, Vince," she says softly, tracing my face with her fingers.

"No, it's just so hard for me to understand how you are here. I don't know what I would be doing right now without you. I have never had this—someone to help me, you know?" I say.

"I kind of figured. I really don't mind sitting here straddling you, but I know you are hungry because your stomach just rumbled again. Let's go into the kitchen together and make something. I just bought all those groceries. I can make a sandwich better than what you get at Sammy's. Hell, I'll even unbutton my blouse a little and shake my ass while I cook," she says. Then she looks down at her tank top and adds, "Well, I could take this off."

I laugh and kiss her, then finally allow her to stand up. She doesn't step back. Instead she reaches down to pull me up. We walk into the kitchen together and make peanut butter and jelly sandwiches. She pulls out a bag of Fritos and waggles her eyebrows at me.

"Do you trust me, Vince?" she asks.

I narrow my eyes at her as she waves the bag of chips. "More than I should, maybe," I respond, making her laugh.

She layers a bunch of Fritos on the sandwiches and smashes the bread together. My eyebrows can't go any higher as I watch her take a bite.

She moans and rolls her eyes in pleasure, and I feel myself getting hard, like that first night at Sammy's.

"I gotta tell you, watching you enjoy a meal is one of my favorite things," I say. She smacks me in the arm and laughs.

"Try it and let's see how you do at containing your joy." She looks at me with a smug expression.

I pick up the sandwich that is now lumpy and bumpy from the Fritos stuffed between the slices of bread. It takes me a second to take a bite without losing half the chips, but when the combination of sweet jelly, smooth peanut butter, and crunchy chips hits my mouth, I moan.

Fucking hell.

"Why is this so good?" I ask her, then quickly take another bite. "You are a fucking genius, Heather. This should be on a menu somewhere."

She just laughs and continues to eat. I get the milk from the fridge, then grab two glasses, pouring us each some.

"Oh, that's perfect," she says, gulping down the milk.

I look at her. She has peanut butter on her cheek and a bit of milk on her chin. "I have never seen anything more perfect," I say.

Light pink flushes her face, and she smiles at me. We finish our meal in silence, then I sit at the table and watch as she cleans up the dishes. When she is done, she grabs my hand and leads me to my room. I kick off my work boots and slide my jeans off, while she pulls at my T-shirt.

"Do you want to take a shower?" she asks.

I shake my head. "I probably should, but I am just so damn tired," I say.

I climb into bed, and it's not long before she is wrapped around me. She took off her shorts, so she is just wearing that tank top and a pair of white cotton underwear. The last thing I remember is my hands trailing over her soft, warm body.

## THIRTY-ONE
## HEATHER


HOLLYWOOD, California
Hugh's Auto Body


I DIDN'T GET a lot of sleep last night, but I am not complaining. Vince never let me go; even sound asleep he kept a tight grip on me. He wrapped his legs over me, pinning me to him as he slept.

My heart has never felt this way. Broken for him and his pain, but so damn happy that I am the one here in his arms. I like being needed like this—for comfort instead of a sober ride home.

I shift a little and smile when he just tightens his grip on me. Looks like I am staying here for a while longer. I have no idea what time it is, but I am pretty sure I heard Tony opening the garage downstairs.

"Thank you," Vince says in a hoarse whisper.

I pull myself up so I can look down at him. "I am glad I could be here for you. Do you feel better?"

"Yeah, actually. I don't think I have ever slept that good," Vince says.

"I can come right back, but I really need to use the bathroom. Can I get up?" I ask, and he chuckles.

"Yeah, sorry. I didn't mean to wear you like a shirt all night." Vince finally lets his arms fall from my body.

I roll away quickly and dart into the bathroom to take care of business. When I come back out, he is no longer in the bed. I can hear the coffeepot starting and the front door open.

"I'll be down in a bit, Tony. Thanks for opening up," Vince calls down the stairs. I hear Tony's muffled reply as I step closer to Vince.

"Want me to go down and tell him what happened? I am sure he would understand if you don't work today," I say.

Before he can answer me, the phone rings and Vince and I both look around for it. I spot it under the table and grab it, then hand it to him.

"Hello? Yeah, this is me. No, I haven't spoken with her yet. I'll call her now. Can I call you back?" he says into the phone, then thanks whoever it is and hangs up.

"I guess I will take you up on that offer. I need to call my mom and deal with stuff. You sure you don't mind?" Vince asks.

"No, of course not, unless you need me here with you when you call?" I ask.

"Nah, I think I will be okay. I like knowing you are close, Heather. Thank you," Vince says. I wish he would kiss me or reach out to me, but he just pours himself a cup of coffee, then sits at the table with a sigh.

I take that as my cue and walk out the door, closing it gently.

I expect to see Tony under a car since that is where he usually is, but instead he is at Vince's desk on the phone.

"Okay. Yeah, thanks. Probably just today. Hey, I gotta let you go. She just came down. Yep. Thanks, man. See you soon." Tony stands as I approach.

"Hey, Tony. Vince will be down soon. I am not sure if he wants to be the one to tell you . . ." I pause.

·   ·   ·

TONY BLOWS OUT A BREATH. "WHEN?" he asks.

"Yesterday afternoon," I say quietly. I don't feel right about telling a story that isn't mine.

"Fuck. I figured it was close given what an ass he was being. Terrence is coming to help with the shop today. He said he can stay tomorrow too," Tony says. He takes out his red bandana and wipes his face. "I can't believe he's finally gone. I'd never tell Vince this, but I kept praying he would just let go, you know? I mean fuck, Vince should have been the one to get drafted. Gio doesn't deserve that half as much as Vince."

I know this is something that bothers Vince, but he won't really talk about it, so to have Tony confirm it makes my heart ache. Since I don't know what to say, I just give him a small smile.

We both turn when we hear the door of the apartment upstairs shutting. Vince jogs down the stairs and comes over to us, draping an arm over my shoulder. He squeezes me closer in a side hug, then steps away.

"I owe you an apology," Vince says. Tony steps closer and pulls him into a hug. I watch as Vince collapses into his friend. He looks small wrapped in Tony's tree trunk arms with his giant hands patting his back. I have to look away so I don't start crying. No one needs my tears right now.

"You don't owe me shit. Go take care of things. Terrence is on his way. He's got a friend that needs a brake job on his Ford, so he's driving that over. We can handle any drop-ins. Tomorrow too, okay?" Tony has Vince's face in his hands now, and he lets one hand fall to his shoulder.

"Hugh was a good man. I've been missing him for so long it's hard to believe he is really gone now," Tony says before letting Vince go.

"Yeah, thanks. I know. It has been a long road." Vince turns to me and gives me a sad little smile. "Can you come with me to the care home? I have to sign some papers and get his things."

"Of course," I answer. Vince walks out the back door, so I follow him. He stops and hands me the keys to his VW. "Can you drive? I just don't think I should. My brain isn't working right."

"Sure, Vince. Whatever you need," I say.

We pull up to the facility after a quiet drive, and Vince hops out before I can say anything. He walks to the front, and I expect him to knock, but he waits until I catch up. We stand there together for a minute or more, neither of us moving. I finally knock on the door, unable to tell if that is what Vince was waiting for.

"Hi, come on in," the nurse says as she pulls the door open wide. I glance around the front room and recognize some of the same people I saw when Mr. Chin and I sat and watched TV, but he's not here. I wonder if I should go back and tell him goodbye while Vince is signing papers.

"Right this way, Mr. DeLuca. The director has everything in her office."

We veer down a different hallway, opposite from where the residents' rooms are, and I glance back over my shoulder, wondering if I should duck out now.

"Excuse me. Would it be okay if I went and spoke with Mr. Chin while Vince is signing the papers?" I ask, and Vince gives me a smile, like he appreciates my idea.

The nurse freezes in her tracks and turns slowly to us. "I'm so sorry. Mr. Chin passed away."

"Oh, gosh. Okay. I am sorry to hear that. When?" I say, fighting past the lump in my throat. It's so dumb. I didn't know him at all, but the thought that he's gone hits me. I had things I wanted to tell him, things I haven't even had a chance to tell Vince.

"He passed shortly after your visit, actually. He fell into one of his quick naps and just never woke up," she says.

I smile weakly and say, "He was a really nice man. Did he have family in the area?"

"No, his partner passed years ago. As long as I have been here, I never saw a visitor for him. He seemed happy though. I don't want you to think he was lonely. We all loved him." Her smile reminds me of the nice nurse I met outside this place when I came to check it out for Hugh.

"That's good. Thanks for telling me that. I am glad he is at peace now and back with Michael," I say, and she nods.

"Vince, she can see you now. Just go on in." The nurse waves her hand toward the office, and I watch him go, not noticing that I have stopped.

"Can I ask you another question?" I ask the nurse.

"Sure. What can I do for you?" she answers with a big smile.

"Do you know if you are hiring for a housekeeping position? I am looking to move here permanently, but I need to find a job." I try to sound confident.

"Oh, sorry. No. This place has no turnover. I think our two girls that clean have worked here for ten years or maybe even longer. It's like that for the nursing staff too. I was lucky to have a friend get me this job. She was moving back East and told me to come in with her when she gave her notice." She chuckles.

"Right. I kind of figured but would have kicked myself if I didn't ask. It seems like a great place to work. Thanks for your help," I say.

"Sure. Good luck to you." She smiles again, then walks back to the front desk.

I let my shoulders droop and sigh before going in to sit with Vince. I don't want him to see me discouraged when he is in the middle of dealing with all this stuff. I spoke with Margaret at the library, and she said they only hire people who are in college or have their degree, so that dream died. Then she crushed my dreams further by showing me rental places that are way out of my price range. The hotels and care homes around here pay a little better than back in Chico, but the cost of living is higher. I called and stopped by eight different places yesterday, and all of them said they weren't hiring. I could go further from Hollywood, but I will need to ask Vince where it's safe.

I slide into the chair next to Vince and wait as the director explains everything. She pushes papers over for him to sign, and I see his hand shake as he takes the pen.

"Did you get a chance to speak with your mother?" the director asks.

"Yes, she said he has a plot in Palm Springs. How does that work? How do we get him there?" Vince says with a shaky voice.

"The coroner can arrange to get him there. You just let us know when." She says it with so much kindness, it's like she is family. I wonder when he spoke with his mom. It must've been this morning, which means it was a quick call. God, I hate this, but there is no place I would rather be. I hate the thought of him doing this alone.

He stands and extends his hand, thanking her, and before I know it we are back outside. I unlock the car for him, and he climbs in.

"Can we go to Palm Springs now?" he asks. "I need to see my mom. I'm sorry to drag you along, but I can't do this alone."

He's staring into his lap, shoulders sagging, defeat written all over his face. I place my hand on his leg. "Of course, Vince."

---

VINCE OFFERED to drive back after we visited with his mom and saw the cemetery plot. Mary DeLuca is a nice enough woman. It is obvious she loves her son. What I will never understand though is how she can love Vince so much and yet let him carry this burden all by himself. She was not very helpful when he asked about a funeral or who to call in the family. After seeing the plot and speaking with the people at the cemetery, Vince decided to just do a small graveside service.

"Mind if we go to the beach instead of back to the shop? I can't be inside right now," Vince says. He barely turns his head to me when he asks, and he hasn't touched me since we left the care home.

When he introduced me to his mom, he said I was a friend from out of town. That hurt, but I tried to ignore it because I know how hard this is on him.

"I have never seen the ocean, so I am going to say hell, yes, we can go to the beach," I say, hoping to get a smile. He just nods and drives us to Santa Monica. The traffic is terrible, and I am grateful to not be behind the wheel. It's past dinnertime when he pulls into a parking lot, and I know he must be as hungry as I am. I glance around, not seeing any kind of restaurant.

"I'm starving. Let's go down to the pier and get a hot dog or something," Vince says as he helps me out of the car.

"Oh, thank God. I didn't want to complain, but I am about to eat my own shoe," I say, grateful when Vince laughs.

"Sorry. I kinda got in my own head today. The worst part is over I guess." He grabs my hand and leads me down a path. We pass girls in bikinis roller-skating and guys on skateboards. When the path dips down and turns a corner, I see the pier and a row of shops with T-shirts and flags fluttering in the breeze. It smells like coconut and sand and saltwater. I look at the ocean in the distance. I can't see where the water touches the sand yet but hope to once we get food. I try and control my excitement about seeing the ocean because I am starving, but also it doesn't seem like the appropriate time to yell something like, "Look, waves!"

Vince steers me to a shack with a line of people. Everyone is barefoot and in shorts or bathing suits ranging from skimpy to modest. Vince and I get in line and wait with everyone else after we put in our order. I try several times to start a conversation with Vince, but all my topics fall flat. I am half tempted to yank off my shirt and run into the water to see if I get a reaction.

Instead, I just people-watch until his name is called. He grabs the food, and I take the drinks and follow him as he wanders away from the crowd to an empty spot on the beach. He sits cross-legged without dropping the hot dogs, and on another day I would have clapped, but he is not in the mood.

I hand him his soda, then sit next to him. When he hands me my hot dog, I grab his wrist. "Vince, are you okay?"

"Yeah, sorry. I should have taken you back. I am not good company tonight." He takes a bite of his hot dog.

"It's okay. I don't need you to entertain me. I just want you to know I am here if you want to talk or anything," I say.

"Maybe after we eat you can tell me more about what you did yesterday. I know you went to the library, and I meant to ask if you learned anything," Vince says. He takes another bite of his hot dog and a big drink of his Coke.

"Oh yeah, I learned a lot actually. I was looking forward to talking to Mr. Chin today, because I think he would have had even more information."

"Eat, then tell me. I know how you get when you're hungry." He winks. It's the flirtiest he has been in days, and my heart reacts immediately.

We finish up, and Vince takes our garbage over to a can, then comes back and sits next to me. "Okay, spill. What did you learn?" he asks.

"Well, I guess it doesn't really matter now that he passed, but I am ninety-nine percent sure that George Chin was right. Iolet thought he murdered her Albert. She followed him everywhere, including your neighborhood, like Mr. Chin said. He made the costumes for all of those movies, and the props in the boxes were from his films."

"Are you sure? Did you find his name in the credits?" Vince asks, and I nod.

"So get this. His partner was actually his business partner too. His last name was Hadley, so they had a business together the H&C. Their company made sets and costumes for hundreds of movies and plays in the Los Angeles area. It was George Chin who came up with the idea for the hat in *Gone with the Wind*. That's probably why Iolet ripped the foot off. Oh, and I think Michael had the idea for the bathtub couch in *Breakfast at Tiffany's*, but George made the cushions. He also made all of Holly's outfits for that movie. He was very talented," I explain.

"Wow. But we know that George didn't kill Albert. I believed him at least," Vince says.

"Yeah, there is no way he killed him. I believe George that he loved Albert, but we will never really know if that love went both ways. I found a few articles written before Iolet appeared on the scene, and they all talked about how inseparable the two men were. Of course it was framed like they were men on the town looking for potential wives, when in reality they were just going on dates. At least that is what George thought," I say.

Vince shakes his head and says, "I can't imagine that...being in love and not able to be together. That sucks."

"It really does. I think there were people who understood, but Albert's family wouldn't have been among them. I read up a little about them and Iolet's family too. Both Albert and Iolet were only children of superrich families. Albert's mother's family was in the oil business, and she married a man who was almost like royalty. They were a big deal in Hollywood in the early days of silent film," I explain.

"You did learn a lot. Any chance you know who killed Albert?" Vince asks.

"Not a clue. It was probably someone that didn't like his lifestyle. Could have been someone in his family or just a random person."

Vince blinks slowly and shakes his head before saying, "So all of this was just a wild goose chase?"

"It seems that way. Iolet was sure it was Mr. Chin, and his family being involved in the film industry probably made Iolet jealous. She wanted so badly to be a movie star," I explain.

Vince whistles and shakes his head back. "Damn. I wish you had been able to talk to Mr. Chin. What would you have asked him?"

"If he knew about Albert's conservative family and if he thought one of them murdered Albert. I bet he did. He didn't seem surprised by Albert's death. I think he worried they found out about him being gay and couldn't handle it."

"You should be a detective, Heather," Vince says.

"No, I don't think that's my dream. I don't know what it is, but chasing leads that end up being dead ends over and over sounds like a nightmare." I try to laugh but it falls flat.

"What's wrong?" Vince asks.

"I just feel bad for Iolet. She spent her whole life chasing this theory, and it was wrong. I think Mr. Chin probably told her it was wrong and why, and yet she chose to ignore the facts." I pluck at the hem of my shorts. I probably wouldn't feel so bad about all this if it didn't mean it was over. I thought I would have more time to figure out what to do. I really don't want to go back to Chico, but I can't find a job or a place I can afford here.

"Yeah, but she had a pretty cool life, Heather. She was in hundreds of movies, met some amazing people, and had fame of sorts. Plus, from everything I remember and what people have said, I think she was kind of nuts. Maybe she knew on some level and was just having fun?" Vince says with a smile.

"Maybe. Thanks for that. Sorry you had such a rough day," I say. I lean over and rest my head on his shoulder.

"It's okay. It's over. Next week we will have a small service for him, and then I can get back to work." Vince's voice sounds hollow.

# THIRTY-TWO
# VINCE



THE WEEK FLIES by faster than I expected, and before I know it Heather and I are driving out to Palm Springs for my dad's graveside service. I am wearing the suit from Iolet's costume closet, and she found a black dress for herself that I am pretty sure is the one Holly wore at the start of *Breakfast at Tiffany's*. Any other day and I would have enjoyed ripping it off her, but I am drowning in all the family drama that comes with a funeral.

Family I haven't heard from in four years have been calling me with opinions about the graveside service, like why was I doing that, and why wasn't there going to be a mass at the church? Part of me thinks my mom didn't help so I would botch this. According to my cousins, she hasn't answered her phone all week. Once again it all falls on me, and I screwed it up.

We get out of my truck and walk towards the crowd that has already gathered by Hugh DeLuca's final resting place. Where were these people over the last four years? My stomach churns, and my chest feels tight. Heather reaches for my hand and weaves our fingers together. She gives me a little squeeze, and I know I have blown it with her too.

I thought when my dad passed it would get easier, that he was holding me back. Turns out that wasn't the case. I blow out a breath, and Heather moves her hand up my arm, holding me closer to her. She leans in and whispers, "I am here," and all I can do is nod.

We take our place in the chairs that face his grave. I went with a simple black coffin with no embellishments. They asked if I wanted an open casket, and I said no without consulting my mom. No way I want to see him in that state. It was hard enough to see his lifeless body when he was still alive.

The priest starts the service, and it is a blur of words and genuflecting. People walk past and pay their final respects, and I want to kick each and every one of them. Instead, I sit, not moving or even responding when people talk to me. My mom, however, soaks it all up like she is the grieving widow. Heather is quiet by my side, her hand on me the whole time. She touches my leg, my arm, holds my hand, and at one point, she leans over and kisses my cheek softly. I don't deserve her.

"Do you want some time alone with him?" Heather asks, and I look at her, then back at the casket. Everyone is gone except a few people standing by their cars. My mom is talking to the priest, and I see him help her into her car.

"No, I said everything I need to say to him before he passed," I say, guilt at what I told him gnawing at my gut.

"Okay, well, if you don't mind, I want to say something." Heather stands and walks to the casket. She places her hand on the top lid and lowers her head, taking a few moments. I can't hear what she is saying but I catch my name a couple of times. When she turns back to me her eyes are shiny, like she might cry.

"Ready?" she asks, and I nod. We walk off in the opposite direction of everyone else because I parked in the wrong area. Heather reaches in my pocket and grabs my keys, and I don't fight her. Instead I just wait while she opens the truck, and I climb in the passenger seat. She climbs in the cab of the truck and turns to me.

"You have until the end of today, then you need to drop this shit," she says. I snap my head to her, shocked at what just came out of her mouth.

"What?" I sputter.

"You heard me. This quiet, feeling sorry for yourself shit has to stop. You have climbed so far into your own head I don't even recognize you anymore. This is what you were waiting for, Vince. You can do what you want now. You don't have to stay in Hollywood. Move back to Palm Springs. Or hell, enroll in college somewhere. Do *something* now that you can do anything!" she yells, throwing her hands in the air.

I just look at her and blink a few times, not sure what the fuck I am supposed to say to that. Instead I slump in my seat and stare out the window. She can't understand. She has no ties to anything, not even me. I watched her fill out job applications and look for apartment all week, so I guess whatever we had is over. It sure seems like she has moved on.

I'm not paying attention to where she is going, so when she pulls into a parking lot and stops, I sit up and look around. "Where are we?" I ask.

"At the base of the Hollywood sign. Come on. There is a trail that way, and we can walk right up to the letters!" She grabs a brown paper bag off the floor of the truck. She doesn't wait for me, she just gets out and starts walking. She's wearing little black flats that look like ballet slippers, and her hair is up in a twist, showing off her long, graceful neck. She's wearing pearls and a pair of big black sunglasses. Damn, she looks just like Holly Golightly. I look down at my suit and smile. She did that on purpose. We match. She knows how much I love that movie, and she probably wore that outfit to chip away at the fucking wall I built. I shake my head and climb out of the truck, jogging to catch up to her.

We walk quietly down the trail to the sign. Usually there are at least a few people out here, but today it's empty.

"Here," she says, and I look at her. She is holding a camera out to me, and she has a smile on her face. "I want you to take a picture of me in front of the sign, but not the whole sign, just the Holly part, okay? Because in case you didn't notice, I am her today." She does a little dip with her hip and lifts her hand above her head. She looks fucking adorable.

I wait while she scrambles up by the letters, and I walk down the hill so I can get her in the shot she wants. I take a few pictures, making sure I get a good one, then climb back up to her. When I hand her the camera, she doesn't look at me. It feels like a punch to my gut.

She walks over and sits by the O, then reaches in the brown bag and pulls out a bottle of wine and a corkscrew. I chuckle as I watch her struggle to open the bottle. I take it from her and pull the cork.

"Here you go," I say. I am towering over, her not sure what she wants. Do I sit with her? Do I leave her here to drink her wine in peace? Thankfully she pats the ground next to her and says, "Sit, Vince. You are freaking me out standing there."

I sit and she hands me the bottle. I take a long drink, hand it back to her, and watch her do the same.

"Losing a parent sucks. You lost him and so much more. Not today, but four years ago. I am probably the only person at the funeral who understands that besides you," Heather says. She takes another drink and hands me the bottle.

I am not sure what she wants to hear, so I drink and stare out across Los Angeles. Well, what I can see of it. The smog is laying low today, like a brown blanket covering the streets. Suffocating. That's how I have been feeling, like I have been smothered.

"I spoke with the attorney. We have an appointment tomorrow," Heather says and reaches for the bottle. She takes a swig and doesn't hand it back.

"Okay, what time?" I ask, like that matters. Tony has been covering my ass at the shop. Well, him and Terrence.

"Eight a.m. I know that is early, but I have an interview at ten, so I was hoping we could see what he has to say before that," she says.

"Where is your interview?" I ask.

"Don't laugh, okay?" She glances at me quickly, then looks back over LA.

"I would never." I reach for the bottle she is hogging.

"Sammy's. I have zero experience waitressing, but they also have a line cook spot open. Something I also don't know how to do." She laughs and leans back, resting her hands on the hill behind her.

"Why apply then?" I ask

"Because, Vince, I have applied to everything within an hour of the shop, and I have only gotten one interview. And I didn't get the job because when I made it clear I didn't plan on putting out, the interviewer told me the position as his assistant had already been filled."

"Jesus, Heather. Who was it? I'll go kick his ass," I say.

"No need. It doesn't matter, Vince. I just need to find a job this week or I have to go back to Chico. I am almost out of cash," she explains.

"Right, okay" I say. Fuck, I don't want her to go. How did I screw this up so badly? I take another swig from the bottle and pass it to Heather, but she waves it off. She stands and stretches, then brushes off her dress.

"I always thought Los Angeles was this magical place, you know?" she says, but I am not sure she is talking to me, so I don't answer. I just wait, and she continues.

"I thought it was filled with beautiful people who drove fancy cars and lived their best lives. But look, the smog is so bad I can barely see the street down there, and the only nice cars I see are the ones that come into your shop. No one is magical here. They are just people. This town is like Chico. Everywhere in this whole damn country is probably just like Chico. The one good thing about this place? My mom isn't here. I don't have to worry about going to pick her up from somewhere, and she can't ask me for money every damn day."

With that little speech Heather turns and walks back down the path toward my truck. I watch until I can't see her anymore, then I take a big drink of wine. I tip the bottle on its side and let it roll down the hill, watching as it bounces and spills its contents as it goes.

The next morning Heather is up and downstairs before I even get in the shower. When I finally make it downstairs, Tony and Terrence are chatting with her, and she is laughing like they are a fucking stand-up routine.

"Seriously, if that interview doesn't go well, let me talk to my mom. The bar might be hiring, or maybe you could pick up shifts when people call in sick, you know?" Terrence says.

"Ready?" I ask, stepping in front of her. I don't want her working at that shithole bar, or at Sammy's. I hate that it has been so hard for her to find a job. It makes me feel even worse because I have never had to look for work. I always had the shop. The shop I resented. God, I am an ass.

"Yep! I'm ready," she says, then steps around me and pats Terrence on the arm.

"Thanks, Terry. I will let you know." I watch my friend's gaze drop to Heather's ass as she walks out the back door.

"Fucker," I mumble under my breath. Tony just laughs, and I hear him slap Terrence.

"Come on, Terry. Let's get that Mustang up on the lift," he says, mocking the way Heather said his name wrong.

Heather and I are both quiet on the way to the attorney's office, and when I park and she gets out of the car, I have to jog a little to catch up to her and hold the door open.

"Thanks," she says as she ducks under my arm and into the office.

"Welcome, thanks for being punctual," Mr. Daniels says as he stands from his desk. I notice he still doesn't seem to have a secretary since the desk is still a mess.

He holds a big envelope in his hands as he motions for us to sit.

I pull out Heather's chair for her and sit next to her.

"I have to say, I didn't think I would be seeing you so soon, but what Heather described to me does seem like you reached the end," Mr. Daniels says.

"Did Iolet give you any idea what we were supposed to be doing?" I ask, and he shakes his head.

"No, she was very vague. She just said that when it's over, I would hear from you both. She also said the police might be involved. That is what made me a little worried. I have to admit, and I don't like to speak ill of the dead, but Iolet Merryweather was a little . . ." He trails off.

"Nutty," Heather and I say together.

He laughs and nods. "Yes, that sums it up. Okay, so here is what she left you." He reaches into the envelope and hands us each a key. I look at mine, then at Heather's. They are old bronze keys that look like they belong to an ancient door. Before I can ask any questions, Mr. Daniels pulls out a document.

"This is the deed to her house, which now lists you and Heather as equal owners. Her bank account has also been fully transferred into to your names, as well as the pink slip to a car. I can't say that it will be of any use, however, since it has been in storage since she left New York in 1935."

Heather and I both look at each other, then back to him.

"What? Did you say New York?" Heather asks.

"Yes. I am sorry. I thought I mentioned that on the phone when we set this up, Heather. She owned a brownstone in New York. It has been unoccupied since she left, so I can't guarantee the condition, but the family attorney and I have been in touch, and he assures me that the outside at least has been cared for."

"Family attorney?" I ask, and Heather takes a sharp breath in.

"Is this a joke?" She is pointing to the paperwork that Mr. Daniels slid over to her.

"No, that is the balance of her account as of yesterday. I just received that document via fax this morning. When you meet with the lawyer in New York, he can go over all the other things, like the stock options and whatnot," Mr. Daniels says.

I lean over and see numbers that make no sense to me. What the hell, Iolet?

"That is ours? And the house in New York?" I ask slowly.

"Yes. I do need your signatures on a few things. I must say I am really glad the police were not involved." He shuffles his papers, finds the ones he was looking for, and hands us each a copy to sign. We do this several more times until he announces we are done. He stands and extends his hand to me first, so I shake it. My whole body feels numb. I look at Heather, and her face reflects exactly like I feel.

We walk out of the office and head to my truck. I open the passenger door and wait for Heather to climb in, then I walk to my door. I pause, my hand on the cool metal of the handle, feeling like my world is spinning. I glance down the truck and see the rust and Bondo spots and all the places the paint has chipped off. I yank the door open and sit behind the wheel.

"Holy shit, Vince," Heather says in a whisper.

She is clutching the key and the papers. She turns to me and says, "We are like Richie Rich rich. Like I could buy that building right there. What the hell?" A strangled laugh bubbles out of her, and all I can do is cover my own mouth with my fingers.

"I know. I don't know what to do right now," I say. I scrub at my face with both hands.

"Let's go back to the apartment and buy a first-class ticket to New York. We can hire a car to pick us up from the airport and take us to whatever the hell a brownstone is, now that we own it!" She squeals and bounces in her seat.

"What? I can't go to New York," I say, still shocked at all of this.

"Why not?! Why on earth do you need to stay here? There is nothing for you here, Vince. Hasn't this last week shown you that? I told you yesterday that you had to stop this moping around, and I meant it. You just got handed the biggest fucking gift in the whole world and you're not going to take it? What the hell is wrong with you?" She is practically yelling now, and I can't deal with it.

I start the truck and speed off to the shop. She can go. I will take my share of the money and stay here. Maybe I can add on to the garage, make it more like what I wanted when I thought this was my after-baseball plan. I can do that now.

"I take it you aren't going to the interview?" I ask like a fucking idiot when we pull into the shop's back lot.

"No, Vince. I am going upstairs to buy a plane ticket. The sooner the better." She gets out of the truck and slams the door, stomping off to the back door. I follow her and ignore the guys as they ask how things went.

Once upstairs, she spins on me, pointing her finger. "Are you seriously not going to come with me? You are going to stay here?" She spreads her arms wide at my dingy apartment. "Here?" she asks again, and for some reason it pisses me off.

"What's wrong with here? A few weeks ago you thought it was the best thing since sliced bread! You couldn't get enough of the cozy couch and my wonderful bed! Now suddenly it's not good enough for you?" I yell. I know it makes no sense. I feel like an ass even as I say it.

"Listen, I would have already left if my fucking roommate hadn't let my mom move into my room. I have nowhere to go back to in Chico. I lost my job at Serenity Falls. That asshole I worked for said I was in violation of our agreement since it took so long down here. Which makes no sense because I haven't even been gone as long as I told him I would be! I don't have a place to live or a job, and until a half hour ago, I thought I was going to have to live in a box under the freeway!" she yells.

"What? When did all of that happen?" I step toward her. She takes a step back, and I feel my heart pinch.

"Last week. You were on the pity boat and couldn't be reached for comment," she says, and her eyes flash with what looks like regret as soon as the words are out. She looks down, then wrings her hands together before saying, "I'm sorry. That was uncalled for. I am going to call the airline and get my ticket. I'll be out of your hair soon."

She stops, then turns back to me and levels those intense brown eyes at me. "Vince, there is a story that my therapist told me when I was struggling. I didn't know how to stop taking care of my mom and start taking care of myself. I have been thinking about that story a lot since I came here. It's about this guy who walks down a road on his way to work and he falls in this deep hole. No one hears his cries for help, and he struggles and struggles to get out of the hole. Eventually he does and he goes on with his day, but the next day he falls in the same hole. This time it doesn't take him as long to get out, but it is still a struggle. This goes on for a week, him falling in the hole and struggling to get out. The next week do you know what happened?" she asks.

I shake my head no, unable to answer. I am still trying to regulate my breathing and calm down.

"Well, the next week he decided to take a different road to work," she says. She blinks at me, waiting for me to understand.

I don't understand. I don't know why she is telling me about some idiot who can't stop falling in a hole. I turn on my heel and walk out of the apartment, slamming the door as I go.

Tony and Terrence are lowering the Mustang off the lift, and I look around at the shop, seeing it a little differently. I could do this. I could expand and make it better. I could add another bay and maybe pave the back lot, put up a new sign, and hire someone that can do the electrical stuff that Tony and I struggle with. I could make it something I am proud of and work for fun instead of for peanuts like now.

Why doesn't any of that make me happy?

# THIRTY-THREE
# HEATHER


HOLLYWOOD, California
Hugh's Auto Body


I DON'T KNOW why I was surprised by Vince's attitude yesterday. I should have known he wouldn't leave. He is stuck here, a prisoner to some promise he made his dad all those years ago. He keeps falling in the same damn hole. Even in death his dad has a grip on Vince's life. I understand a little because my mom had that over me until I came to LA. Taking that different road changed me. I wish he could understand.

Last night he offered to take me to the airport, but I told him I would rather get a cab. When I woke up in the morning, he was nowhere to be found. Tony wasn't in the shop either, so I wrote him a brief note like you would write in a yearbook, not to someone who you feel a real connection with, but I was feeling extra immature.

"It's been real," I wrote, and that is something I am sure I will regret my whole life.

Now, looking out the window of the plane as we taxi to our gate at LaGuardia, my heart aches at what could have been. I sigh as I look over at the little old lady who sat next to me on the flight. She is very sweet and has offered to show me around once I get settled, and who knows, she might end up being my best friend. I have always enjoyed the company of an older crowd.

I don't bother looking around as the car I hired takes me to Iolet Merryweather's family attorney. I am stopping here to sign yet another document, then I will go to her old home. My new home, I guess. I haven't fully decided if I will stay, but right now it feels like the right thing to do. After spending hours taking care of the last bit of paperwork and explaining that Vince would not be coming, I climb back into the hired car, and we head for the brownstone. I still don't know what that is. I look up as the car slows and notice the beautiful street lined with trees. Not at all what I expected of a New York neighborhood.

"This is the place," the driver says, and he motions to the end unit of a row of houses. There are big cement stairs that lead to a single door. The windows on either side are covered in heavy drapes that are closed. I thank him and give him a tip that is probably too much, and he hands me my bag. I should buy myself a decent suitcase when I get settled. I climb the steps, fish out the key to the door, and slip it in the bottom lock. It turns easily, so I move it to the top lock and freeze when it doesn't go in. I jiggle it again and shove it, but it is clearly the wrong key for that lock. I turn the handle on the lower knob. It is unlocked. Damn it.

I slide down the door and sit on the cold cement step. Vince must have the key to the top lock. Of course Iolet would do something like that. I bury my face in my hands and have what can only be described as a small breakdown. I am not sure if I am crying or laughing at first, but it isn't long before it turns to full-on sobs.

I am so tired. I was on the plane for six hours, then at the lawyer's office for at least another two. I have no idea where I am, and now I have to walk around until I can find a phone to call who? Who do I even call?

I let a loud sob escape and jump when I feel a hand on my shoulder. I wipe at my face and sit up. "I'm okay. I'm sorry if I was—"

"Don't apologize, Heather. I should be the one apologizing," Vince says.

"Vince! What are you doing here?" I ask, looking up into his face.

"Let's talk about it inside. I assume this goes in the top lock?" He holds up his key. I stare at him, unsure if I want to kick him or hug him.

"Yes. I should have known Iolet would have been weird about this too," I say, still wondering what would make me feel better, the kick or the hug. Vince pulls me up without stepping back. He puts his hands on either side of my face and lowers his lips to mine. He brushes his mouth against mine in the softest of kisses.

"I am sorry, Heather. You were right about everything, and I was an ass," he says.

"Yes. Yes, you were." I laugh, grabbing him and pressing my lips to his, claiming him in a rough and passionate kiss.

"Jesus, let's get inside before we get arrested," Vince says. He puts his key in the lock and turns it, then pushes the door open, revealing our new life.

"Welcome home, Heather," he says with a cheesy smile.

THIRTY-FOUR

# EPILOGUE

ONE YEAR Later

To my worthless family,

    I have gone to the West Coast where they will no doubt love and revere me. The role I have in the movie Top Banana will, of course, earn me an Oscar. Albert and I shall be married, and all of you will finally see me as the successful woman I am. You will not be invited to the wedding or my movie premiere, and I hope this letter makes you feel as lousy as you have made me feel over the years.

    Yours, in absolute disgust,

    Violet Merryweather

I SIGH with a little sadness when I reread the letter we found a year ago. We finally figured out what the list of movies meant. Iolet had amassed costumes and props all from shows that George Chin had designed, but the first letter of each movie on the list of films she gave us contained the first letter of her clue. Like *Gone with the Wind*, *The Maltese Falcon*, and *Breakfast at Tiffany's* meant GTB, or Get the Bastard, as we suspected. Once we knew that, that she suspected poor Mr. Chin, the rest was easy. I wish she hadn't spent so much time chasing that theory, but mostly I wish we had found who actually killed Albert. She died believing George killed him. She chased George all over LA, auditioning for and securing a role in every film or commercial he had a hand in. I wish I knew what she hoped to accomplish by stalking him. Detective John Fitzpatrick said George Chin was never a suspect because he was out of town the night Albert was murdered. Maybe she was just jealous because Albert loved George and never loved her?

The day I found Heather on the stoop of what would become our home was filled with so much emotion, and even though it was rough, it will always be a favorite of mine. That was the day I told Heather I was sorry I fought what my heart wanted, not just with her but with my own life. I had put myself on the back burner for so long I didn't know how to move the pan. I warned her that I was probably going to screw up again, but she just wrapped her arms around me and kissed me senseless. It was what my battered heart needed, but it wasn't the only thing it needed. I didn't realize I created an unforgiving standard for myself when my dad had his heart attack. I was devastated about my dream of playing ball at the college level withering away in front of my eyes.

I was the best pitcher, I got straight As, but I was also a damn good mechanic, so I stepped up. I put aside my feelings, shoving them under the rug over and over, year after year. As time went on, I didn't know what my life was supposed to be outside of the shop. My thoughts are interrupted as Heather's voice comes from the other room.

"Are you going to come help me, or do I have to drag this thing down myself?" Heather yells from upstairs.

"I'm coming!" I yell back and put the letter back on the desk. My mom arrives later today, and Heather has been trying to make the guest bedroom on the second floor more presentable. Apparently, that means getting rid of the hundred-year-old mattress. I swear it was made with rocks and sewn with hatred. We've tried to move it before but gave up each time. Heather has spent the past year going through each room carefully to ensure there were no stolen items from Broadway. I think she misses the mystery that brought us together. I have been encouraging her to take some classes at the local college. She really would make a great detective.

I bound up the stairs and laugh when she comes into view. She is just as scrappy as the first day I met her, and somehow more beautiful. She is holding one end of the mattress, and her hair is sticking up everywhere, like she went to war with the damn thing.

"We have to get it to the curb before they get here with the new mattress and furniture. They said they haul away old mattresses, but I don't want to give them the chance to back out." She huffs and reaches up to tame her hair.

I lean in and give her a quick kiss on the lips, then grab the other end of the mattress and pull as hard as I can. We manage to get it outside just as the delivery truck pulls up.

"Hi! Thanks for coming so quickly. I'll show you where that stuff goes," Heather says as the guy hops out of the passenger side of the cab. The driver gets out and walks around to open the back of the truck, which is filled with a new bedroom set. I step aside and wait as they unload it, then watch as Heather leads them up the stairs.

When they have finished, I casually point to the old mattress and tell them, "Here's the old one you agreed to take."

"We could have brought that down for you," the guy says, looking at me for the first time. "Hey, aren't you the new pitcher for the Renegades? You're Vince DeLuca! Fuck, man, you have quite an arm on you. Free agent? I am impressed. You better know there is no team that will treat you as good as the New York Yankees. Keep playing like you are and they will call you up in no time. You could win us a series!" The guy pats my back like we are old friends.

"I'll try my best. Thanks." I pause because I am not used to being recognized as a ballplayer. No one cared about the city league I played with, and they sure as hell didn't recognize me in the street. Now that I am playing in the minor league, it's like I have oxygen again. Part of me wants to take this guy out for a drink so I can hear about how awesome he thinks I am again, but my more logical side steps up, and I say, "This mattress is like a hundred years old and it weighs a ton. My girlfriend didn't want you guys to refuse to take it, so we brought it down," I explain.

"You better not hurt that throwing arm, DeLuca. We got it. Marcus, grab that end, would ya?" The man bends down, and he and his friend wrestle the thing into the back of the truck.

"Jesus, you weren't kidding," he grunts. When he finishes, he pulls out his wallet and finds an old business card. He pulls the pen from behind his ear and asks for my autograph.

"Sure, man. I appreciate your support, and you taking that thing out of here." I sign the card and shake his hand. The other guy must not be a baseball fan because he just climbs in the truck without a word.

I go back inside and climb the stairs to the second-floor bedroom. My mom is planning on staying for a month or more, and for the first time in a while, I feel excited to see her. After the funeral and learning about the windfall that Iolet left us, I cut everyone off. I didn't speak to her for a few months, and I only started talking to her again because Tony wouldn't get off my back. Mom kept showing up at the shop begging him for information. I didn't tell Tony the whole story when I left, so he didn't have much to share, but eventually it all came out.

Three months after I left him in charge of the daily operations of Hugh's Auto Body, I sold him the shop for a cool $100 and a promise that he would keep the name. He hired Terrence as a full-time mechanic, and they are doing great.

I lean against the doorframe, watching Heather as she makes the bed with new sheets and a matching comforter. When it's made and perfect according to her standards, I tackle her from behind and pin her to the mattress.

"Vince! I just made the bed." She laughs, and I lift up so she can turn. God, she is so beautiful.

"Let's break it in," I say, wiggling my eyebrows at her. I lean down and kiss her softly.

"I am not christening your mother's bed, Vince. What is wrong with you?" she says, laughing and pushing at my chest.

"Okay, then get downstairs to our room and take off those clothes so I can ravage you before she gets here. We all know how loud you are when you are getting the good stuff," I say, kissing her again. This time she melts into me and runs her hands up and down my back.

"You do give me the good stuff, don't you?" She sighs.

"Iolet knew what she was doing. That saint of a woman sent me everything I needed to be the happiest man on earth," I say, making Heather's cheeks turn a little pink.

"I love you, Vince," she whispers against my lips.

"I love you too, Heather."

# ABOUT THE AUTHOR

Pamela Dean is an emerging author of romantic comedies. This is Pamela's second book.

If you haven't had a chance to read *And I Love Her Still,* it is available on Amazon and Kindle.

https://a.co/d/1dO2PK8

Follow Pamela Dean on Facebook for updates on her next book.

Email with questions or comments at PamelaDeanWrites@gmail.com